the
dark
trench
saga

A STAR CURIOUSLY SINGING

KERRY NIETZ

FREEHEADS

A STAR CURIOUSLY SINGING by Kerry Nietz
Published by Freeheads
www.kerrynietz.com

Cover Designer: Kirk DouPonce
Creative Team: Jeff Gerke, Lisa Lyons, Jill Domschot
eBook Conversion and Design: Kerry Nietz

ISBN 978-0-9839655-9-6

Library of Congress Cataloging-in-Publication Data

An application to register this book for cataloging has been filed with the Library of Congress.

To Silas and Natalie
May your future be a million times brighter
than this one

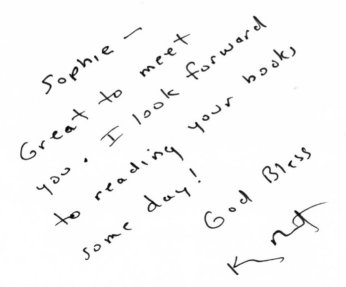

OTHER WRITINGS BY KERRY NIETZ

FICTION

DarkTrench Saga:

A Star Curiously Singing
The Superlative Stream
Freeheads

Peril in Plain Space:

Amish Vampires in Space
Amish Zombies from Space

"Graxin" (short story) appearing in *Ether Ore*

But Who Would Be ~~Brave~~ Dumb Enough To Even Try It?
(contributor)

Mask

NONFICTION

FoxTales: Behind the Scenes at Fox Software

ACKNOWLEDGMENTS

To my wife, Leah, for not letting me give up, despite having written this one "for me."

To my parents, Rex and Helen, for buying me all those books when I was young. See what happens?

To the friends and family who have encouraged me, even when it must have seemed like I was sitting on my hands all day—especially David, Rusty, Jon, and Brian.

To retired Major General Curry. Sorry to make you wait.

To Jeff Gerke, for "getting it" and sticking with me. May you always have full access to the Stream, with no stops in place, either internal or external. (Words can't express, freehead.)

And finally, to the Lord, who clearly wanted this to happen, despite my many faults.

I AM DREAMING, and yet I'm not.

The night is cool, calm—the opposite of the big stew that has just happened. Like the Abduls' god was throwing everything he had down on the city. All flash and action. On the horizon I can still see the bursts of lightning, the power in the moving tempest.

The driftbarges took it the worse, of course. Seventeen of 'em rendered inoperable, according to messages on the stream. Unable to shift their precious cargo from sea to store.

Barges are really land boats—angular hoverlifts on two sides and a large bay in the middle for product storage. The bay is fitted with arms able to lift the product, stack it. They're built tough because they have to be. Anything that travels the streets has to be tough.

I am many stories above the streets. Seated in my personal transport on the strings—the cables that crisscross the upper levels—I scan the cityscape ahead. The streets are the reason for these too. Downriders travel the strings. Shiny, sleek, and compact, they carry people like me, and our glorious masters, to places we need to be. Without complication.

Complication is always waiting for me to arrive. Like the barges.

"Your presence is needed there immediately!" my master's voice says just now in my head.

That will take some explanation, I know. Don't worry, freehead, we'll get to that.

As my downer nears the stockyard, I see the mess the storm has made. To the east—my right—is the great river. A waterway snaking endlessly from north to south. To the west is another sort of river, but this one isn't moving. A long line of dead barges, loaded with valuable supplies. A clogged roadway. Ahead of them, maybe a kilometer away, I can see the receding taillights of the last barge that is functioning. A lumbering automated giant, able to unload itself while Abduls sleep. Useful equipment, when it works.

The yard is still dark. No one has gotten the lights back on yet? Odd, since I'm not the first to arrive. Masters hate stoppage, so everyone who owns a stalled driftbarge has awakened his personal DR and sent them out here. Soon my downrider will touch down and I'll join them. There are nearly a dozen debuggers here already. I can sense every one of them in the stream.

I'm implanted, you see. Got a metal teardrop in my head. Keeps me connected to the information stream, helps me do my job. It does other things too. Things not as helpful. For me, anyway.

The work lights flicker on, illuminating the yard below and the red downrider pylon ahead. Ten downers are nestled at the landing, though only one on the same string as mine.

That's good, because deboarding gets a little shaky the further you are from the pylon, and I'm not a fan of shaky. I'd live at street level if I could. My downer stops, the transparent canopy slides back, and I step out. Reach back for my supply bag...

"Are you there yet, Sandfly?" my master asks, speaking straight to the implant again. He's not as anxious as he may seem. Not really. He just plays the part for appearances' sake. If he were actually upset he would've tweaked my head.

I respond in the affirmative, tell him I'll update him when I can. He goes away then, promising to leave me to my work. He probably will, probably sleep the whole night away.

I take another look at the yard. I see at least three bald heads already scaling barges. For some reason these three have picked barges near the end of the line instead of near the front—those that will need to leave first. Low-level debuggers, I think. Have to be.

Or fixing only what they're responsible for and leaving. Just as likely.

I stream to my nano-enhanced jumpsuit—standard fashion for a DR—and tell it to take the chill out. The nanos make their presence known, singing back an "OK" and making with the heat. I smile at their responsiveness, the warmth my chest and limbs now feel. At least *something* here is working.

The pylon's central ladder is already extended, so I grab hold and slide it to the ground. I make a quick check of the stream. Try to see if I'm familiar with any of the DRs hanging out there. In my mind the words form, becoming part of my personal—implant-created—waking dream. *DanceRate, FrontLot, BerryMast...* Most are vague names to me, newer implants with only a single specialty.

Only the moniker *HardCandy* stands out at me. I know her by stream rep. She's unique, unusual. Better than most, they say. And on top of that—female. Almost unheard of in our world. Abbys, I mean "Abduls," like to keep females mostly for themselves. One with a shaved head must be truly remarkable.

Or real ugly.

To be social, I send out a quick "Hello" to anyone who cares to listen. I approach the mess, reaching the shadow of the nearest barge. This model is immense—maybe three times my height and thirty large steps long. Like all barges, its predominant color is grey, with only a burst of color—a logo or stylized script somewhere—to indicate its owner.

I get a handful of clipped acknowledgments in the stream. No real friends here. I can see bodies in motion on the ground too, though. Bald heads in jumpsuits climbing, running, pawing through their bags.

"Sandfly?" someone says, aloud. A lanky youngster emerges, formerly hidden behind a barge to my right. He's barely half my age, and, since I'm only twenty-five, that's saying a lot.

"Yes?" I say.

"TreArc property, right?" The kid looks nervous, like this is his first big outage. The first time his master pricked his brain awake.

I do a quick check: He's level ten. I frown. Probably *is* his first.

"You have an implant," I say. "Use it."

He waggles his head. "Sorry," he squeaks. "Just trying to converse. I know you're TreArc. Know your rep."

I nod. "And so...?"

"You got three up front," he says. "Part of the bottleneck."

I sniff, squint at the jumbled chaos ahead. "Figures." I sigh at him. "Three! Really?"

He frowns, waggles again. "I would've tried 'em," he says, "but my master was adamant. Only wants me risking on ours. That's pretty much spec for tonight."

Real team effort. "Appreciate the thought," I say.

I pull the bag from my shoulder and break into a jog. I pass two barges parked side by side, and then a third that has somehow gotten itself sideways in front of them. This last has all four loading arms extended and draped lifelessly over its sides, as if it intended to crabwalk its way free. It has a sickly sweet odor to it too. Perhaps the food within is about to spoil. Faulty refrigeration backup, probably. Glad it isn't mine.

Next come two newer models. X3os. Clean and polished, with scarcely a nick in their crossed saber logos. Hardiest drift on any lot, the shills claim. Yet here they sit, dead as the rest. Deceit in advertising. You got nothing against A's lightning, streamshills! I scoff. I hear crosschatter from other debuggers. Someone begging for missed hexspanners. Another whining that they're low on sheets. Someone describing talk circuits.

Talk circuits? No barge has talk circuits. I shake my head. Low levels...

After passing a few more barges, I catch the sound of two debuggers in disagreement. A stream touch gives me their names: BullHammer and ThreadBare.

"Don't know," one says. "Haven't worked on any from before they had skin."

"But you got the specs, right? It is in your head."

I think I know what they're about. Their location is off to my right and not completely out of my way, so I move that direction.

I find BullHammer and ThreadBare—both older than the last DR I encountered, but still fairly young—crouching before a vaguely humanoid servbot. The bot is clearly meant for industrial applications and has about a decade of wear. My first clue to its age is the flexmetal exterior. Since the invention of synthskin, the old flexmetal models are rarely seen anymore. The bot is the color of burnt umber, with an elliptical yellow logo on its forehead. It is roughly humanoid, but with wheel runners instead of legs. Cold eyes stare out at me. Another casualty of the storm.

"I can handle this myself," ThreadBare says to BullHammer. "Just go back to your barge."

"My driftie is like a three nanosecond job," BullHammer says. "Simple fluid sheer and a possible boot rewrite." He raps the bot on the shoulder. "Pointless if this hunk is still sitting here. I'll foul the hovergears running it over."

Knowing my priority is still ahead, I contemplate moving on. I'm not here for a servbot. Still, should I leave it to them?

ThreadBare reaches into his bag and pulls out a rolled flexible *sheet*—a debugger's favorite viewing device. He peels off the stickum that holds the roll together, stretches the sheet taut. He'll kill the bot if he continues.

I can't watch any longer. I send them a "Stop" in the stream.

They turn to look at me, eyes wide. "You're from TreArc," Bull says then. "Your drifts are up front, twelve. Syncs perfectly with what my master always says." He smiles. "Says Tre's get preferential treatment."

I sniff. "Yeah, that's right," I say, dripping sarcasm. "Only the Imam's own mechanicals before ours." I nod at the bot. "What's down with this one?"

"I'm fixing it," Thread says. His unrolled sheet reflects the yard lights above. "Just trying to get a read on what's wrong."

I shake my head. "That a new sheet?"

"Of course," Thread says. "Only the best. Got it at Grim's yesterday."

"But what age is it?"

"Current age, I guess. What does it matter?"

I frown. "Because a current age sheet won't work on this bot," I say. "The skin won't stand it. In fact, you'll probably make things worse."

"How could a sheet make things worse?"

I point at the bot's midsection. "See those ridges there?" He looks and nods. "They're not resistant to sheets. You slap a sheet on that, and you'll plug it for life. Then you'll have to *carry* this bot out of here somehow." I give Bull and Thread a once-over—they're slight in build, but that's not unusual for DRs. All of us are. "I doubt you can manage it."

Bull looks annoyed. "Might as well start pushing now then. ThreadBare is slow going."

Thread raises a fist. "Bull, you blinking—" I see a flash of pain in Thread's eyes and the fist lowers. His whole countenance changes. "Peace be to you, brother."

Bull smiles brightly. "And to you be peace, together with A's mercy," he says. But he doesn't really mean it. None of us do.

I shake my head. "Now that you've got that out of the way, do you want me to give it a pitch?"

Thread frowns. "Rails, man, I got it. How hard can it be?" Returning to the bot, he slides a hand over its chest and midsection. He next attempts to peer into the aforementioned ridges.

"What are you doing?" BullHammer asks.

Thread keeps looking. "Trying to find what's wrong." I let him search a couple seconds longer. "Rails," he says. "I give. How do you see inside this thing?"

I open the side pocket of my bag and take out a small hex pin. I feel along the surface of the bot until I find a tiny depression, work the pin into place. I'm rewarded with an audible *Chunk*.

"Access plate," I say. I find the side of the plate, swing it forward. It opens to reveal the inner workings of the bot. Everything is dark.

I check the bot's specs on the stream, just to be certain. "These things have a hard reset," I say. "Only way to get to it is through the plate. Can't stream it. Can't probe it." I point to a spot below the bot's midsection. "Shine a light here."

Bull and Thread exchange glances, then race to see who can retrieve a light from their bags first. Bull wins.

With the light, it is easy to see the finger-sized hole. I slide a finger in, find the sliver of the reset switch, and trip it up. The bot's eyes respond with a flickering glow. Success!

"It needs a full thirty seconds to check itself," I say. "Then give it the usual ready command and stream it to get out of the way."

Thread looks at Bull, whose smile has long since departed. "That was hip work there, twelve."

"Sandfly," I say. "Twelve is only a level."

Bull flushes, looks apologetic. "Right." Both bow, which I answer with a quick nod of my head. "Keep your bits flowing, boys."

Leaving them to their waiting, I turn toward the mass of dead barges again and run.

"HardCandy is up there somewhere," Thread streams to me. "Be careful."

I almost chuckle at that. Leave it to a low level to notice the only girl in the yard. In our entire universe, really. Not that it makes any difference.

• • •

It isn't long before I'm debugging my second driftbarge. The first was an easy fix. It had partially fixed itself by the time I reached it, in fact. That's the beauty of integrated nanotech. Sometimes the problems erase themselves.

But this second one, well...

This particular model is an X15—a ten-ton behemoth—and it has needed attention for some time. The lightning was just the straw, you know? The final cap.

I'm near the top of the front section, where the bulk of the mover's mind is located. Higher than I like to go without a harness, but I'm okay this time. Both the back and front surfaces are sloped and kept slick to prevent unwanted boarding. For a normal human, that makes things difficult. But I'm far from normal. The barge will extend handholds for those who speak its language. Which I do.

I have a string of sheets laid across a section of its tubular brain pan, and all they're showing me is chaos. Pipes are sheared, pathways fried, the nanos are in a state of panic—scurrying like ants in a downpour.

Working two barges over is HardCandy. I've attempted to touch with her a few times on the stream in the last couple of hours. Mostly casual stuff. Work stuff. But I've been curious to meet her. Had to see what she was like. That's part of being a debugger. We like to *know* things. I can't say the conversation was entirely reciprocal. But that's to be expected. She has inherent stops in her head, just like I do. It is better to be cautious.

Only a handful of debuggers are left in the yard now. Most have finished with their chores and quickly downridden away. Masters keep a tight rein on their investments. Especially in a thunderstorm. Wouldn't want to fry an implant. The barges that were able already headed down the road toward their offloading destinations. Others idle patiently, waiting for me to get my other two out of the way.

For its part, the storm seems to have quieted, moved away. It still feels dark out here, though. Really dark.

I've been listening to the creaks and groans of hindered barges and an occasional curse from a climbing DR. We aren't the most agile. But now I hear a new sound. It is of multiple men—young Abduls—walking between the barges. I hear their footsteps and laughing. They aren't children, these Abbys, they're older than that. Old enough to know the rules.

There is the crash of breaking glass. Something thrown hard against a barge.

"Fix *that*, implant!" one of them yells. Next comes laughter. Giggling malevolence. The voice is far away, but discernable just the same.

I get a message in the stream from someone named FrontLot: "We've got company in the yard, brothers. Careful. I almost got hit."

"There's work to do," HardCandy answers. "Ignore them. Another storm is coming."

"How did they get here?" Front asks. "There's supposed to be a fence..." The dialog goes cold then. There's still work to do.

Shaking my head I grab a handhold, move to the highest sheet I've placed. I think I see the problem. A metal fitting, a blinking piece of hardware, is completely misaligned. I stream for the barge's code, give it a once over. The system could never handle that variation. Parameters aren't there. No wonder the thing is—

"What is *this*?" An Abby voice again, closer now. I can almost smell him. No way can he see me, though. I'm hidden above, atop the barge.

"I do believe it is a *woman* skin," a voice says. "Fellows, look!"

I get a feeling in my stomach. Like I've tasted raw spiders. "Hard-Candy?" I whisper in the stream. "You good?"

No answer.

I pull myself to the center of the barge's top surface. I skirt the bay section in the middle, moving forward. Toward the voices.

"Grab her!" someone yells. "Bring her here!"

There's the sound of movement. A struggle, a female groan.

This is against the rules, and they know it. Hard's master will be ticked. But what about Hard? What about right now?

The next barge is within jumping distance of my own. Barely. It might hurt a little...

I try anyway.

My feet crash against the edge of the bay, but I make it safely, stand tall. There is such a ruckus in front of me that nobody heard. I'm grateful. I have to see. Have to know. I scamper ahead.

I reach the edge of the bay and look over. Nearly ten meters separate me from the next barge, but that is irrelevant. The shadows are long here. And the stench is all below.

One Abdul has a woman—Hard, I have to guess, mainly because she's bald—by the back of her beige jumpsuit and is pulling her backward toward him. Two others are in front, near her wildly kicking feet.

"It is forbidden," she says, almost hissing. "Touch me and lose your hands."

The Abbys laugh. Probably sons of masters. Confident that the law won't find them.

Plus there are three of them. Courage in numbers.

"Where is security?" I stream to no one in particular.

"It makes no difference," FrontLot streams back. "Anyone who can help will be too late."

I watch, feebly, as HardCandy continues to struggle. One of the Abduls near her feet manages to grab an ankle. She shrieks in anger. Kicks harder with the other foot.

The stream has grown completely silent. Like everyone is waiting in fear. A half-dozen debuggers. Frozen. I don't blame them. Stops are fully in place. Tweaks only a forbidden thought away. There is only so much any of us can do. The rest leads to pain.

I glance down at my own slight frame. There's nothing I can do that way either...

The Abduls have Hard gripped tighter now. She's struggling, but it isn't getting her anything. Only seconds are left.

Part of me wants to return to my job. Hide. Leave her to these Abbys who skirt their own laws.

I make a fist at my chest, fight the interference. I glance at the machine in front of me. The one beyond, on the far side of them. Can I reach it?

Not by jumping. No, of course not. That is the machine Hard was nurturing, though. What did she accomplish?

I sing out to her drift barge: Are you ready?

The barge feeds me a list of small problems: unequal lift, slight friction on one arm. The big answer is "Yes." He's ready to go.

"Extend!" I stream. I watch as one of the barge's vertical loading arms grows from the side of its bay. Quiet. Frictionless. So far, so good.

Below, one Abby is looking around. Thinks he's heard something. "What was that?"

I contemplate how nice it might be to have that mechanical arm simply pulverize him into the ground. To leave them all just smelly, hairy spots in the cement. I begin to stream an order to the barge—

Ouch!

A headbuzz hits me, igniting a storm in my synapses. Not enough to debilitate me. Just enough to make its warning clear: the mental path I'm traveling down is filled with danger. Stupid "stops." That wasn't an external tweak from my master. Only the inherent stops from the implant. The bridle on my brain.

I grit my teeth, shake the feeling off. Make myself go calm. This is only a test. I'm doing diagnostics on a malfunctioning barge. I'm not trying to harm anyone. Really.

"Now," I stream, keeping my mind carefully neutral. "Drop."

The arm bends at the large joint. The lifting surface—a silver articulated fork—plunges straight down for seven meters and impacts the pavement behind the group.

Clang!

"By the light of A!" I hear, followed by a dark curse and the sound of scrambling shoes

I don't dare look. I can't. But I want to.

I tell the arm to retract now. It does. Because it can hear me. Because it must obey the debugger.

"Drop!"

Another clang. This time from farther away. On the opposite side of them. I'm not completely sure of their location, but I'm fairly confident. I feel a bit of pain for the uncertainty. Nothing I can't live with, but real pain nonetheless. I can sense where HardCandy is, though. Thankfully. I know *she's* safe.

"Is she doing that?" someone asks.

"They're not allowed to hurt us," another says. "Can't. Now help me."

"Drop!"

I risk a glance. Two of the Abbys have let go of Hard completely. The other—the one who grips Hard's arms—is looking wild. He glances up. I roll away, out of sight. Just in time. Stupidly frightened.

I hear a klaxon in the distance. Could be that someone called security, or could be mere coincidence. Regardless, it works.

"Bluecoats!" an Abdul screams. "Let's *go!*"

"Will she...?"

"Forget it. Let's go!" The claps of running feet on pavement. Abdul sounds and smells diminish.

I'm still huddled on my back, hiding in the bay of a barge. I feel the coward. I turn and glance over the edge again. Hard is on her feet, brushing at her sides. Her arms wrap around her then, squeezing. I hear a sniff—could be crying, but I'll never tell. She's free and I got through it without a major tweak. All told, a major success.

I creep away, back toward my personal task.

I get a message. A touch of glowing warmth. Only her mind to mine. She knows what I did. She could sense my nearness. It's her way of thanking me. She sends me something else too—a mental gift. "A taste of freedom," she streams. "In case you ever need it."

There is pain in her sending it, probably, but she feels I'm worth it. It stirs me a little. Makes me all out of spec.

"What is it?" I ask, even though it's obvious. It is a location.

"A special place," she says. "Where there's a little more truth."

I thank her, tuck the location away secure in my deeply buried implant.

• • •

All that at the loading dock—it happened two nights ago. But in chute sleep, it is like *right now*, replaying perfectly. The occurrence bothers me still, toys with me. The question is "Why?" Why am I still thinking about something I can never have?

Another problem I have to solve.

IT IS HARD TO DESCRIBE, this buzzing in my head. It wakes me, obviously. But it is hard to clarify for someone like you—at least the type of person I assume you to be—someone with a free head. We haven't had true freeheads since before the date change, and that's really before I remember. Before I'm allowed to remember. I'll try to be lucid, though, in hopes you can follow along.

Anyway, the vibration wakes me from chute sleep, meaning someone needs a debugger. It rarely happens anymore, but it happens. So early in the day. Crichton, I hate early. I blame that on the buzzer itself, but I could be wrong there. I mean, you'd think they'd want me to sleep. Otherwise, how can I perform?

So, I'm up. I stumble from my glossy onyx chute, across the narrow wedge that is my home, and make for the screen. It is difficult to ignore, since it is pulsing red. They talked about banning red once. That would be nice. It would be much better if it was a warm orange, don't you think?

I reach the screen and hover over it, the flashing reflecting in my eyes, I'm sure. Maybe off my head too, since no debugger has hair anymore. Everyone else, hairy. Debuggers, never. Stand out in a crowd, you know. Never be lost. Never run away.

I place my hand on the screen and watch the color change. It flashes blue now, extending from the circle around my hand. Pulsing, living. Then the blue dissolves, becomes a face. A hairy human face.

My master. He nods the required blessing. "Peace be to you, DR 63. You slept well?"

"Sandfly," I say. "I still like 'Sandfly.'"

Lips part, revealing perfect jewels. "You're fortunate I protect you, Sand. Otherwise..."

"Lashes ten," I say. "Wouldn't be new."

Another head bow, another flash of teeth. "You aren't my best. You could be decommissioned."

"But you woke *me*," I say. "I assume there's a reason." It is better to be short with Abduls. Sometimes, it is the only way to get things done. They rarely understand humor, anyway.

The face turns to the side briefly, as if studying something on another vidscreen, then his attention returns to me. "It is good for you, this task. It will help with your journey. Put more good works in the scales, Sand. You should be grateful."

It is just like an Abdul, trying to tie everything to some eternal comeuppance. I don't need it, don't believe it. "What I'd be grateful for is more sleep," I say. It was a trifle sarcastic, and I know it. Actually feel a twinge in my head for it too. The Abdul hasn't moved though, so it wasn't his doing. Sometimes, after you've felt enough of the tweaks, you start to expect them even when they haven't happened. They become a false conscience.

I suppose that's the point. Tweak 'em to keep 'em!

"So what's the task?" I ask. "Another interchange lose its mind? Barges down again? Need me out on a hopper?" A hopper is a mechanical device—nano powered—that rides atop our freeway system mending strings. It represents the most exposed of our jobs. That's why I hate it. I don't like wind. Or heights. Not going to tell my master that, though. Wouldn't give him the pleasure.

Another head bow. I'm growing tired of those too. "No," he says. "You should come to TreArc so I can brief you in private. There will be...special considerations. You will need to prepare."

I resist rolling my eyes. "Aren't we friends?" I ask. "Stream it to me."

"I'm sorry, Sand, I cannot. You should come in."

"Fine," I say, not meaning it. I really want to sleep. "Be there in a few." I slap the screen, closing the connection. That was a little rude too, but for some reason, no tweak that time. Maybe it is all me. Maybe the thing in my head doesn't work that well.

I make for the sanitary, stream out for the cloud, and relax as the purifying steam surrounds me.

I have a stop to make before seeing my master: GrimJack's. Then I'll be right on to TreArc. No problem there.

At least it's no hopper.

THE WEIRD THING about GrimJack's—the cool thing, actually—is that it is situated on a hill. There aren't many of those left since that whole "No land higher than M" thing. Blinking last imam. I wish—

Ouch!

That was a real buzz that time, I know it.

Anyway, GrimJack's is cool. His place sits maybe a story or two higher than the ramshackles around it. We still sometimes get snow here, and in times past I've taken an empty digger thorax to Grim-Jack's and ridden the ground down the hill. It isn't much of a ride, but for a few quick seconds I get a thrill. Taste freedom for a bit. No way can the implant get me for that either, because it doesn't know. No way could it—because I don't think about it. I only laugh.

I arrive at GrimJack's on my downrider. Swinging in on a star, you know.

Oh yeah, you probably don't...

A high level debugger devised the solution—about 1950 AH, maybe—and it took little time for adoption. We needed to get people off the street. It was dangerous down there. One thing about Abduls, they can't drive.

Downers were the right tech at the right time—an A-send, the Abduls would say. They come in single and two-ped configurations, with the riders aligned one behind the other in the latter variation. Their lines are all sleek and compact, with the most notable feature being the place where the top surface curves up over each passenger compartment. One hump or two, just like camels.

I pull into the landing pylon and who do I see? HardCandy!

I'm startled at first, but I manage a simple stream greeting and a smile.

But does she look at me? Even give me the time? No. Only a cold flip of her delicate bald head, like maybe a fly landed there, then she turns her brazened self on me, mounts her downer, and up she climbs. Like she never even...

Now in truth, I admire her. I'm infatuated, really. She's placid, you know. For her to survive as a debugger—takes real guts. Beats the alternative all to bits: being wife seven of some hairy master. Lots of bits. But to turn her back on me like nothing had happened at the driftyard. Well, that just rails.

I remember the location she gave me. If it were written on paper, I'd be tempted to take it out and hold it. Make sure it is real. I still have it in my implant, though. Safe. As real as anything I've ever known. I was hoping maybe it meant something. More. Anyway, I need to get to that special place. See what "a little more truth" tastes like.

But enough of my problems. I leave her shadow behind and reach into the downrider for my c-card, still plugged into the rider, and climb my way to GrimJack's.

The building itself is all red brick and stucco. Grim says it was something called a "comic book" store once, and says it with pride. I have no idea what that means, aside from the fact that it has this heavy musk scent about it, like maybe a cat got locked in a steamer. With a bottle of wine.

The door is solid wood, disguised in green, and heavily furrowed by time. It has a mechanical brass knob that I resist thinking about. I don't want to know how many have touched it before me. I simply make it work, clanking and shaking the door free.

Within, the store is like a second home. Placed prominently near the center is a big ol' cushion chair. It is maroon, and real ugly. Grim needs the extra support, though. He's like two of me, with the second Sand-weight wrapped firmly around his middle.

Circling behind that chair is a pipe organ of shelves, spindles, and tubing—dispensers of those things that make a DR's life possible. The interior walls are lined with remnants of Grim's various endeavors. His electro-mechanicals and copper wires. Shells of machines that have lost their function. Experiments gone awry.

Maybe that explains the smell.

As I enter, Grim emerges from behind a stack of what look like screen casings. But ancient. He has a magband slung across one eye, making the eye look all large and fishlike. He must've been deep inside something, looking mighty close.

"What are those things?" I ask.

"Plasmas, from like the late 1400s," he says. "I'm trying to refit them for live optic. Think I could sell them high. Maybe earn myself a lift ride."

Ugly, I think. But "Good plan" is what I say.

Smiling, he makes a little back and forth with his head, clearly pleased. Because of his past life, Grim's hair matches mine. Once they clean it, it never comes back. His scar is another story.

"You see Hard?" Grim asks.

"Yeah," I say. "Ignored me."

He shakes his head—harder this time. "Don't take it personal, Sand. She doesn't like men. Not allowed to."

"So I've heard." Though I suspect different.

"No sense of humor with that one either," he says. "I dredged up an old word today and spun it on her. Told her not to go all 'movie' on me. She just fed me a cold stare. Said she doubted I knew what the word meant, and if I did I wouldn't go talking about something so old it would get me lashes. Some strange flak like that." Grim has a prominent scar along his left temple that he scratches at nervously. "She's bent, that one."

He swipes the magband from his eye and moves to his oversized chair. It wheezes under his weight. "Anyway, so what you needing, Sand?"

"Got a job," I say. "Need a sheet."

"Got sheets galore," he says in a bored tone. "So routine." He reaches to his left and starts rummaging, eventually producing a silver canister. "How many you need?"

His attitude is critical, but I know sheets are his mainstay. Without them he'd lose house and hill. "Maybe two. Three, max."

"Take five. I'll deal you." He draws five transparent sheets through the canister slot and rolls them into a bundle. He then slaps a piece of blue stickum on them, and hands them to me.

I hesitate.

Grim bends forward, attempting to search my eyes. "Something *more* then?" A look of hopefulness now. He *must* be bored.

Returning to Grim's after I've started a job is a real pain, you see. I don't like the distraction. So, sometimes I'm slow at this point. Slower than someone like Hard would be. It is the one time I calm my mind enough to really search it. To inventory exactly what I might need. Have to anticipate.

"Maybe a nano-scanner," I say. Even though my master *said* it wasn't a hopper, it could be something nearly as bad. I got picked for a digger once. That was real bad. No sheet going to work on them. Can't see nothing with a sheet. Too much shielding. Has to be shielded, though, doesn't it?

"Nano?" Grim asks. "Now you're singing my language!" He frowns, shakes his head. "But no can do."

"I don't know what I'm up against," I say. "I may need one."

He spins to his right, grabbing one of the telescoping vertical tubes behind him. Turning it, he shoves it upward. "Banned, as of the third. Imam's orders."

That news I missed. "What are they doing?" I ask. "Expect us to work with bare hands?"

Grim smiles. "To match our heads, you mean?" The smile dwindles. "They don't know us, Sand, and they don't care."

"A pure regression," I say. "Why?"

"Afraid someone might use 'em on a servbot."

"Like *any* mechanical."

"Can't," Grim says. "Apparently they got souls now."

Robots with souls? "Since when?"

"Since they don't need plugging anymore. Independence is identity, Imam says."

I want to grab my plastiweave jumpsuit and rip it, but I know I couldn't. Clothing is near indestructible now. My fingers would split before it did.

Still, it was always this way with the Abduls. Never understand us. Couldn't. But they keep us because they need us. Tolerate, but rarely help. Do those in power *ever* help the guy getting things done?

"Loony..." I mouth. But even though I spoke softly, I feel a buzz again. I hate that. I grit my teeth against the pain, against the disgust.

GrimJack shakes his head. "Careful, Sand. Keep walking that wall and they'll take *your* soul." His finger traces the scar. "You'll earn one of these." The man is usually stone, but a tremor has entered his voice.

I glance away, toward the parking lot. The view is better. I don't know what I'm up against—and to ban my best tool...? "I only have three specialties," I say aloud.

Grim's voice feels my pain. "And servs are clearly the most chic," he says.

When compared to driftbarges and hoppers? By bounds!

"I can give you a light probe," he says. "Might show you something if you end up stuck."

I frown, but what choice do I have? "Sold," I say.

Grim finds a dark canister and opens it. Within are small bronze capsules. He wraps one in brown paper, stickums it closed. I hand him my card. Credits gone and forgotten.

"Ease, Sand." He says as I leave. "Walk in ease."

My back waves to him. I'm still railed.

TREARC'S HEADQUARTERS ARE near the center of the city. Fittingly, because that's where the temples are. My master's company, like most businesses these days, is somehow linked to the temples.

The downrider takes me past a dozen of the ornate domes before reaching the shining obelisk of the TreArc building. I go directly to the downer pylon near the building's top, ending a few stories short of the nearest temple's gold and amethyst roof. If someone were sitting on the pinnacle, he could roll a ball right down on me.

Within, the TreArc building is nothing special. Most of the special went out about 1500 AH. The building *does* have a central skylight, so that's something. Lets a little morning clouds in for the upper ten stories.

My Abdul's working quarters are situated along the center, which is a bad thing to them. They prefer to be out near the temples. Not me. If I were an Abdul, I'd want to be in the center. Give me those clouds.

Briefing meetings are always crazy. Whenever I'm present my master splits the room in half with a big nano-curtain. Me on one side and him on the holier side. All I see of his hairy face is about a seven-centimeter rectangle around his eyes. Yet I see his full face on the vid at home. It makes little sense to me. Like my breath is going to disturb his eminence. Add weight to the wrong side of his scale.

Too bad the curtain isn't airtight. Then I wouldn't have to smell him, either.

Regardless, my side of his office is all business charts and framed piety. His side is mystery.

I find my usual spot in the floor—a place where the marble tile shows a hairline fracture—and stand over it, head bowed.

"Peace be unto you...Sandfly." His voice from behind the curtain.

"And to you be peace, together with A's mercy."

"You took your time," he says.

I raise my bag of supplies. "A debugger has needs," I say, now looking forward.

"Of course," he says, and I think he bows too, because I lose his eyes for a moment.

"What is the job?"

A long pause follows—so much that I think maybe the Abdul is praying. There's so many prayers to be said in a day, and time is short. "Have you heard of DarkTrench?" he finally asks.

I touch my temple and hear a click inside as I contact the bitflow—the stream—within the room. It is only a moment before I reach it. A groan escapes my lips.

"You know of it?" he repeats.

"I'm getting it now," I say, still sampling data. "Conical design, heavy plated, ultrafast connections."

Much more to it than that, though. Much more. DarkTrench isn't just any old construct. It flies through space. You miss so much while you sleep. I had no idea the Abduls cared about such things. There's no trade in space, after all!

Been awhile since they conquered anyone. Maybe that's it.

There isn't much on the stream about DarkTrench, other than bare schematics. Doesn't even say where it goes. My bet would be somewhere where there is stone. All those temples—we need more stone!

"Space travel?" I say. "Why?"

My master's eyes fall away. "None of your concern... Sandfly." I sense a smile behind the mask. I want to smack the curtain, I swear.

"You woke me," I say. "I can't do anything without information. Something like DarkTrench will take lots of information."

There is a chuckle this time, an honest-to-A chuckle. "You will not be working on DarkTrench. No need to discuss *those* specifics."

"You brought it up." Abduls try to be so in-charge and sophisticated, but sometimes they're obtuse angles.

"Only for context. Though it is my understanding that you know some of the people involved." A pause, in which I guess he's looking at his desk. Abduls don't see the bits like me. They have to read. Takes them longer. "Is a 'TallSpot' and 'Handler' known to you?"

I insert a pause of my own. I know them, of course. But not in a good way. Abduls all. We met before any decisions had been made about our lives. In that innocuous ten years before they applied the salve to my head. Before the implant.

TallSpot was gregarious and commanding—a real imam in the making. Handler was often Tall's shadow. A worker bee, an enforcer, but still popular. You sort of knew they were going to succeed.

"Been much time," I say. "I doubt I'd recognize them."

"They are two of DarkTrench's four crewmembers. TallSpot is the pilot, in fact."

Cheers for him. "So why do they need me then?" I ask. "Need some tips? Design opinions cost more..."

"The costs have been accounted for," he says. "You will need to go to them for more information."

Go to? I'm sure I'm not hearing that right. I can't be. "Where are they?"

My master's eyes disappear. Then through the rectangle I see his forefinger, pointing straight up. My stomach moves the other way.

"That's hazard," I say. "Can they afford hazard?" I'm trying to be smooth, but I don't feel it. I know if they can build a ship, they can probably afford hazard. Still, I've got to try. I don't want this.

"Of course," he says. "Your way is completely set."

"Will my level hold up to it?" I'm level 12—a midlevel, but higher than most. Something like this should require a lot higher. It would be a way out for me, anyway.

"You will require an upgrade," he says. "Your card, please."

I slide my card through the rectangle. I hear a hum and see a flash of purple. Upgraded. Unbelievably. It means 4K more credits a month. To start.

Now I'm *really* nervous. The card returns to me, still feeling warm.

"Be at the lift in CA by day 37 at 9 a.m. local," he says. "Any questions?"

I attempt to clear my head—a hard task when half your brain is searching for more information than the bitstream can give it. DarkTrench? Come on. Need more bits, man. Need something to get me out of this. I'm allergic to lifts. Don't want space! Masters don't expect questions, though. Not really. At least mine never does.

"Can you tell me where they went, at least?" I ask. "Where DarkTrench is going?"

Another pause. I think he's praying again. "Anywhere they like, Sandfly. They can go anywhere."

The rectangle closes. I feel a vibration in my seat and a corresponding nudge in my head. This nudge isn't from my inherent stops. It is generated from my master's golden controller, still clutched in his hand, I assume. Time for me to go.

CA lift by nine in the morning. Rails. It really rails.

I HATE THIS, the not knowing. Debuggers are used to *always* knowing. We're plugged. If the information is available, we find it. Through the stream we sample the bits of billions. Trillions of bits! Almost we can feel them, but not quite. There is always some coldness. Cold bits.

I have one place I can go. Not GrimJack's—there is nothing more for me there. Someplace a little out of reach.

I ride the downrider to the bay, all the way to portside. If it weren't for the air refiners I'm sure I could smell the salt. There is still a tang of something in the air, though. The refiners never quite get it right.

The downrider touches earth and I step free. Around me are the remnants of an archaic parking lot, now more grass than crumbling asphalt. I'll be alone here probably. Really alone.

The place has the feeling of forgetfulness, like good memories have been driven away and trampled. There's no landing pit at all, just a broken circle of concrete, scarcely large enough to keep my feet from wearing sand. There's a high yellow fence that obscures the sea and an overgrown path leading through it. Still made of stone! Hard to believe the stone hasn't been reclaimed for temple work, but there it is.

I gingerly walk that path, a bit disturbed by its hardness. There is no give whatsoever. The walking surfaces I'm accustomed to are textured, painted, remanufactured. I never knew how firm *real* stone can be. It surprises me, causes me to move faster than I expect.

Sixteen, thirty-two, maybe sixty-four steps later I reach the spot HardCandy described to me. The place where there's supposedly "a little more truth." I stand beneath an old structure, remnants of an iron bridge the many peoplemovers used to traverse—moving humans slowly across the sea. The same way the Abduls arrived.

I listen to the ocean's pulse. It overshadows the distractions in my head, makes me feel almost placid. There is a hot zone nearby, though. I can feel it in my implant. I'm on the edge.

I think of HardCandy. I know she doesn't owe me anything. I don't *want* anything. Still, I remember the night I saved her—the real version, not the remanufactured version the chute fed me. It still dredges my emotions. Makes me uncomfortable. Makes me wonder if what I did was right.

Another step and I'm in the glow, exactly the spot I'm looking for. One solitary LED still dangles from the structure above. Instructions from Hard had been bundled with the coordinates. "If you stand there," she wrote, "the bitshield is weak. You might be able to see a little more. Reach out and touch a little more."

I look...

Bingo. I find the stream here. But it's odd here. A little... sharper than I'm used to. Tweaks my nerves. I wonder where the nearest booster is. It can't be far, but boy, is the signal unusual.

DarkTrench, what are you?

They say there are places—like in the OuterMog or something—where everyone has a freehead. That is hard to fathom. I wonder if those places generate to the stream. I wonder if they'd know anything that would help me.

The other benefit of this place, Hard's hidden spot beneath the bridge, is that it takes much of the sting out of the implant. There is freedom in that, a feeling of elation that I have to work to contain. The muting is necessary, really good, because I don't know what I'm getting into here. I need to not be distracted. Not be prodded as I explore.

DarkTrench was built last year. Someone knows that, at least.

I continue to search, pulling hard.

Now, this is interesting...

I assumed the ship was for trips here and there between the

local rocks. Moving the oh-so-precious ores from Nep or Jup. But there's more than that here. Lots more.

I close my eyes to the burning. A warning that tickles my cerebrum. They got that implant tied so close, so hard, it hurts my eyes sometimes. Bits are flowing, flowing...

Then I see the ship. All sleek and magical. Very few angles. Not Abdul-looking at all. There must have been many debuggers on it. The work would've kept me buried for months. That's why I wasn't asked, probably.

You're level 13 now, right?

I won't get my hopes up. I'm flush out of hope.

DarkTrench again. More magic. Sleek, black magic. It's ultra-solar—the first. Able to flip! There is a time element too.

The phrase "Back to go forward" is mentioned. It is technical talk of a type I'm not aware. Not in the normal training. Maybe if I was able to chute sleep long enough, I'd catch it. If they'd let me.

Maybe they let level 13s...

Flipping. That's an interesting term. They take the matter—DarkTrench matter—and they flip it. Makes the ship something that can slide from point A to point B.

I think of TallSpot and Handler...and whoever else mans the trip. Did they know what was being done to their substance? Did all their training prepare them? Folded, compressed, elongated, dropped through a window of time...

Abduls are easy that way. They take it for the team. Scales...all about balancing the scales.

I don't know that they went anywhere, do I? Did they go? Somewhere? Alpha Benditzone or something?

The stream shifts some, growing even sharper in my head. I shake it off and move a few paces to the south. I re-find the sweet spot. There's got to be something else, something more...

Not a whisper. Plus I get this jittery feeling from my implant. Like it is worried about me, thinking I might be planning something dangerous. I drive whatever notion—anything that could make it suspicious—out of my head.

I think about HardCandy again. I wonder if she said anything to anyone about that night. The way she shifted me off at GrimJack's makes me wonder. Not that it would matter. If she said anything, they would've decommissioned her anyway. I know, I've seen it before. It doesn't take much.

She never said, "Thank you." Not really. Still, she sent me warmth and a picture of this under-shadow place. Did that mean she liked me? Thought I was special in any way?

I'll get nothing more here.

I turn toward the path again, back toward the business at hand. I shimmy my way to the downrider.

Rain is coming, I can taste that too—feel the flux in the local stream. I insert my card, and the downer rises into the sky. I dread what's coming next, but I gotta do it. I have no choice.

It will be okay, Sand. Like riding the cable to Bristol.

But not like that. Not like that at all.

CA USED TO BE CALLED something else. I don't remember. I'm a zone over, so I have to leave early. No chance to learn anything more before I go. I pack my supply bag with the few things I'll need, plus the stuff from GrimJack's, just in case. Can't find anything that will calm my nerves, though. I touch the stream for a soothing audio, something by TeaTim, but even that doesn't help. The bells only increase my anxiety.

Getting to the next zone is fairly easy. Downrider North to the flash train. Four hours by flash, then another hurdle by airstream. I'm there with plenty of time to spare.

I'm in no rush, though. I wait two hours in the studiopad—watching the saucer-shaped lift travel down the ribbon. Thousands of tons descend, loaded. Thousands of tons return, loaded. An elevator to the stars.

It is like the old days, I tell myself. Like an expectant lover watching a mate arrive by ferry. Slow and steady—except this time it doesn't go horizontal, it goes vertical. Up, up, shifting with the winds, but still going up. All the way to black, where only blue hangs below.

I don't like any of it.

Debuggers don't ride lifts. They don't go to space. That's for tourists and bots. Thrillseekers and the ironclad. I know the ride is supposed to be smooth, supposed to be safe. But that's all theory to me. Plus there's the pending darkness.

Some of us did it, though. They must have or none of it would work. How did they manage?

Finally it is my turn. Either go now or be tardy. I couldn't handle the headbuzz for being late, so I go. Hoist my supply bag, follow the rest of the passengers onboard.

The lift is big—large enough that you don't have to look outside at all if you don't want to. Most do, though. As soon as we're onboard they rush to the windowed sections to watch.

Not me. I hit the stream for the lift's specs: raw tonnage, last time of service, number of bots present. Answers: 6,560, day 23, and twenty-six—with seven being servbots of various models, manufacturers, and press dates. I head for the lift's center.

I feel the lift begin to ascend. Due to acceleration dampening, the change is minimal—I doubt most humans would detect it. Would even pause in their stride.

I'm more sensitive than most. I know our measurable speed is increasing and the safety of the base tower—and the attached studiopad—is quickly sliding away. Soon all that will prevent us from plunging to Earth will be an absurdly thin ribbon. A tenuous carbon string.

My life is spent on strings.

The lift provides a small shopping area on the inside. A "mall" is what they used to call it. Rows of goods and shinys enclosed in glass. Little of what is sold here appeals to me: reading materials, clothing...hair products! I frown at the things that warrant the average Abdul's attention and credits. For a people so concerned with the next life, they seem eager to collect a lot of ballast in this one.

I walk the nearly empty corridors, my face a mask. Most of the merchants are still setting up. They expect that passengers will spend the first hour of the journey gazing outside, I reason. A few of the shopkeepers look surprised to see me walk by. I ignore their lingering stares. In the past, a bald head signaled age, sickness, style, or rebellion—now it's a sign of slavery. Not physical, but mental.

The stream is available to me here too, of course. I could find a corner to park in, close my eyes, and lose myself for hours. Delve into whatever subject piques my interest. Communicate with other DRs, peruse the new spec tables.

I choose not to, though. Mostly I want to distract my mind from the subtle shifts I feel, the indications that we are indeed moving upward, no matter how gravitationally dampened. If I keep myself moving, keep my eyes observing, then maybe...

I pause at a store that caters to pets. In the window is a cluster of puppies. Cautiously, I stoop to look. There is a mixture of breeds within, a smaller shorthaired variety and a larger huskier one. The smaller ones, the shorthairs, mostly clump together around the food and water. The larger ones are more gregarious—walking the window, yipping and jumping, biting at each other. A welcome diversion. Minutes go by as I watch.

Finally, the most boisterous husky approaches a shorthair and places a paw squarely on its forehead. It is a motion I know well: submit now or else.

GrimJack's scar.

Expecting a belly-up surrender, I shake my head and stand up. Nearly walk away. I give a final look at the confrontation—and smile. The small pup is on his feet now, looking the large one in the eyes. The latter is only playing, but I don't think the small one is. He only wants to be left alone.

Unconsciously I raise a fist. Then, frowning, I put it down. No buzz yet, but I know it is always a possibility when thoughts become action.

Eventually the lift has risen far enough that the sightseers begin to make their way to the inner mall area. Family groups, all in their robes, turbans, and burqas, troll the places I've already been, filling the mall with new noises and smells. I start to stick out, evidenced by the increasing stares. They need me but they don't want me—not in their everyday. That's how my life is.

I consider finding a place to stream now. I could use the time to catch up on things I've missed while living in the physical. The controlled stream is so often like a rice dish, though—an occasional bit of meat or sauce covering a mound of bland. There will be some things that interest me, of course, but those can be difficult to find. I wish for the bit of freedom I touched under the bridge—in Hard's Outer-Mog spot.

I feel a tiny lurch then. Grit my teeth.

An Abdul approaches, self-assured, fine linens, all the proper tucks and creases. Full length umber robe, shiny gold vest. I think of turning my head, acting like I don't notice. How bad would it be if I simply ran away? My kind are known for idiosyncrasies, for our "quirks." It probably wouldn't be that bad.

Instead, I watch him, humorously.

He stops, straightens himself, gives a subtle shake to move everything into place. "Debugger," he says directly to me, "I require your services."

"I'm on a job already." I can't help myself. This Abdul needs my ire.

His eyes widen, and I swear, a lock of hair springs out of place. Mission accomplished.

"Here?" he asks. "On the lift?"

"Discussion of my current job is forbidden. You should know that." I touch the stream with this guy's image, just to see if he shows up on any important lists, like *Abduls Who Beat Debuggers*. He doesn't.

He seems even more bothered now. To compensate, he smoothes the back of his head. "Listen, I need your help." He reaches into his vest and produces an ivory-colored crescent. He shows it to me, then wraps his hand around it. "I have a controller."

It certainly looks like a controller, which is bad news for me. I don't need any more head buzzes today. By law—current law—he doesn't have the right to use it. I'm on a job already and thereby disqualified from any ad hoc duties. This guy looks itchy, though, and the chances of me protecting my rights here on a lift are slim. I search the immediate area. Others are staring at me now. Even the nearest shop owner has paused in the midst of dispensing creamdots.

That's another part of my problem: any of these others might get the idea they can ride this guy's controller. Repair my personal steamer, debugger. Fix the reception on my headpatch. So I've got two choices: run—and risk the controller—or go with this guy quickly.

Frowning, I nod. "Show me."

He pockets the controller and turns. I assume it will be a short walk, but I'm mistaken. This guy actually has some credits. We end up at one of the lift's few apartments.

A lift's journey to space isn't long enough that most people feel the need to have a place to stay throughout. When the tourism and shopping is done, there are numerous lounges to sit in, plus entertainment of the streaming and non-streaming variety. But not this guy. He has a habitat. And by the looks of the heavy door and thick blue carpeting, it is a nice one.

I sense that there is one servbot within, along with two petbots.

"It is my spouse," he says as we enter the sumptuous main room.

I stop. As plugged in as I am, there's little I can do for the living.

In typical Abdul fashion, there are many small Abduls nearby. Four swarm from an adjoining room to greet their father, but go ice when they see me. Dark eyes become chasms. The senior Abdul ignores them, leading me instead to a bonafide bedroom, complete with a veiled canopy bed and matching divan. The colors are blue and gold.

I didn't even know they had sleeping arrangements on lifts. Of course, lifts aren't one of my favorite subjects. This Abdul definitely has means.

His wife is lying on the bed, fully covered in a black burqa, including over her face—as I would expect.

"It is her heartpiece," he says. "I believe the programming has deteriorated. She feels too tired to get up."

"You need a med-op for this," I say. "A med*bot*, at the least." DRs are versatile, but there are some things we're not to work on. Human appliances is one of them.

"It is the programming," the man insists. "You can fix it."

I shake my head. "No, I can't. Not in my primary. Not in my files. Can't." Medical implants like the one his wife has would require me to be in close contact with her anyway and I doubt he would want that. We're like lepers, remember.

The controller reappears. "I *will* use this. Without hesitation."

Now all I want is to clock the guy, except with all the kids around I figure that is a no-go. While I'm still mulling, he dismisses them. They filter out, having said little since they first saw me. Then I notice another person in the room, a bigger person. A bodyguard standing silently behind a velvet curtain. Odds here for a flyweight debugger don't seem good.

Who am I kidding—I would've gotten buzzed anyway.

Time to use reason. "Listen, you don't want me messing with her. I could seriously make things worse. I'm sure there is a med onboard somewhere..."

Another wave of his controller. "I found you first. Help her." The curtain ripples as the man behind it steps out. Big lotta Abdul. His face is clean-shaven and expressionless. Don't need expression when you got muscles. Or a voice.

One more try. "I would have to get close to her."

The man's eyebrows lift. "Close to her? " he says. "How close?"

Bingo. "I may need to touch her to interface with the heartpiece," I say, keeping the emotion low. "Usually the port is under the left breast."

That brings a definitive head shake. "No," he says. "It is forbidden."

Knew that would work. *Knew* it.

The head shake continues. "It is not necessary, debugger. She broadcasts into the local stream. You can get a reading from there. Work your magic."

Rails. Really rails. "Her heartpiece sings to the stream? Full band?"

"I don't know the banding," he says, "but she has the top of the line. Installed last month." That brings a smile to his hairy face—talking about his wife like she's the latest bit of vid equipment. If there were a gold-plated model, I'm sure he would've sprung for it.

I feel a deep longing for my chute right now.

"Try it," he says with an assuring nod. "You will see." His eyes move to the top of my head, then back to meet my own eyes, hard. "Stream, debugger," he says. "Just stream."

I glance at BigUgly in the corner. He hasn't changed one iota since I looked last. Same position, same expression. I hate him now.

Without closing my eyes, I touch the stream.

Most people think we have to close our eyes to do so, but we don't. No way am I closing my eyes on these two anyway.

I get a sense of a nearby machine. Not biomed... something strange. Whatever it is, it is interfering. "You have something else switched on?" I ask. "Something that broadcasts? Something that pulls?"

The man with the controller looks surprised for a moment then snaps his fingers. Smiling, he motions to BigUgly, who pulls out a small rolled item—an organizer of some sort—and unrolls it. After a few moments of playing with it, he nods. His boss smiles and nods, signaling I should try again.

Which I do. The big disturbance is clearly gone, and I *do* get the sense of his wife's heartpiece...I think. The nanos in it are singing out. But not loud enough.

"This won't work," I say. "The signal isn't strong enough. I can't tell anything."

The man glances at my supply bag, the one I've had slung over my shoulder the entire time. "You have nothing with you that can help? I understood debuggers have instruments they can use."

I almost smile at that. A sheet would likely *stop* her heart by mistake. And a light probe? I have no idea what that would do, but it wouldn't be pretty. "Nothing that wouldn't hurt her."

He glances at the floor, stumped.

I give him a little help. Don't want to get myself on some *Bad Debugger* list I wasn't aware of. "You know where the broadcast comes from? Is it under her breast as well?"

That brings a derisive sneer. Probably all the talk about his wife's breast. I think maybe he'll go ahead and use that controller anyway. He doesn't say or do anything, though. Just thinks for a moment. "I believe it is on her leg," he says finally. "On her left leg."

I nod. Now we're getting somewhere. Sooner I find that heartpiece the sooner I can confirm I can't fix it. "Can you uncover it?" I say. "It should help."

He hesitates. Come on, Abdul. I'm not going to touch her. Don't worry.

Finally, after an inordinate amount of time, he reaches out and pushes the black material up, exposing her left leg to the knee. I'm surprised by what I see, and in that slightly altered state I step forward. It is a big mistake.

Startled, the husband raises the controller and presses it.

A line of pain connects my ears. Crying out, I stumble forward, but closer to his wife—which I'm sure he doesn't want. He begins to babble in one of their obscure languages. Something I could easily translate if there weren't this little catastrophe going on in my head. My hands come to my ears, clawing for something they'll never reach.

Stupid, Abdul. Rails stupid.

I pry my eyes open enough to see that I'm now kneeling at the bedpost. The wife's uncovered leg is right there in front of me. *Right there!* I could almost touch it. The skin is colored gold and mottled with—

The pain stops and large hands grip me, bring me to my feet and away from the bed. Someone, in a gruff and thickly accented voice, commands me to "Stand!" and I'm fine with that. Glad to be farther away from all of them. BigUgly moves past me, returning to his normal subservient position.

I still hate him.

"See, debugger, I told you I would use it."

I close my eyes and massage my temple. It isn't where the pain was, but somehow it feels good. I'm really railed. "You expect me to help you now," I say. "After that?"

"You almost touched my wife," he says. "I told you..." He looks more nervous now than ever. That's not so inexplicable. I have a fair idea why. Those "discolorations" on her leg.

His wife begins moaning, which is the first I've heard from her. She still isn't moving, though.

The pain is fully gone now. I want to get this done and over. I put a hand up in surrender, touch the stream...

There it is, the nanos from her heartpiece singing out at me. It is a random, arbitrary tune—a dark symphony. In the background is the beat of a drum, the amplified sound of her heart. But even that is a jumble. No wonder she doesn't want to get up. What is it, nanos? What's the story?

Her implant does more than keep a human heart in rhythm, I discover. It is doing part of the chore. It mostly involves the muscle on the right side...

I go stream wide for more information. The right side collects the oxygen-starved blood from the body into the right atrium and moves it—pumps it—into the lungs for a gas swap. CO_2 out, O_2 in. *Got it.*

Her muscle on that side is weak, and the implant is supplementing it somehow. That isn't working, though, not quite. Now I need some datasheets. I need to see what bits the implant is following. It's difficult, because the individual nanobots are playing together loosely. Part of them are singing well, the rest not so much. Code, I need some code! I grab a singer, roll his stream, look for his markings. There!

There is a problem. Her implant is reacting to high levels of stress. It shouldn't be. She's prone—there should be little stress.

Wait, of course!

Pain. It would make sense considering what I saw. Abduls—are there any decent ones left?

I search for the heartpiece manufacturer. Recalls, studies, something that could help with the fix. Most of the biomed stuff is closely guarded, though. As it should be.

"Do you know something?" the Abdul asks, oblivious to how we work.

I'm trying to fix your problem here. I shake my head, close my eyes tighter. Not now. *Not now!*

I find something. There is a fix out there. I can't believe this, can't believe I'm actually thinking of doing this. I'm a conduit now. Filling myself with data. I examine the code line by line. Get a good sense for what it is doing. I call out to the singers in her heartpiece again, get them to listen to me. They ask for identification.

Bites. I open my eyes. "Her normal med-op? Do you have an ident?"

He stares at me, looking lost. The missus moans again, louder now, and I know why. Some of the important nanos are freewheeling. Getting totally out of sync. Gotta fix that. Fast!

Abdul finally wakes up and runs to a nearby dresser. Opening it, he pulls out a stack of circular cards. Hands one to me.

"What is this?" I ask.

"Ident," he says. "Med-op ident."

I hope he's right. I focus my attention on the card. It looks legit. I find the information I want, then briefly wonder where he got it. Lots of credit, this guy. I sing out to the nanos again. They accept the ident.

Straighten up! Pull into sync! I transmit the changes. Push them along.

The song shifts, and for a moment I think I got it wrong. Some of the little movers signal they're ceasing. That can't be right, can it?

No!

Yes, yes, it is right. They're returning to form. The ones out of sync had to stop to get back in rhythm. Some had to pause to find their rhythm, is all.

I hear the lady gasp—a breath of cool, fresh air.

Move, little soldiers. Strengthen, pump, move that gas along.

With the fix in place I lock it down. Clean any messes I've made along the way. Not a lot of space in those little guys. Don't want to waste anything. Are we good? We're good. "I'm leaving now," I sing to them. They ignore me, but they understand. They'll do their best.

The woman's response is immediate. She rises in her bed and looks at me. I can only see her eyes through the burqa, but they are wide—scared? I hope not, not too much. My changes are solid, but they're not completely proven. I'm not a med-op!

Lay down, I think and put out a hand. I still don't know what language they speak. I look at her husband, who now seems genuinely relieved. "Tell her to relax," I say.

He immediately follows with a burst of speech. The woman remains sitting, though, staring at me—which I'm normally used to, but this time it is troubling. Her eyes soften and the skin near the corners wrinkle. I think she is smiling. That's good. Good for you, lady. Glad I could brighten your day, because I think you probably need it.

"You've done it?" the husband asks, as if the woman sitting up isn't enough of an indication. "She will be all right?"

I stifle a shoulder shrug, though it is my first impulse. "Seems like." I back up, instinctively searching for the door. The room has small windows in the far side wall, which I hadn't noticed before. The view outside is almost pitch-colored. If I looked longer I might even see stars. I don't *want* to look longer, though.

"Wait, debugger," the man says, and begins to ruffle through his vest pockets.

I feel a shot of fear. This guy is not the caring husband and father he might have others believe.

I saw.

My fears are bogus, though. He pulls free a golden disk and hands it to me. "This for your help," he says and gives me a look that is one part gratitude and two parts threat. BigUgly grunts from the corner. That is probably all parts threat.

I take the disk and look it over. It is engraved, has the silhouette of a woman on one side, a bird on the other.

"It is a *coin*," he says. "A solid gold coin."

I can't help but frown. What am I supposed to do with it? Give it to GrimJack? Let him slag it for his experiments?

"It is worth many credits," he says, and I believe him by how he says it. "Many, many credits."

Nodding, I slip the coin into the chest pocket on my jumpsuit. The pocket automatically seals it within. The man returns to conversation with his wife, the focus of his full attention now. That's my ticket to leave.

A short time later I'm back at the mall, searching for a place to eat in the few minutes before the lift reaches the top-end station—silently hoping the guy doesn't beat his wife again before I can get off.

THE LIFT ARRIVES right on schedule. I'm told they always do. I join the mass of people as they exit the lift and move to the sandstone-colored causeway leading to the station.

The atmosphere is all controlled here, but they can do little about the slight bounce to our step. No matter what they learn about gravitons, they still can't quite make space feel *right*, like home. I'm not speaking from experience, of course. This is my first time up—first time ever on a lift.

I'm not wild about any of it.

Furthering my distress is the fact that somebody forced—and I say *forced* because I can imagine no other way it would happen—the designers to put windows in the causeway floor. That's real nice...*if* you want reminded that you're a thousand kilometers high. I don't, and it is all I can do to make myself move forward, keep my feet enabled, you know?

I spend most of the traversal staring at the ceiling, which someone had the foresight to paint sky blue. Comforting, except there are small windows there too. Space is much darker than you might think.

The station itself is minimalist. Light colors and few things to attract someone's attention. No shops, no ads, no animals. That's fitting, though, because it is a mere pass-thru for most people. A means to a better destination. There is only a small sampling of the "prosperous life" posters one would see everywhere down below. Pictures of bountiful harvests and fattened livestock. Lies filled with color.

Soon after boarding, I feel a slight tingle in my head. Nothing unpleasant like a full-on buzz, only a reminder that I'm here for a reason, that I'm not out of their reach. I wonder if they've been playing that tune all day for me, or if they knew exactly when I'd arrive.

Probably the latter. Debuggers tend to be predictable.

Regardless, after the tingle comes a summons. Directions travel with the signal so I follow them perfectly. This means I leave the tourists behind. They will board another craft on their way to a low orbit cruise or fancy hotel. Somewhere pretty and wonderful.

But not me. I'm brought instead to a hallway that traces the station's exterior wall. After ten minutes of walking and "window avoidance" I'm brought to the far side and another surprise.

I reach a set of double-locking doors—the kind that take a high clearance level to enter—only to have them whisk open before me. I pause a moment, cautious and thoughtful. I then remember my promotion to level 13. The upgrade must have cleared me for this door. There is no other likely explanation. I walk through and they snap closed behind me.

Beyond the doors, the hallway widens to three meters. Large enough to move heavy equipment around. Clearly such width is no longer necessary, though. The hall is completely empty aside from me. There is no decoration. Only white walls and checkered floor. It shouts a simple message: do not linger here.

Streaming now, I sense devices in the ceiling. Sneaky devices—nasty devices. *Security devices.* They might not kill a man, but they would sure make him hurt. I also detect recording mechanisms, cameras...loudspeakers. I'm in a restricted area, of that there is no doubt.

A short, naturally-balding man approaches me. He's dressed almost entirely in orange—like one of those historical spacesuits I've streamed about—except it isn't quite right. There is no puffiness to the material and, more importantly, no bubble helmet. Wouldn't want to be consistent! The fact that he's bald is a little unusual too. Most non-debuggers have that fixed these days. The only thing truly normal about the man's appearance is his skin color: a warm brown.

"You are DR 63?" the man says. "Excuse me: Sandfly."

I nod.

The man extends a hand. A gloved hand, but a hand just the same. I hesitate, stare at the hand, contemplate what it would feel like to take it, and then, when I think I might actually do so, the hand is withdrawn.

The man smiles as if nothing has happened. "You may call me Scallop," he says, "*if* it makes you comfortable." The smile is reassuring, seemingly genuine. "We try to be as informal here as possible."

Scallop isn't his real name, of course. He's an Abdul too—a high-ranking one, judging from the rainbow of decorations on his lapels and the gold com device on his chest. Normally, only masters have those.

"We have only a small group here," Scallop continues. "Security and enforcement, a few service personnel..."

And a fair share of bots. Hundreds, if I read the stream correctly. Glancing up, I notice a duct for the station's circulation system. Inhabiting that hidden maze are dozens of fist-sized mechanical crickets, responsible for keeping the airways clean. In addition, I stream location idents from over forty servbots, both of the humanoid and non-humanoid variety. Medbots, squat maintenance bots, heavylifters...even a few exploration snakes.

"I assume you know all there is to know about DarkTrench?" Scallop asks.

"I was told very little," I say, the absolute truth. "My master said it wasn't necessary for me to know."

He gives a quick nod. "Formally, that's true." He indicates the hall ahead, motions for me to accompany him. "But as I said, we aren't completely formal here."

We travel some distance in silence, both trapped within the stark hallway walls. Then suddenly, ornamentation breaks out, but still in an austere fashion. Tiled mosaics fill the walls on both sides. The mosaic on the wall to our left is a portrait of the reigning Imam. He is dressed in black robe and turban—white beard perfectly trimmed, eyebrows dark and furrowed. His expression is one of intense study. The wall opposite is a picture of a spiral galaxy, an oval cloud filled with stars of orange, white, sapphire, and red. Our galaxy, I assume. A smorgasbord of potential stone.

We arrive at a silver moving walkway, which Scallop immediately enters. He leans on the side rail and lets the machine do its work. I get a chirp (stream-wise) indicating that the walkway is in need of repair, which causes me to hesitate before stepping on. But I decide to let that go and join him. As long as it doesn't accelerate me through the station walls, I figure I'll be all right.

As we slide along, Scallop talks—reiterating information I already know: DarkTrench is experimental, ultrasolar, able to flip, go places beyond dreams.

"Why?" I ask, halting his narration.

Scallop looks up at me quizzically, blue eyes burning. "Expanding the kingdom, of course." He nods. "Is there a better reason?"

I bow my head. "Of course not."

He smiles. "And there is the promise of additional resources, certainly."

We certainly need more of them. If it hadn't been for the discovery that petrol was renewable, things would be much worse than they are. Of course, Abduls had effectively won the world by then anyway. Then came the Engineers' Rebellion, the falling of Eiffel, the global purge...

The walkway makes a turn, and we pass another row of windows. I avert my eyes, but Scallop steps from the walkway and immediately grasps my elbow. "You must see this," he says.

The sensation of his grip is unfamiliar, unnecessary. I can't remember the last time I was touched, even by my own kind. There are few I'd *want* to have touch me. Maybe only one.

Hesitating only briefly, I let Scallop lead me. His grip is strong, regardless.

The darkness of space fills the window, equally alarming are the pinpricks of light—they're everywhere, and brilliant! More shocking than a clear night at home.

I shut my eyes. I want to close off, fall into the stream. The stream can be soothing, like a warm mental blanket.

"Look," he says. "There!"

I pry my eyes open. Squinting, I peer through the window, even as I try to keep as much of the void as possible diminished in my mind.

Then I see it. DarkTrench. Conical, shining, frictionless—a tapered cylinder flaring into a starburst tail.

"It is wonderful," I say, eyes now agape.

"It is," Scallop says, almost worshipfully. "An angel of the deep."

I shut my eyes again, searching the stream, hoping to touch the construct across the void. But of course I can't. It was an irrational desire—a lust, almost. I anticipate the buzz of correction, but it doesn't come.

"Who has made this?" I ask.

"Oh, many, many minds have worked on it. Some of the best DRs available—levels fourteen, fifteen." He smiles. "An occasional thirteen."

I nod, returning my view to the ship. A long umbilical connects the station to it. Clearly that is a foreign thing—stark white against DarkTrench's slate coloring. Yet it looks large and sturdy enough for transit. It must be how you get there from here.

Within, DarkTrench must seem like a symphony, a smorgasbord of singing machines...

Scallop touches my elbow again, coaxing me away. I politely remove myself, but manage a smile anyway. "DarkTrench has a problem for me to address?" I ask, hopeful. We return to the walkway and continue toward another set of doors.

"No, no," Scallop says. "DarkTrench is working perfectly. Completely in sync."

The walkway ends and I find myself tossed gently to the right. Thankfully, there is a handrail present. I correct myself without much embarrassment. We then proceed to the second set of doors, and pass through with little pause.

"In fact, DarkTrench just completed its maiden voyage," Scallops says. "Perfectly."

New information to me. Exciting and wondrous. "DarkTrench has gone out?" I say, stopping midstride. "It works?"

"Absolutely. As I said, she is an angel. She completed a trip to Bait al-Jauza."

It takes only a stream touch to understand. *Bait al-Jauza* is a corruption of the star name "yad al-jawza," which translates to "hand of the central one" in Old Standard. The literal meaning, though, comes closer to "armpit of the central one." Interesting choice, Abbys!

It is also known as Betelgeuse. A large red star.

"It is four hundred and twenty-seven light-years from here," Scallop says, smiling. "The trip was accomplished in less than a week."

I am impressed. Any debugger would be. Speed is where we live. "And Ab—" I start, then correct: "Humans were onboard?"

Scallop nods. "There were four in the crew," he says. "All returned safely."

He leads me through a labyrinth of white corridors. They all look the same to me. I hear unseen machines singing to me from everywhere. Finally he stops at a stream-aware grey door. He presses his palm to the lock.

I'm restraining anger. I had to ride a lift! Don't they understand how out of spec that is? "So what am I here for?" I ask. "If there is no problem with the ship, and the crew returned safely, why am I required?"

"There was another member of the crew," Scallop says.

The door slides open, and everything becomes like diamond. Shining and clear.

ON A TABLE in the middle of the room lies a servbot. In pieces.

I approach it respectfully, as if approaching a casket, and lay my hands on its pale oval head. My fingers drape over its endlessly staring eyes. Bowing my own head, I try a rudimentary communication link. All is quiet, though. The bot is as "toes up" as I've ever seen.

Servbots were my first specialty. They're as close as bots get to being human while still being primarily a mechanical device. Under current rules even that distinction has blurred. They are made to appear human. On the outside, a mostly realistic-looking synthskin is wrapped to make the servbot more approachable, able to cradle a baby if required. At a distance, you might not be able to tell robot from man. Much of the face is inanimate, though. For bot speech, a tongue is a terribly inefficient organ. Within, they are glass, metal, plastic, carbon, and lots of nanos dancing.

"What happened to it?" I ask.

Scallop frowns. "We're hoping you can tell us, of course. This is how it returned."

I pan the room for the first time. Nearly everything is white: white walls, white cabinets with countertop near the door, an off-white floor. The examination table itself is brown cushioned leather, as is the circular stool beside it. There is a silver wheeled cart near the table, an archaic moving-hands style clock on the wall near the cabinets, a diagnostic wallvid (stream-linked to the table), and a single piece of ornamentation on the wall opposite the door: a framed picture of a planet.

Because you can never have too much *space* represented.

"From the flip?" I ask. "This bot was on DarkTrench when it reached Bait al-Jauza?"

"Absolutely," Scallop says. "We wouldn't make such a trip without one."

His response is true on a number of levels. Abduls are heavily dependent on servbots. The heavy credit Abbys, like the wife-beater I met on the lift, usually have a houseful of them. Every menial task is performed by servbots. If programmed right, they can alleviate much of the need for a debugger. They can address the easy things, anyway. Makes sense they would take one on their way beyond our system. I'm surprised they didn't take more—and I say as much.

"It was only a there-and-back," Scallop says. "Proof of concept. When we return we'll take more. Many more." He studies the mess before me and shakes his head. "We hope to, anyway."

I can't resist trying to stream to the bot again. No-go, though. *Rails!*

"And the crew saw nothing?" I say. "They have no idea how this happened?"

"TallSpot and Handler were in the pilot's nest, nowhere near the bot. The other two, the scientists, were running tests in the lab adjoining the room where the robot was found. They say they heard noises—repetitive thumps—and then nothing."

I nod, and make a brief summary of the bot's parts. One leg has been amputated above the knee. The other is attached, but discolored. Both arms are severed. They lay on the left side of the body. There are tiny scorch marks on the thing everywhere, potentially from circuits having fried. I feel under the head, searching for something important.

I find only an abscess. I turn the head over to look. There is a large gash over an empty, two-centimeter slot.

"Where's the headchip?" I ask. Even early synthskin models like this one had headchips. It is central to the bot's functioning. Every primary process runs through it, every pathway touches it. The chip also acts like flypaper for everything the bot perceived, both audibly and visually. It is crucial to discovering what happened.

"We are not sure," Scallop says. "We believe the thumping noises account for that. The bot was found lying next to a steamer. We think it pounded its head on the duct."

I don't know whether to laugh or frown. I choose neither. "The robot ripped part of one leg off, disconnected both arms, then hobbled over to the steamer and cracked its cranium until it stopped functioning. Is that the story?" It would be near-schizophrenic behavior. I find it ridiculous.

Scallop shrugs. Not helpful.

I scan the bot again. "This is a model 19." I remember something about them. "Early on they had a recall because some of their fluids were ill-mixed." Could that create such behavior?

"It is clearly odd," Scallop says. "An answer is high priority."

I move to examine the bot's arms. They show little sign of abuse, surprisingly. They are simply disconnected. "All my jobs are high priority," I say, managing a smile. Especially when the customer holds a controller, as Scallop no doubt does.

Scallop nods. "But this time the whole DarkTrench program is at stake."

Blinking *what?* "I've never seen an operation like this held up because of a bot," I say. "Certainly you have another—"

"Regulations require that we know exactly what happened before we continue. The crew isn't allowed to leave the restricted area until we know. In fact, they still wear their suits." Scallop pauses. "It has been a few days already. They are getting anxious."

It has always been this way, even before the implants and the controllers. Whatever the situation, a debugger's work has to be done immediately. I can't help but sigh. "There isn't much to go on here. No headchip...no streaming..."

"We need an answer."

I glance at the framed picture. It is not Earth, that much is certain. It is a blue-shrouded monstrosity.

Challenges are what we're made for, Sand. They keep us useful. Not decommissioned.

And DarkTrench. It deserves to fly...

Scallop takes a step toward the door. "I have duties to attend to. And so do you."

Another part of my psyche, a hidden part, stirs, and for an instant I wish they had called someone else. Deep down I've always known I'd come upon a task somewhere that is too big for me. Is this it?

Shouldn't they have gotten one of the debuggers that worked on the project? "I was level 12 only a few days ago," I say. "Why me?" I don't expect a proper answer, but I have to ask.

He shrugs. "No offense, but does it matter with your kind, really? Aren't you nearly interchangeable?"

I shake my head. "That's a common misconception. We have levels. Areas of expertise."

"But you are all connected in the same way. Touch the stream equally."

"I suppose that's true—"

"And servbots are in your area of expertise, are they not?"

"Yes, but..."

He shrugs, takes another step toward the door. "Consider yourself lucky then. You are one of the few who has seen DarkTrench. Even those that worked on it had limited access to the whole operation. You will be unlimited in your investigation."

What there will be of it. I can't imagine finding anything new. This bot is dead.

"Unlimited?" I say, grasping the scope of Scallop's words. "Even the ship?" That wondrous, amazing ship...?

He nods, smiling. "Yes," he says. "Even the ship, if necessary."

I glance at the bot. "But my master said—"

Scallop raises a hand. "And *I* have said that station formalities are different from those below." A reassuring smile. "Not to fear, Sandfly. I am the master here. No one will stand in the way of your investigation. No one will pursue repercussions later."

I stare wide-eyed for many moments before finally managing a single head bow of gratitude.

Scallop mirrors the bow. "I will go now."

I return my attention to the bot. I barely hear the door close.

I DROP MY SHOULDER, shake the supply bag loose, and let it descend my arm to the top of the wheeled cart. I make use of the stool. I sit there for three whole minutes, just appraising the mess. Eyes stare blindly at the ceiling. Tendrils of discoloration everywhere. Arms lined up like dead white eels.

I shake my head. The sight makes me uncomfortable, a bit below level. What do I do now? Where do I start?

I hear GrimJack's voice from earlier days. "Eliminate the cripples!" he would say, by which he meant "Fix the easy problems first." Sometimes that helps get the brain moving toward the bigger target. Sometimes not. Regardless, the saying has relevance here. The bot is as crippled as they come.

I unzip my bag, curling the edges back so I'll be able to see within easily. I reach for the bot's left arm, check the fingers, test their flexibility. All seem to function. I examine the ball joint on the other end. Whatever took it off did so cleanly. It is virtually undamaged. I even detect the shine of viable cohesion nanos still on the surface. Shrugging, I lift the arm to where it fits into the bot's shoulder. Give it a shove.

Thwup! The arm moves into place. A small success.

The right arm is equally pristine, but a portion of the shoulder socket is not. There is some scoring, a clear marring of the smoothness. I pull a slipshaper from my bag. The handle of the tool fits snugly in my hand. The working end has two prongs, between which an adjustable molding arc is generated. I set the appropriate concavity and grit setting and put the tool to work. There is a slight flash as the arc works the rough spots into the socket. A few minutes later it measures smooth.

I bring the arm up and shove it into the shoulder. No connection. Another trip to the bag, this time for a small bugwedge. I press the wedge to the socket's edge. Try the arm against it. The arm goes in. No sound this time, though.

The leg is another story. The knee socket is completely missing. Again, I am struck by the amount of overall damage. My impulse is to disbelieve Scallop and his assumptions about the crew. I can't imagine the bot doing all this damage itself. More likely, the Abduls got bored and decided to have a knockdown on the only thing available. A couple weeks away might do that to a person, especially to someone without streaming abilities. Rails, those Abbys attacked HardCandy, and they weren't even in space.

I glance at the clock, watch the second hand steadily advance.

I wonder what this "flipping" would do to a body. To a mind—human or synthetic. Had sufficient testing been done? Or were they in such a hurry to get "there and back" that they didn't give latent repercussions a second thought?

Best not to linger on Abdul motives for too long. The mental lash is always waiting. And I'm certain these highlevel debuggers Scallop mentioned *would* think of such things, even if their Abdul masters did not.

I return my attention to the leg. Can I manufacture a new socket? I reach into my bag and bring out a packet of plyagel. It is a staple for debuggers, an item we always carry. The packet is hermetically sealed and divided into two chambers. When the seal between them is broken, a malleable plastic is formed.

I break the seal and press the resulting substance into the hole at the base of the bot's thigh. I make use of the shaper again, reshaping and accelerating. Finally I think I have something that might work. I next break out a carton of generic nanos. I stream, looking for the proper instruction set, and feed them that. After smoothing the nanos themselves into the new socket, I pull the calf section close and shove.

Twhooop! Leg attached.

Not bad, Sandfly. Might earn your credits today, after all.

With some effort, I reposition the bot on the table so it is sitting up. The eyes stare straight ahead, mindlessly. I wish for the nanoprobe I'd asked GrimJack for.

Stupid Imam, stupid leadership, stupid rules...

I feel the sting of caution and wince. The new rules are a part of my control matrix already. Not surprising.

"So, what do I do with you now, bot?" I ask aloud. "You look presentable, but you've got no life, and no headchip..."

I lean forward and trace one of the scorch marks. It starts at the neck and works down to the chest. Servbots are normally dressed in servant wear—robes of green—but not this one. It is completely exposed. Naked. The normal robes hide little, of course. Servbots may look similar to humans, but they have none of the things that people hide. The robes are for ornamentation, and to make masters comfortable.

The scorch marks are pathways that have fried, I'm confident now. This bot is ready for disposal.

Sighing, I cross my arms and straighten in the stool. I stream out for the nearest communication hub. I need to update my master. No sense wasting time.

I find my outgoing message blocked.

The door slides open and Scallop enters. "Were you trying to send something out?"

The question surprises me, because that would be a lot for him to know. And so quickly.

Nasty, sneaky machines on this station.

"I was," I say, frowning. "I need additional instructions from my master. This bot is unserviceable."

Scallop looks sympathetic. "You will not be able to message out from here. The facility is protected."

"Protected?"

"There are stops in place. Messages cannot be transmitted from here to the outside. It is the rule. Too much data may be present." He gives the bot a protracted look. "You've made some progress, I see."

"Meaningless progress." I stand, letting a hand fall onto the cushioned table beside the bot. "I can do little more."

Scallop's stance tightens. "An answer is required for why the bot has malfunctioned," he says, sounding a bit severe. "No one can leave until we know."

I feel for them. Really, I do. Stuck so far above the Earth. There's no way that can be comfortable.

Empathy isn't a specialty of mine, but I force some anyway. "I apologize..." I pat the bot's repaired knee and frown. "Even debuggers have limits." I drift toward the door.

Scallop remains in my way, unflinchingly. "I am sorry too. Perhaps you misunderstood. This mission is of the utmost importance. You are here at my request. If you can write this off as a natural phenomenon, or explain it in some way with a high percentage of certainty, then we can close the case and you may go home. But until that time..." He smiles. "It is late," he says. "Perhaps if you slept on the problem." He stretches a hand toward the door. "We have facilities for you here."

Scallop has a push I don't like, but his offer has merit. "You have cinder chutes available?"

He pauses, searches for words. "No, I—"

Bites. "Then I doubt sleep will help."

Scallop looks at me blankly, hand dropping to his side.

I start my best freehead analogy. "Imagine a vid projection that plays non-stop for twenty-four hours a day," I say. "It may even be something that you enjoy. The content doesn't matter. It plays continually all day, every day. Now imagine it plays in a sealed room, and it plays at a volume that cannot be ignored. That's the room we live in." I force a smile. "Except we can't shut our eyes or plug our ears."

"But you control your connection to the stream, correct?" Scallops says. "Turn it off and on at will?"

"That's true," I say. "But not while we're sleeping. You'd think the designers would've thought of that, found a way for us to be truly off-stream, but they didn't." I shrug. "Even chutes don't remove the stream's flow completely. They just mute it enough to make true sleep possible."

Except it probably isn't what he would call true sleep either.

Scallop does a little nervous bounce. "But won't the stops I mentioned help?" he asks. "Reduce communication?"

I sniff. "Outgoing stops?" I say. "Hardly."

So like an Abdul. Never researching, never thinking things through.

"But don't block the stream completely," I add, feeling a little nervous now too. "If you want your problem solved."

Scallop raises his eyebrows. "Completely?" he says. "Oh, no, I wouldn't do that. Couldn't. I didn't realize..."

How could he not? "You had debuggers on the station before, right?" I say. "Working on DarkTrench?"

Scallop glances at the bot, nods. "Yes, of course. But conditions were different then. I didn't think that such a short period of time would make your extended sleep requirements necessary."

I look at the counter behind him, noting three transparent cylinders there. "Chute sleep isn't just an extended sleep requirement," I say. "It refines memories, filters essentials..."

I watch for a bit of recognition, some sympathy in his face.

I get nothing. More analogy needed.

"You know how you can be thinking about a problem before sleep and have the solution appear—large and obvious—when you awake?" I ask. "Multiply that by a thousand. That's what chute sleep represents for us. It's an integral part of our usefulness. As important as the tools we carry."

It *is* possible for us to sleep without a chute—sometimes there is no choice. That is a fits-and-starts proposition, though. Information circles our heads like a vulture, waiting to invade our dreams at any time.

Imagine riding an elephant in the Congo when a modern building suddenly drops into your path. Or leaning in for your first kiss only to have her head change to lettuce. Alarming!

Hallucinations are only part of the problem. There are longterm risks, as well. Stories of debuggers who have expired from what they've seen...

Scallop is still thinking, his inherent slowness beginning to show. "You do get fatigued, though, don't you?" he says. "Like the rest of us?"

"Not like the rest of you," I say. "*Never* like the rest of you." I force the edge away. "But yes, I get tired. I feel tired."

He smiles, holds his hand out again. "Then perhaps, if you rest." He steps forward and touches the wallplate, opening the door. "Come, I'll show you to your room."

THE ROOM SCALLOP GIVES ME is clearly painted in such a way to give the illusion of one direction being "up." The wall coloring—a soft blue—varies slightly from ceiling to floor, with the lightest shade being on top. A remnant from when the station was lacking proper gravity, I assume.

Not having a proper *up* direction can be confusing for some people. I may be one of those people. I hope never to find out.

Otherwise, the room is unremarkable. It has a standard Abdul bed, medium firmness; the common lavatory implements—a rectangular full length steamer, a circular wasteunit; and a small simulated-wood desk. The predominant color is silver. Silver with a hint of rose. Weird mixture, I know, but that's how it is. A touch of incense, a pomegranate blend, is in the air, doubtless customizable for personal taste.

In one corner of the room stands a white sajada tube—a cylinder used for the storage and cleaning of prayer rugs. The presence of the device makes me smile, because even if I wanted to use the rug it contains, the direction the designs on the sajada would traditionally point—toward M—would pose a bit of a problem. Maybe not in zero gees, however.

Plus, we debuggers are exempted from the usual prayer requirements. "Our work is our prayer," they say.

The room has a small, rectangular porthole window. I'm sure many see that window as a benefit, something you pay extra for. But the last thing I want to do is look outside. To do so *accidentally* would be truly frightening.

Unless...

This is weird, because even though I categorically don't want to look outside, I feel drawn to the window anyway. Abduls speak about the first man and a garden with forbidden, yet irresistible, fruit. The tug I get from that porthole must be similar.

Perhaps some of their stories are true.

I walk to the window and glance out—squinting, of course. Reducing one's vision is necessary because the Earth fills half the window's vista. It is really bright.

I quickly turn from that, avoiding disaster, and focus to my right. There I can see the back half of DarkTrench, moored to the station. The ship's starburst section is one of the few parts that isn't perfectly smooth. It has a wave pattern to its surface. Difficult to describe adequately, and a bit disorienting to stare at for long, but remarkable just the same.

Leaving the window, I return to sit on the bed. Am I a prisoner here? The notion worries me a bit. But I'm something of a prisoner no matter where I go. Always at someone's beck and call. Only a head buzz away from submission.

I feel a weight in my chest pocket. Touching the clasp mechanism to release it, I pull out the coin Wife-Beater gave me. Holding it up, I stream at it absently, as if it will respond. It is relaxing to push out a stream. There is a certain warm feel to it, a release. And the coin is as good an object as any to push on.

I get no new information that way, though. So I resort to regular optics.

One side of the coin has a drawing of a bird on it. I know because I recognize the wings. Beneath that is what looks like a sunrise. Above the bird are words, but those are mostly worn away. All I can definitively make out is "States." On the other side of the coin is a standing woman. Actually, she could be walking, as her right leg looks shorter than her left.

Just like the broken bot, I think and smile.

So the coin woman is either walking or has a leg that is malformed. There is a lot of wearing on her side of the coin as well. I think the woman once had hair and was holding something in her left hand, but those details are completely gone. She's missing a hand and nearly bald. I think of HardCandy. The word "Liberty" is inscribed above her.

"'It is worth many credits,'" I say aloud. "'Many, many credits.'" With a sniff, I tuck the coin away.

HardCandy! I wish I could touch her—streaming, of course. Aside from that one instance when she let her guard down immediately following the driftbarge incident, she's been completely cold to me. Out of reach. Got her shell up big. I have a gleam that she's softer on me than most, though.

At least, so I thought before GrimJack's.

Now, I know what you are wondering, freehead. You're wondering if debuggers are like other humans in regards to the opposite sex. You might even be wondering if we are "sexed" at all.

How base-10 of you.

Physically, I assure you we are completely normal. But, due to the head noise—due to our "place in life"—that fact becomes almost trivial. We live so much of our lives "serving" that we have less time for those pursuits that others find natural. And less drive for them as well.

Then there is that little issue of the head buzz. Can't leave that out of the picture. Omnipresent, always judging—or bringing the sting of rebuke. Actions can hurt!

Everything is arranged these days, anyway. Abdul marriages are arranged. Debugger marriages are arranged—arranged not to happen. "You don't have time for such things," they say. And they mean it. We *do not* have time.

I think about the bot, wondering if I could get it switched on again as it stands. Sure, it would have none of the critical memories, but if I could get it moving again, that would be significant, wouldn't it? Show more forward progress.

The model I'm dealing with here is the RS-19. Those went into service before I was born. I've never actually debugged one before. But many servbot systems are standard, predictable. For instance, there aren't too many ways you can engineer an eye. Someone came to that conclusion about human eyes long ago, I think. Change too many things, maybe anything, and the system falls apart. Becomes a big white ball of goo. Same holds true for a servbot. Some things are optional, some things change, but many, many things remain the same.

Still, there are thousands of models.

I hit the stream, testing Scallop's blocks again. They still won't let me communicate, which rails me, but they have left most of the general information available. That's good, because I have something I need to check.

I find the quadrant for the botmaker—Elipserv. A big conglomerate they are. I check the stats of the RS-19, and dive into the service records. Good marks, that model. Explains why they took it on DarkTrench. The joke's on them, though, because theirs is busted now.

Better to bust an old model than a new one, Sand. Credits don't come cheap. That much is demonstrable, that much is true.

Some of the Elipserv models have a streamside backup system, which keeps the important information safe and comfortable. Would this model have one of those? Could I get that lucky?

I'm not hopeful, but I check anyway…

Rails! No fortune for me. Streamside backup started only four models ago. Long after the RS-19. Another wall of stone.

Now I wish I had someone like GrimJack or HardCandy to touch with, bounce ideas off. I feel really alone.

Or maybe I'm tired.

I slide down in the bunk, knowing it will only be a short nap. Stupid Scallop!

A little sleep might help, though.

I think.

THE NIGHT WAS BETTER than I expected—not great, not satisfying—but not terrible, either. I woke only three times. The first was because my head collided with the wall. That's not unusual, really—the chute has a track for our heads. The second time was because I had a dream about traveling in a two-ped downrider with the reanimated bot. He told me about his flowerpot named QuarterThree and his hexadecimal friend named QueenElizabeth before I awoke.

How could anyone sleep through that?

The third time I awoke was after my second dream, which featured cauliflower stalks. They were everywhere. Growing in a vat of cheese that could also stream vids. Nanos were carrying the signal...

Dreams are weird without the chute.

I glance up at the window again. From this perspective there is nothing but blackness visible. That's good—it helps me refocus.

I get a head buzz from Scallop, inviting me to the refectory. I'm fine with that. I stream him my intentions to join him, and disrobe, throwing the jumpsuit into a hamper at the foot of the bed. I step into the steamer, adjust the aroma to something citric, and let the steam fly. It envelops my body, coating, purifying, energizing.

My clothing is not ready when I emerge. I have to wait a few minutes after exiting the steamer. I pace nervously, avoiding the window. Finally I hear, both audibly and via the stream, a chirp signaling that my robe is ready. I stoop and remove it from the hamper, now clean and wrinkle-free. Ten minutes later I'm on my way to the refectory.

Locating the refectory is simpleton's work since Scallop packaged directions with his invitation. I stream check the station map anyway. It confirms that he isn't sending me out an open airlock by mistake. That makes me happy.

The refectory is less antiseptic than my room. There is mock wood paneling and bright colors—even an artificial plant or two. It isn't what I'd consider "homey," or even comfortable, but it is casual. Country diner is the theme, I think. The dominant smells are cinnamon, nutmeg, and butter. The room has seating for thirty people, but I count only two other patrons, both with their backs to the entrance. I won't stand out here... much.

Waiting just inside, Scallop sees me right away. He leads me to a table on the far side of the room. The tabletop has the semblance of a red checkered pattern to it, but as we sit, a portion of the pattern is replaced by an image of the menu. Scallop immediately touches the table's surface and begins moving through the choices.

The table sings to me, of course, telling me it is stream-accessible. I wouldn't need to touch the surface at all, and in normal circumstances I wouldn't. Why risk contagion?

Still, I'm unsure whether Scallop will see my using the stream as pretension or not. So I make an exception for him. I physically interact with the table, certain that bacteria from the last Abdul are invading my flesh.

The menu itself is sparse, with only a few choices that would appeal to a debugger. Most of us are "easy to digest" people. It goes along with stream immersion. Though we're wired for it, a full-on stream search can still be unsettling, even to a level 15. Wouldn't want to lose your lunch while solving something big. After a brief period of weighing choices, I make a selection.

Scallop seems happy. "The food is actually quite good here," he says. "I'm sure you'll be pleased."

"I'm sure." The refectory has a trail of horizontally-placed windows on the far wall to my left. They are distant enough that they aren't a huge distraction, but because of the planetary glow beaming through, it is hard to escape the feeling that we're literally sitting on the world.

"So, any new ideas this morning," Scallop asks. "About the bot?"

I shake my head. "Not really. I've checked the bot specs, but found nothing useful. No inherent defects, no recalls..." I emanate logic. "I need outside access. The only way to move forward."

Scallop's shakes his head now. "Not possible. I would like to make an exception for you, but I can't. Quarantine rules."

Always more rules.

It takes a moment before his use of the word "quarantine" registers. In earlier times, quarantine against biological contamination was important when charting the unknown. But in my realm, where information flows seamlessly around the world in an instant, a streaming quarantine makes sense as well. How could I have missed that? So low level!

"I'm able to audit the flow discretely," I say. "There's no way I could pass something out."

"We cannot afford the risk. Especially with a servbot having been damaged."

The implant notifies me that I have a message from the outside. I file it away for future access. Scallop notices nothing.

"Would it help to talk to the crew?" he asks. "They have very little to do right now. I'm sure they wouldn't mind."

I frown. By definition, standard human interaction is not a specialty. And I'm not a blinking gumshoe. But the idea of seeing TallSpot and Handler again—that's even lower in my preferred event queue. "Doubtful it will help," I say. "Especially if they weren't nearby, have no actual records."

"You don't like our kind, do you?" Scallop says, startling me with bluntness. It suggests a common Abdul myth about debuggers. The answer is much more complicated than "not liking" something.

A servbot approaches, carrying the food we ordered. It is a fairly late model, female version. Part of a hybrid line where "servbot" is a borderline designation. Its top half appears as human as any servbot, but the bottom half is a tripod, with each "leg" ending in high-traction wheels.

I'm grateful for the distraction. My meal—a salad made with lots of radishes and lettuce—looks much better than I expected. The station must have a greenhouse onboard.

Curious, I stream the station map again. There's one on the upper level! Impressive.

Scallop's meal is placed before him. A plate laden with meat and gravy. Remarkable he stays so small.

The bot streams a siren call and the tabletop transforms again, shifting into an ornate design approximating a temple niche, with the pattern drawn in such a way as to give the impression that the niche concaves downward into the table. The true direction of M from space, of course.

Scallop bows his head. I bow too, not because I want to but because it is expected—that, and the fact that the bot has turned to watch me.

"In the name of A, and with the blessing of A," Scallop says.

"Feed him who fed me," I answer, "And give him drink who gave me drink."

Scallop raises his head, as do I, careful to hide my distaste for the whole scene. Technically we're all true believers—born that way, they say. But I can't help wondering what things were like before beliefs were mandated by the state. A time I never knew.

"As I was saying," Scallop says with a smile, "you don't like us, correct?"

"I wouldn't say that." I skewer a bite and raise it to my lips. "I am different, because I have to be. Consequently, my perception is different."

"And your perception of me?" he asks, raising an eyebrow.

I chew, thinking—wishing—I could bury myself in the stream. "You seem to perform your duties adequately."

Scallop smiles, gravy wetting his lips. "But you have no strong feelings about me, one way or the other. Just that I perform adequately." He chews vigorously, still smiling. "Certainly you have emotions, Sandfly. Those haven't been removed?"

I shake my head. "The implant has little bearing on how I feel. It discourages certain thought patterns, but emotions are ungoverned. Emotions are often a detriment to good work, however." I shrug, taking another bite. "I keep them controlled."

"Always?" he says. "You suppress yourself, make yourself like a servbot, through force of will?"

The subject of free will is tricky. Borderline tweak-worthy. Yet I can't help myself. "My will has never been my own," I say. "Not fully."

No tweak! Maybe because I'm only stating facts.

"So, do you feel jealous of the rest of us, then? Angered that we're not like you?"

I sniff. "Your behavior is controlled too," I say, "but at a different level." I indicate the table. "The call to prayer, for instance." That brings a warning tweak, but I don't care. I force a smile.

Scallop doesn't seem to mind. He outright laughs, in fact. "You have a good sense of humor for someone who controls his emotions."

The bot rolls by our table, a steaming substance on its tray. I get a whiff of chicken bouillon.

"I don't always control them," I say. "For instance, when I'm streaming wide, they are fully present." I smile, reflecting. "It can be quite satisfying. Sometimes sorrowful too. Maybe even maddening."

Scallop listens attentively now, his fork halted.

"Again," I say, "it is hard to fully explain...to someone like you."

"Yes, yes...someone like me." Scallop smiles assuredly, resumes eating. "We are always different. There will always be a wall, a boundary that cannot be crossed."

I shrug. "I suppose that's true."

The wall is a necessity. When the Abduls won the "war," which was as much about birthrates as battles, common thought became mandated. Mass executions, torture, mutilations—all geared toward making sure everyone was on the same codepage. The laws were changed and everyone officially became of the same faith.

Careful, Sand, this reflection might hurt. And pain won't solve anything.

I look to my food again and am surprised by how little is left. That is a blessing, though. I hurry the last few bites. "I should return to my work."

Both eyebrows rise. "You know how you'll proceed then?"

I nod. "There are a few more things I can try with the schematics available. But after that, I don't know." I pause for effect. "Again, it would be good to have full streaming capabilities."

Scallop frowns. "I wish there was some way I could accommodate you. Perhaps a written letter could be arranged. Difficult, but it may be possible."

I dislike having eyes on anything I write by hand. It is a form of violation. As for contacting my master—if he sweats a little over me, that's almost optimal.

The bot has no headchip, though. Going to be tough without that...

"Not right now," I say. "I might have something later."

Scallop stands, allowing me to do the same. "If there is anything else that will make your job easier—more comfortable—just ask." We walk together to the refectory door. "We have an adequate parts room, if you need hard supplies." He puts a hand behind me, smiles. "I'm sure you can find it."

I mock his smile with one of my own. "As long as you don't lock down the map."

"Oh, I won't do that—"

"And I will need a cinder chute if this takes more than another day."

Scallop lightly touches my elbow. "Better get busy then." He means it as a joke, but I'm not having any. He seems to catch my mood too, because his next statement is more formal: "I'll see what I can do."

ON THE WAY to the examination room, I review my message.

Messaging itself is worthy of explanation, freehead, especially since this particular message was sent FI. Speaking simply, and perhaps a bit pejoratively, messages can be sent with different impact levels.

Easy Impact (EI) is what you might call a "text only" message. It contains simple written characters and nothing else. Though commonly used by Abduls, this method is completely *non grata* for debuggers. We would use EI if we had to—it works in a pinch. But so does stale bread. And nobody wants to live on stale bread...

Extended Easy (EE) is text coupled with sound. The sound helps because you can glean more of the sender's implied meaning. Experientially, it is like the sender is reading the message to you over your shoulder. There is still room for misinterpretation there, however, which is why most of my kind prefers at least the next level.

Impact or Standard Impact (SI) is text, sound, and video imaging. The video clearly adds a lot over EE. With the image of the speaker you can discern all the emotional cues that humans are so fond of using: hand gestures, head tilts...you name it. SI has downsides too, *especially* if the sender is someone you don't particularly like to see. But at least there's no smell...

And finally there's Full Impact (FI), the imam of messaging levels, primarily because it is only available to debuggers. With FI you get everything the sender can give you—text, voice, video, and emotion—all packaged into a warm bundle. And all possible due to the wonders of implant-to-implant communication.

There is no room for misinterpretation with FI. It is like being joined at the head. Because you are. A freehead could never handle FI, sorry. It would fry your synapses, leave your head an empty husk.

The message I received while dining with Scallop was sent Full Impact, which insures that it is from someone like me. Given that FI messages can occasionally be disorienting, even to DRs, I decide to find a place to tuck myself into while I digest it.

Noting an apparent connection between the amount of use a hallway on the station gets and the intensity of its lights, I duck into the darkest one I can find—

Only to have the hall brighten around me. *Not cool.*

After a quick stream check, I discover that the lights are strictly motion activated. I slide to the floor and remain as still as possible. I'm grateful when the lights dim out again, masking me in an early morning gloom. I turn my attention to the message...

HardCandy's full figure comes into view, lithe and sleek, with an arms-crossed stance of toughness. Her almond-shaped eyes look straight ahead, piercingly, stunningly. She's trying to hold back her emotions, I can tell, but there is still a bit of unease beneath the shell, a bit of worry. As she begins to speak, my spine tingles.

"Not sure if you're streaming this, Sand. GrimJack said he hasn't seen you since Day 36, so I don't know. I hope you're still active." She looks to her right and then down, searching. "Never know these days, do you?" She pauses, as if I might respond. "Anyway, stream says you got promoted. Hope that's going well. Also says you were called out for something big. Not sure what that means exactly, but..." Her stance shifts, and her eyes avert briefly. "Don't take my behavior the other day personal, you know?"

That part she meant, I could feel it. My spine tingles again and I feel this slightly heated...flash!

"I won't forget what you did," she says. "I *haven't* forgotten." Another glance to her right, away from my virtual eyes. "You're the closest thing I have to a friend," she says. "That's not saying much now, I know, but...well, I get the feeling you're like that LED at that place I showed you." She looks forward again and leans. "Is that you? If so, take care, Sand, care. I don't know where you might be, but it must be important." An ambiguous smile. "Anyway, give me a touch if you can."

Then the message is over. A hundred nanoseconds of Hard-Candy's brain connecting to mine. Wasn't enough, even at Full Impact. Never is.

And there's no way to respond.

I stand up, and the light notices, brightens. "Have to get down," I say, not really knowing why. "Sign off and get back to Earth."

I REACH THE EXAMINATION ROOM to find another surprise. Looming over my bot is another Abdul. He is taller and darker than Scallop, hair full and long. He wears the same monochromatic suit that Scallop does, except his is red. More noticeable is the fact that there's a transparent bubble over his head. I'm sure that isn't comfortable.

But it is consistent.

"So, have you got this figured out yet?" he asks.

TallSpot has changed little since I saw him last, over ten years ago. Taller, yes, and his voice has deepened. But the handsomeness and self-assuredness? Still the same.

He smiles within the bubble, appearing genuine. "They tell me you like to be called 'Sandfly' now," he says. "Good to see you again." He extends a hand, which of course I don't take.

This job is like a sea of discomfort.

All of us, Abduls and debuggers alike, attend the same schools through age ten. That's where I met TallSpot. He was a class ahead of me, part of a group of children mapped out as gifted. "Ready to lead," they said of him. "Quick decision-maker!"

Now I know what you're thinking. Why wouldn't someone like *that* be chosen for implantation? Isn't that the kind of person you want solving the world's problems? Fixing broken things? Intimately connected to the stream?

The answer is "Absolutely not!" Debugging is a solitary profession—it has to be. Debuggers make terrible leaders, with little exception. And vice versa.

"I have to say, you look different without hair." TallSpot is still smiling. Oozing people skills. "How have you been?"

Crichton, even through the suit he seems strong, robust.

I pause, contemplate an answer. Debuggers were born of necessity. We're the ones with free access to information. We're allowed to think outside the norm on most every subject. Compared to what most Abduls know, information-wise, we're like birds in the sky—which is why the occasional tweaks. There had to be someone like us, though, because the rest of humanity has lost the ability to think differently, to think fluidly.

So, is my life good? Better than it would've been? Perception is everything.

"Fine," I say. "I've been fine." I force a smile. "Aside from the hair."

That brings a hearty laugh. I expected it would. *Gregarious* describes TallSpot accurately. Unfortunately, he also ran with the toughs in school. I wouldn't say he instigated anything, but he never *stopped* anything either. In my mind, that's just as bad.

I stream-check his record. He's had a long list of accomplishments since childhood: valedictorian, class president, track star, soccer star...test pilot, planetologist, speech expert. Well-rounded and successful—no surprise there. He has only one wife. Unusual. No children. Wants some, though.

"So, when are you going to produce a sire?" I ask, as if we'd been discussing the subject. "Or have you been too busy with your speech and planet studies?"

He goes expressionless for a moment, then smiles again. "I almost asked how you knew that," he says. "That's incredible. Really. What else do you know?"

The temptation to stream deeper—to look for something that actually might sting a little—asserts itself, but I ignore it. There's always time for temptation later. Strength is in the holding back. The implant helps with that. Instead, I recount the mundane details of TallSpot's accomplishments.

"All absolutely correct," he says. "Incredible."

I just nod. It seems appropriate. "Here to check on your crewmember?" I visually inspect the bot. It appears to be exactly as I left it. Sitting upright on the exam table. He hasn't tampered with it. Yet.

TallSpot shrugs. "Got little else to do. I've read everything I want to read, seen every vid I want to watch..." Hope enters his eyes. "You going to clear us soon?"

If the mission report I read is accurate, they've been back a week already. Probably getting itchy.

"I'd like to," I say, thinking of HardCandy's message. "I'd like to be back down as soon as I can. Still not one for heights."

TallSpot shakes his head slowly. "No?" he says. "I didn't know."

An incident from our childhood: TallSpot's gang chased me up a tall piece of playground equipment. I panicked when I realized how high I was. Fell.

"It's not something you should remember," I say.

He watches me closely, back braced against the table. "I have a wife to get back to..." His voice trails off. I can see he's thinking.

My eyes drift to my supply bag, still open on the cart. It looks untouched too. Have to inventory it later.

"Do they let...?" Tall begins.

I shake my head. "No," I say. "Never." I shrug, attempting to keep it light. "Two implants sharing the same abode? Doing life together? Much too dangerous."

He nods, draws quiet. Undoubtedly, he is trying to find a subject we can easily connect on. There can't be many. "Have you seen DarkTrench?" he asks then.

"I have," I say, allowing myself a smile. "From the outside. It appears...very sleek."

A chuckle. "It is that. Especially during flips. And the stars, Sand, they're amazing." He raises both hands, begins moving them freely. "Bait al-Jauza was massive. Dominated the spectrum. We discovered things we never expected. Quantum fluxes, the debris field was almost a light-year across, there was a large section of rocky matter too. We think perhaps a planetary system began to form there once. Tidal forces destroyed it, of course—al-Jauza is much too large."

He looks to the ceiling, his mind now 427 light-years away. "It has this ultra-hot patch on the surface—a circular storm pattern. Similar to Jup and the other outer planets..."

I listen attentively. Human conversation is slow, but an interesting topic helps. "Flipping," I say finally. "What is that like?"

He pauses, and I can see his breath collect on the visor for the first time. Perhaps the suit's breathing mechanism needs adjustment. "None of us knew," he says. "Going into it, none of us knew what to expect. It is like nothing you could experience otherwise. Not unpleasant, certainly. Weightlessness? Not really. More like the feeling after a good meal. Or somewhere in between. Weightless *and* full."

No real information there. "How about your thoughts? What did you think about when you're actually traveling? Flipping? Are you active on the ship?"

"Oh, that..." He stares off again, as if searching for words.

I wish he could stream, then he could FI me the whole experience.

"Not that different," he says finally. "I mean, you can think and do things. But there are lots of periods of...déjà-vu, I guess. Periods where you're sure you did something before."

I try to imagine what the bot onboard was going through, whether time lapses, either real or perceived, would affect a system trying to orchestrate the movement of nanos. Would it influence the bot brain itself?

I quickly consult the specs again. Nanos are only ancillary to brain function. Might explain the missing appendages, though...

I approach the bot and touch the socket of the arm thoughtfully.

"I've briefed the administrator already," TallSpot says. "I don't see why the bot's malfunction should keep us here. It's only a machine. Why quarantine us?" He nods my direction. "Your people will put your heads together and have it figured out in short order. I'm confident of that. Then we'll correct it for the next ride. No problem."

I sniff. "Bots have been given souls now," I say. "So says the Imam. I guess they ran out of potential converts." That remark earns me a buzz—gentle, but persistent. I suppress a grimace.

"Did you just get disciplined?" he asks.

Perceptive guy. Guess that's why he's a pilot. "Only a warning," I say.

He approaches the door. "I guess we both have our prisons now, don't we?" He taps the side of his headbubble. "I'm hoping to walk away from mine soon." A gentle smile. "I'm counting on you, Sand. *Please* get me out of this!" The smile broadens before he turns and exits the room, the door sliding shut behind him.

Then one of us will be free.

I SPEND THE BETTER PART of two hours metaphorically running in place. I make little progress on the bot, and more than a few times I contemplate returning to my quarters to stare out the window. That's how bad it is.

Now, I know what you're thinking. You're thinking that I don't like TallSpot (and maybe Scallop either) and so have little incentive to move ahead on my task, that I'm stalling to make their lives more uncomfortable.

Such is not the case. In fact, if I really didn't want to see them anymore it would be in my best interest to get done quickly, now wouldn't it? To get them out of my hair...so to speak?

Most debuggers wouldn't let such emotional entanglements affect them, anyway. Even if there were no credits involved, there is still the ego of the thing—there is still a problem here that *has to be solved!*

I glance at the examination room's solitary picture, realize the depicted planetary surface isn't as solid as I thought. There is a hint of banding. Horizontal strings of lighter and darker blue.

Much of my current interest isn't with the Abduls or the Dark-Trench mission anyway. It isn't even with the bot. My stream-hampered head keeps returning to HardCandy and her message.

She told me to be careful! That means she cares, doesn't it?

Debuggers are effectively neutered. Not biologically, but mentally. And possibly socially. Contemplating the opposite sex won't get me buzzed, but I'm quite sure that pursuing the act of procreation would. And it wouldn't be gentle.

So why this fascination with HardCandy?

I don't know. The meaning eludes me. Like my marveling at DarkTrench, like the pet store on the lift. Some things grab my attention and won't let go. It isn't an obsession, really. It is extreme and dedicated interest.

I think about HardCandy's place under the bridge. I wonder if we went there together whether the loosening of the implant's correction mechanisms—those nagging internal *stops*—could allow for more contact between us. I wonder if she's ever thought about such things...

She said I'm like that LED under the bridge. Why? Because I use less power? Because I'm outdated? Because I'm lonely? Because I'm smaller than—

Okay, now I'm obsessing.

The wall clock's minute hand slides forward.

The new "Guidelines for Bot Interaction" are stored in my head, but I've been putting off reading them. I really don't care what the Imam feels about bots, or what he thinks about how I should do my job. He's a man from the right family who happened to get a lot of Abduls to blindly follow him. Powerful people.

Careful, Sand...

Sighing, I close my eyes and have a look at the guidelines anyway. It is filled with spiritual edicts and pithy sayings. I ignore all that, skimming through with only a few neurons assigned the task. What I really want to know is how it affects me, what it costs me in lost time.

Then I find it.

"If the mechanical entity is able to be examined using purely interactive means, then it should be. Only those without ability of auditory communication skills can be probed using those means normally reserved for lesser mechanicals..."

In other words, if I am *able* to talk to the bot for a solution, then that's the route I have to take. This also means that the more invasive tools of my trade—a nanoprobe, for instance—aren't allowed. Sheets, which are essentially read-only viewing devices, are apparently still permissible. For now. It is a good thing I didn't start right in on the bot again. Saves me some shocks.

No matter our effectiveness, there is always someone trying to restrain us.

The bot stares into the room, thoughtless and soundless. Standing, I approach it, turn its head and look at the gash on the back. The abscess isn't as large as I originally thought. In fact, much of the damage is superficial. The elastic synthskin has been torn, but that is easily reparable. The big problem is the loss of the headchip.

I make a perfunctory check of the bot's appendages, just to see if everything has healed properly. The knee bends now, the socket performing exactly as it should. The shoulders both rotate completely as per spec. The fried pathways? Well, those would be bypassed *in situ*, if...

I check the bot's schematics again, paging through gigs of technical data in my head. It seems there is only one thing standing in the way of a fully functioning bot—sorry: *entity*. I stream out to the station, check for the hardware storage Scallop mentioned. Do they have what I need onboard?

No such luck. Clarke and crichton! Stuck again!

I message (EI) Scallop, telling him of the part I need. He comes back with an apology and a promise to get one. I recommend trying GrimJack's and using my name. He thanks me for the suggestion and says he'll look into it. I'm hopeful he follows my suggestion. It would at least give someone an idea of where I am. I inform him that I'm stuck until I have that part. Scallop says he'll get right on it. That's good behavior for an Abdul.

So now what?

I contemplate returning to my quarters. The effects of the lack of chute sleep are starting to hit me already, the flow of information being restricted by my own fatigue.

Maybe a nap will help.

IT IS SHORTLY AFTER my tenth birthday. A weekend, a day away from school. My parents and I have just finished the afternoon meal, one my mother has prepared herself. We have no bots for such things. We aren't so fortunate.

We are all still in the kitchen. I am steaming the dishes clean in our silver five-year-old steamer. Father still sits at the table, reviewing the news on his communicator, with the cracked screen. Mother is transferring the leftover salad to a sealable container. The container is odd, however, because it looks like a fireman's hat.

There is a knock on the door. Mother dons her black scarf, goes to see who it is.

It is my school director. He is dressed in proper Abdul garb—long one-piece robe and white head cover, a gutrah. Except the gutrah is bound to his head by a piece of red licorice. After the formalities, I am driven from the room. I stand inside the darkened living room nearby, listening.

"Your son is a prime candidate for implantation," the director says. "His scores are quite high."

We are tested twice a year. A test was given only last week.

"It will be good for everyone if you allow your son this honor," the director says. "For our nation."

Mother looks stoically at my father. He is stoic as well, in his own way. Silently listening.

"It will help with our continued struggle. Our enemies advance."

I smile at the joke. When the Abduls took power it was supposed to mean the end of war, that divisions between men had finally been eradicated. We were finally all "awakened" to our hidden nature, to what we were meant to be. Yet we still fight with other countries—though the Abduls are in power there too. Our *hidden* nature must be worse than advertised.

The director continues his spiel, does a real sell job on my parents. They listen intently throughout, unmoved, unmoving. There is a lot of bowing, hands being clasped, but still little reaction from my parents.

Finally the director leaves. I can see only see my mother's eyes, but I recognize fluid there—pending rain.

Dad puts out a hand for my mother. "This will be good for our son," he says, nodding. "A good thing for us all."

My father was a lot of things, but never a good liar.

A carrot stick hops from the hat my mother placed it in. It walks the length of the table before taking a seat on one end. It begins to whistle.

"A hates those that do wrong," my father says. "And now our son will be unable to do wrong. A will approve of him."

More silence.

"I wish I could go for him," my mother says. "If they would take me, I would."

Father shakes his head. "Scriptures say that no bearer of a burden can bear the burden of any other." He pats mother's hand. "That is A's way." A smile. "We have our own burdens. This is the way it must be."

My stomach revolts. I'm turned inside out. I curse the tests and the director. I don't know why my parents are thinking about abandoning me, but I can't believe they don't love me. They have shown me love in many ways before.

The following morning a tall, slender man arrives. Bald, colorless, with deep wrinkles over his eyes. I play the strong man throughout. I don't hold my mother. Or even kiss her. The skinny man leads me to a black two-ped downrider and we climb into the sky. I never visit my home, school, or parents again.

I should have kissed my mother.

"In my country," the skinny man says to me as we skim across the city, "they used to breed horses for speed. If a particular horse was exceptionally fast—say it could do a mile in two minutes—it would be set aside as a wonder horse. The seeds of that horse would be sold to countless other horse owners, and from them offspring could be produced that would also do the mile in two minutes.

"Unfortunately," he said, "it was discovered that while we could create thousands of fast horses from a single wonder horse—hundreds that could do the mile in two minutes—we could *never* create an even more special horse. One that would break out and run the mile in, say, a minute and a half."

He smiles, guiding the downrider toward the emerald facility where I would soon be implanted. "The breakouts come only by the will of A," he says. "Only when man stops trying to control everything."

The man transforms into a cricket. All I hear is chirping for the remainder of the trip.

A DEBUGGER NEVER SLEEPS longer than he intends. He sets an internal timecheck and wakes precisely when he wants to, with a stern head buzz tickling his synapses. He may decide that he wants to sleep longer after the fact, of course, but at that point it is too late. He will be up.

No word from Scallop yet on the replacement headchip, but that's my next step. Replace the headchip and start talking to the bot. See if that leads me anywhere. Not sure how it could, because the bot's memories are essentially whacked. Still, it would be something. The bot would be fully functional.

What do I do until then? Can't just sleep and eat.

I sit up in my bed, clench my hands into fists, and stretch them high above my head.

I could examine the bot's internal code. If I stepped through some of it, I could see where things might have gone awry. Possibly.

Where do I start, though, if I really don't know what the problem is?

Symptoms: the bot went crazy, its arms and leg came loose and it bashed its own head. Killing itself. End of line and good night.

Climbing from my bed, I glance over at the window. Though imprisoned, Scallop did say I had full access. I stream out to Scallop to see if he is available. Unfortunately, he is not.

TallSpot? Also occupied, surprisingly. He suggests I talk to Handler.

Images of Handler flash through my mind. Squat barrelchested kid. Thought he was infectiously funny. A menacing clown.

Frowning, I find his ident and send him a message.

"I need a tour," I say.

WE MEET BESIDE A DOOR outlined in scarlet and clearly marked "Danger." It leads to the umbilical I'd seen before. To Dark-Trench.

Handler is an inflated version of the child I remember—still stocky and short, with crew-cut hair. An appearance that will forever scream "Bully" to me. Like TallSpot, he wears a red pressure suit and a bubble over his face. Handler's bubble appears to be ill-fitting, however, as his cheeks press tightly against the inner surface.

"I know you," he says finally.

"We attended school together," I say. "Until I turned ten. The age when implant recipients are gathered."

"Right, right," he says, and manages a smile. "Your eyes, something about them seemed familiar. You changed since then, though, huh?"

I bow my head. "You could say that."

"You're a DR now. That's very, um...honorable."

I decide against checking Handler's past. I'm sure he's fortunate to be where he is. Probably got an assist from TallSpot. Handler's kind always need someone to cling to, someone to pull them up.

"Does it hurt?" he asks, pointing to his bubble-enclosed cranium. "That thing in your head, does it hurt?" Surprisingly, he looks genuinely interested, perhaps even a bit concerned.

I shake my head. "The surgery was painless. Not even a headache after."

He nods thoughtfully. "But now, I mean. Does it hurt? Having that thing inside all the time?" He squints. "Is there pressure even?"

I don't mention the head buzz—it would only make Handler ill. "Can't feel a thing," I say. I nod toward the hatch. "Can we...?"

"Sure, sure," he says, looking embarrassed. He raises his right hand and applies it to a square panel beside the door. His hand is outlined in blue and a secondary, more-elevated panel slides open. An amber light shines out, briefly connecting the panel to Handler's eye. There is a snap-hiss then as the hatch door unlocks and begins to move.

"Usually we don't need this," he says, motioning toward the upper panel. "Usually we match DNA. But because of the suits and all..." He frowns. "It's a hassle."

I follow him into the docking tunnel. Thankfully, there are no windows here. Only a solid white accessway—a bridge from station to ship.

"I'm glad these have gravity now," he says. "When I started, they didn't. It was a real pain, walking. We train for it, of course."

I can't help but smile. School reunions must feel like this—everyone trying to resolve past sins through extreme politeness. No sense ending the civility. "I'm sure it was."

It is a short walk to the other side. Only a small portion of Dark-Trench's hull is visible where the umbilical joins it, but even that delights me. It is obsidian—like dark marble—and as sleek as it appeared from my quarters. There's another hand panel there that Handler makes use of. No shot of light this time, though.

Then finally we're inside. The first room is as visually plain as the accessway. Beige in color, rectangular, with benches along either side. It reminds me of a small locker room—without the smell, thankfully. The scent here is sterile. On the opposite side of the room is another sealed door.

"Airlock," Handler explains. "A necessity when we're in space. Never know when you might have to leave."

I notice the presence of the ship's stream. The transition is like falling from a waterfall into a placid brook. There is no change in the amount of information flow, but what I receive feels smoothed out: predigested and warm. I sigh with satisfaction.

Handler frowns. "Sorry it takes so long." He is speaking of the interior door, which is beginning to open. The room beyond is darkly lit. Glowing blue panels—fully interactive, I assume—the only sources of illumination. When the way is clear and we have stepped through the door, Handler calls for light, and the room explodes with it. Shades of blues and black dominate—a welcome contrast to the airlock and tunnel.

"This is the disembarkation area," Handler says.

A fact I already know because DarkTrench has told me. The stream is so finely tuned here it feels like it is anticipating my wants.

The door shuts behind us. On either side of it is a section of large cupboards and shelving. *Pressurized passive storage*, the ship calls it. Containing those items most convenient to have near the exit. One cupboard holds additional suits like the one Handler has on. I see racks of handheld equipment, oxygen tanks, emergency supplies. Everything tidy and contained. Clearly marked.

Beyond the storage section the room opens up into a small control center. *Ancillary Management Center*, according to DarkTrench. The exterior wall is lined with those interactive panels I noticed earlier. Beneath them is a seamless countertop—also interactive—and rigid preformed seats.

Handler walks to the end of the room and stands near the wall. Each panel is a vidscreen—alive now, actively displaying an image. Most are exterior shots of the ship and the station beyond. Others are diagnostic in nature, with updates both frequent and dynamic.

"It looks like you could run the ship from here," I say.

Handler's eyes pan the room. "Pretty much we could," he says and smiles. "Not being implants, we need duplicate control areas. Information always available." He nods toward the airlock. "This area doesn't get used for that much, though. It is for emergency situations. Evacuation, or when docking and loading."

DarkTrench feeds me the emergency evacuation procedures, tells me how to pull together a suit, attach oxygen, activate the airlock...

"There were no DRs on your flight," I say, in the way of actually asking.

"That's right," Handler says, smiling. "Your kind made it easy for us, though." He pats the nearest wall. "This baby could almost read our minds. Smooth as silk to fly." He pauses, shrugs. "I'm sure some will come along eventually."

The debuggers that assembled DarkTrench certainly thought so. That might be only my own hopeful impression, though. Admiration mixed with jealousy.

"What do you want to see first?" he asks.

"Whatever you'd like to show me."

Stop, Sand. You're regressing, becoming a child with a new toy. Handler doesn't notice my feelings, but he probably shares them. "I'll take you to the nest. That's where the real action is." He leads me down a short hall to a circular and silver-floored lift large enough for three to stand abreast. We ascend to the upper level.

For a test ship, the DarkTrench is larger than I expected. I mention as much to Handler.

"Part of that has to do with the engine." He makes an odd, two-fingered hand gesture. "The flip. It requires a certain amount of mass to set up." He shrugs again. "It's technical." A weak smile. "And secret."

"Of course."

We enter a larger control area. The main bridge, I assume. It's a semicircular room—comfortable, but not spacious. Four people could occupy the space with little trouble. There are banks of screens here too, along with a number of desks with manual controls—the sort of stuff Abduls would require. The seats are cushioned leather.

Hanging from the ceiling near the front is a curved and elongated vidscreen, a focal point for the crew. Below that and offset a meter either direction are two large removable panels. *Transparent sections of the hull, DarkTrench teases.* Windows to the darkness beyond. Thankfully, they are closed.

It all seems inefficient and backward to me. A room full of screens and controls, when a midlevel debugger could probably do it all in his head. Two DRs certainly could.

Handler activates one of the screens and runs through the ship's coordinate structure, along with its basic operation. "You can't just point at a star and hope to get there," he says. "Time is an important factor. As important as distance, actually." He swirls a finger in the air. "You see, the whole galaxy is moving. Both rotationally, like this..." the finger stops, stretches toward the wall... "and directionally, like this." A smile. "We use both in our calculations."

Handler's lecture continues. Clearly, more is going on in his head now than it appeared there was in school. That was a long time ago, though.

Meanwhile, the ship is querying me, giving me options. It streams me an FI tour that I regretfully have to ignore in order to give Handler the proper level of attention. It moves on to list the data it has received since the start of operations.

"...it is like that saying, 'the only thing constant is change.' That's how it works, you see. No matter how you built a ship, there will always be a time difficulty."

I focus on what Handler is saying. He sounds like he thinks it's important.

"Let's say you see Alpha Centauri from a telescope and decide you want to go there." Handler manipulates the vidscreen again, resulting in the display of a star chart with Alpha Centauri labeled and circled in the middle. Earth's sun is labeled in the chart, as well.

"It is almost five light-years out, right? So, you get in your spaceship and travel at the speed of light. You get there in five years, more or less. But the Alpha Centauri you reach won't be the one you saw from here. It will be one five years later. Or ten, actually, since the star you saw before you left was light that had taken five years to get to your telescope. Same thing with the return trip. The world you'd return to wouldn't be the one you'd left. Years would have passed.

"Time is as much your enemy as distance, see? And any ship you build needs to deal with that. At least, if you want to reach that other star and have it be similar to the one you saw from here. Your ship needs to be able to cross time, right? It's both a spaceship and a time machine, see?

Handler smiles, stretches palms out like a beggar. I simply nod to show I'm following.

"One of our scientists, Grackle, has a saying. A way of describing how DarkTrench moves. 'Back to go forward' is what he calls it."

"Meaning?"

"Meaning that though the ship may travel backward in time—which it must do to beat the speed of light—its position in space relative to where it began is always forward." Handler rocks assuredly on his heels. Happy with the knowledge. Proud to finally share.

I don't get it, but at least it explains the bit I gleaned from the OuterMog. Back to go forward. Gotcha!

Still, the science is exterior to my specialties, and way beyond my level. I'm reminded of something I streamed once. "Isn't there an issue with moving clocks running slower?" I ask.

Handler stares at me, blinking. "Isn't that relativity theory?" he asks. "From the 1300s?"

He returns his attention to the screen, silently touching and searching before picking an item from a list. Again the image changes. This time to that of a diamond-shaped object in space—the representation of a spaceship—and the circular globe of a planet. The diamond departs the globe, moves swiftly into the depths. The single letter "C" follows in parentheses.

I shrug. "Possibly."

"It deals with the effects on time the closer you get to the speed of light. To a stationary observer, it would appear that clocks on a ship traveling near light speed are running slower than his own."

"That's probably it." Yeah. Levels of expertise beyond mine.

Handler smiles. "Your statement is a bit of a myth, though."

"How so?"

"In space, there are no stationary observers," he says, "excepting A, of course." He gives a slight bow of his head, points at the image of the globe. "Any *stationary* observer isn't really stationary from the moving ship's perspective, right? To anyone on board it appears that the observer is the one moving away near the speed of light, and that *his* clocks are running slower."

"I see," I say, not really seeing.

"It is all moving," Handler says, waving his hands in the air. "All of it..." He tucks his hands behind his back and smiles. "Your personal state of reference is what's important." He indicates the controls, the array of screens. "The way DarkTrench travels steps beyond the rules of relativity. Outside it." He points a finger at me. "Doesn't mean there aren't rules in place, of course. There are. Just different ones."

Definitely more going on in Handler's head these days...

I remain silent, absently scanning the controls. Handler's description makes me think that if the crew wasn't responsible for damaging the bot, then the method of travel itself must have been. All this flipping, back and forwarding, there's no way a bot was designed for—

The ship chirps at me again, describing the available meals on board. I *am* hungry. I had taken little for the afternoon meal, my mind being too preoccupied to break. The ship must sense that somehow, possibly performing a pull operation on my implant.

I'm also feeling fatigued. I sometimes wish I had the kind of nano-soup running through my body that bots have. I wouldn't fatigue so easily.

Of course, if I had a chute to sleep in.

I query the ship about the trip they took, wondering what information it has available. Were there any recording devices...?

There are, but unfortunately there are no visual devices in the *incident* room. Not surprisingly, all such recording devices are focused outward.

Still, that room would be worth investigating...

"The room," I say. "The one the bot was in when it malfunctioned. Can you take me there?"

Handler nods. "Of course," he says. "Do you want to go now?"

I nod, and without further comment he leads me past the lift toward the rear of the ship. We step through a doorway that sports a locking metal door. "Security for the pilots," Handler says. "A tradition we still maintain. Even in space."

Next comes a hallway. There are rooms with doors on either side. *Systems storage*, the ship tells me. My first guess would've been crew quarters, but DarkTrench informs me those are on the lower level, and are much smaller. I smile, wondering if they are big enough to hold a cinder chute.

DarkTrench says *No*.

Finally we arrive at a room with stainless steel sinks around the perimeter and a black, two-level table in the middle. There are wall-mounted vidscreens here as well, along with sealed hanging cabinetry and other pieces of equipment I can't immediately identify. Many of the latter are freestanding near the wall, while others are placed prominently on the table's lower level. I ask the ship about the large, saucer-shaped device on the table in front of me.

A phase disrupter, it tells me.

"This is the prep room for the lab," Handler says. "The bot was here when we found him." He scans the room briefly before taking two steps forward and crouching low. "The arms were laid out here and here." He indicates two locations, about a body width apart. He straightens and moves to stand beside a meter-high black box with visible piping exiting the top. "The bot was slumped up against the lab steamer here, facing out. We think that's where he messed his head up." Handler looks at me. "You saw him, right? The head, I mean."

I nod again.

"It was pretty bad," Handler says. "I sort of liked that bot. Probably the most reliable one I've ever worked with. Especially for his year and model."

"And what was he used for?" I ask.

"Assembling the experiments. Prepping them." Handler nods toward the rear of the ship. "Cleaning work too, of course."

"What type of experiments were these?"

"All sorts of things." Handler moves behind the table, leaning back against one of the sinks there. "Outlined in advance by your fifteens. Testing animals, ant farms, plant life. Checking us out too, of course." He smiles through the bubble. "Had me exercising for an hour a day with the ship listening. I suspect that was partially because it was good for me."

DarkTrench again suggests some food. It also asks if I wish for the resident bot to begin cleanup duties. I find the last part amusing. If I answer in the affirmative will I return to the examination room and find it cleaned?

"How long after you completed the flip did you find him?" I ask.

Handler thinks, eyes searching the vidscreens. "Not until the third or fourth day after we arrived," he says. "I remember Betelgeuse through one of the windows—"

"Wait, you mean no one entered this room for three days?"

Handler shakes his head. "No, I mean the bot didn't malfunction until then."

"It wasn't after the flip?" Another theory, blown. A multiday latency for a bot problem is unheard of. And the return flip couldn't have caused the malfunction, either, because the problem happened while they were still in orbit around Betelgeuse. What else could make the bot react crazily, aside from the jumps? What other unknown elements were there?

Another head-bubble shake. "No, we were definitely a few days out. The flip went perfectly. It took a few days of checking to make sure. Little got done in the way of experiments during that time.

"But the bot was in full use then. Like I said before, they're reliable. In fact, I had it helping me with star cataloging after we arrived. Lots of data to get down and verified." Handler indicates the ceiling, which is a dark blue color. "The ship is capable of retaining all of it on its own, of course, but we try to get duplicates of the important stuff. Navigation and time readings first."

My attention for what Handler has said is divided. I was so certain that the flip itself was the variable. What else could it be? I call out to DarkTrench, who comes running like a puppy. "What recordings are available in this room?" I ask it. "Show me what you have."

The response is EE—extended easy. I get the temperature readings in the room, the amount of time elapsed since the ship's system was started—but, as DarkTrench warned, no video. "It was how many days after you jumped?" I ask Handler.

"Had to be at least two." Handler thinks for a moment, then slaps his hands together. "No wait, it was after the third day. I remember because of the meal we had that day. Turned my stomach."

I nod and signal DarkTrench to move its recording ahead, to give me everything it has from early the third day. Again I see textual representations of all the readings in the room. Oxygen content, Nitrogen, artificial gravity variances. Next I begin to register subtle clicks and clangs—sounds of the bot at work, I assume. I ask the ship to skim ahead until the sounds cease.

A few seconds later I hear nothing. I see only the textual readouts again. Oxygen normal, Nitrogen normal, Gravity normal. Temperature, Atmospheric Pressure, Humidity, Background Radiation—all normal.

"Was there anything unusual about the star?" I ask.

"Now there's a question," Handler says, smiling. "Depends on how you define *unusual*. Betelgeuse is a variable star, meaning its brightness changes over time. Even the earliest records we have for it—from before the implementation of the AH numbering system—had it varying in brightness over a period of several years. Some years see many variations in brightness, other see few."

"So, there were things happening?"

Handler crosses his arms, the material of his suit making a scratching sound with the contact. "No. Not while we were there, not really. I only mentioned that to tell you that this ship is heavily shielded against all forms of radiation. It would have to be."

Taking that cue, DarkTrench walks me through the onboard shielding. It is quite extensive, able to withstand triple the particles emitted during a solar flare. Again I'm awed by the highlevels that created this void-traveling marvel. I'd message them a bouquet, if I could.

Handler adjusts his lean. The sink behind him lets out a clipped screech. "There are two kinds of particle radiation you have to prepare for in space," he says. "There are the high energy particles that are emitted when our Sun, or any sun, has an intense flare-up. And then there are cosmic ray particles. The latter is always present in space. The danger there is one of long-term effects—birth defects, developing cancer later in life, things like that. The first type is less frequent, but much more deadly. Someone exposed to the radiation from a solar storm would grow ill and die very quickly. It would not be pretty."

I frown. Approaching the phase disruptor, I place a hand on the saucer section. I find it cool to the touch. "This ship protects against both kinds," I say, parroting what DarkTrench has already told me.

"Correct," Handler says. "The solar kind was most important for our trip, of course, but the shielding is built to handle both."

I study the disruptor's simple inlaid controls. "What would either radiation do to a body, exactly?"

"To a human?" Handler says. "Why, it would pass right through." A smile. "Of course, along the way it would tear apart the strands of DNA within cell nuclei."

"Damage the programming?"

Handler nods. "Correct. Makes those cells unable to perform and repair as they normally do." He pauses. "Of course, many of those radiation consequences can now be reversed through nanotech." Another smile. "But again, there are no worries of irradiation here in DarkTrench." He reaches out to pat the wall. "We're safer here than back on the station."

I didn't need the reminder that I'm actually in space. Vulnerable, alone, and with tenuous access to the stream. I force a smile anyway.

I tell DarkTrench to reverse the EE recording, to return to a few minutes before the sounds end. I then ask it to begin playing again. I hear the rattles of the bot's movements in my mind, see the playback of sundry textual details.

Handler watches me closely. "You're talking to the ship, aren't you?"

I keep my eyes open, yet raise a finger for silence. I want to absorb everything. Was the bot streaming anything during the moments before it went non-functional? Was it reporting anything?

DarkTrench provides radiation information. Nothing unusual. No solar flares.

I hear a large clank in the recording, as if something metal hit the floor. The bot must have been holding something and dropped it.

Then I hear something out of the ordinary. Can you magnify, DarkTrench? Reverse and magnify?

The ship complies. It reminds me of my blood sugar level, which I acknowledge. Then I hear the important part, the part I've been waiting to hear. Audio that is not the bot's work sounds or the cleaning of a mess. It sounds a bit like...

Singing?

My vision blackens and my knees fail. I register pain.

I SEE HARDCANDY moving down a green path. In the background I hear the rustling of wind and the happy "tweettweet-aleet" of some avian. Overhead and around us are large trees, larger than I've ever seen. The sky is clear and rosy. Sunset or sunrise, it has to be.

HardCandy raises her hands and spins around—ecstatic, jubilant, triumphant! She looks back at me and smiles, reaches out to touch my cheek. The stream is...absent. I'm puzzled. I stop and raise a hand to my temple. I feel empty, lost, afraid.

Everything is precisely right, and yet precisely wrong. I stagger forward, following Hard. We reach a clearing in the forest and the light becomes brilliant, all-encompassing. I look up and stare at the sun. It fills my vision. I'm blinded! It is red and angry—vengeful, but merciful. Radiation fills me.

"Are you going to be all right?" Hard says. The birds' tweeting becomes frantic. "I can't fix you. Are you going to be all right?"

I awaken to Scallop's face. Where did he come from?

Scallop is leaning over me and squinting severely. I see the thick hairs of his eyebrows distinctly, and the individual pores of his nose. In his right hand is a light, the beam of which ends somewhere near my top lip. His breath smells of peppermint.

"Ah, so you're up," he says. "I was certain we would have to decommission you, but TallSpot said to be patient. To let you rest."

I frown and reach out for the stream. It is there. I look for the diagnostic that's hidden in my head. I find it, and start visualizing a rainbow in reverse and pair-swapped order. That begins the process.

Forty seconds later I'm assured that the implant is in perfect functioning order. I lift my hands and bring them together, touching only the fingertips. Sitting up, I roll my shoulders, blink twice, and curl my toes. I check my internal time with that of the stream.

All is correct.

We're in another examination room, I realize, identical to the one I've been using for the bot, excepting two obvious differences. One, the solitary picture here is of a stony red planet—Mars, I think—and two, *I'm* the one being examined.

"What happened?" I ask.

"You tell me," Scallop says. "We don't have the proper facilities to check you here, of course." He glances over his shoulder. "The medbot tells me you are suffering from low blood sugar, slight hypertension, fatigue, and dehydration. There is also a small welt on the back of your head from where you struck the floor."

I touch the back of my head, wince at the tenderness there.

"It wouldn't have been as bad if you had hair," Scallop says, smiling. "Poor Handler, you surprised him completely. He feels awful that he wasn't able to catch you."

I nod. "So do I. It surprised me too."

"If I were allowed to wager, I'd say it was the blood sugar level that got you. You really should eat more."

I try to run through what I remember. The intense flow of diagnostic information, the sounds of the bot in action, DarkTrench's nagging...

"I could've sworn there was something else," I say. "Something I heard."

Scallop straightens. "Something on the ship? Handler assures me you were the only two onboard..."

"Really?" I wince again. "I wasn't aware."

I look to where the white medbot reclines, near the door. It is a rolling tripod model, with an adjustable forward wheel able to extend independently of the back two. There are three appendages above its waist also, all segmented and blistering with instruments ready to go. The head is conical and slides up and down on a telescoping "neck." The model is an ME-42, but the slang term is *Lipstix*, mostly because of the head/neck functionality. The 42 is at least two years dated, and would know nothing about a debugger's implant regardless—just as Scallop suggested.

"You have a 42 model," I say, frowning.

Scallop shrugs. "Is that what it is?" he asks. "I wouldn't know."

"Another debugger I know, ThrillRide, works on medbots exclusively," I say. "He claims he wouldn't let a 42 within twenty feet of him. 'Just as likely to end your life as save it,' he always says." I grin weakly. "Or at best, attach your leg to your shoulder."

Scallop's face whitens. "I wouldn't know." He sets his light on the nearby counter, beam end down. It rocks and falls over. Turns 50 degrees before stopping. "Always functioned adequately for us," he says, still watching the light.

I stream to the medbot. It reports a faulty bearing in one of its wheels and a missing pinion in its middle arm. "It could use some adjusting," I say.

Scallop nods. "Send me a list of necessities."

"I'll do that," I say.

Something isn't right here. Any debugger worth his implant would've corrected these things. Even a new implant—a level ten.

"Why are there no DRs now?" I ask. "On the station, why no debuggers at all?"

"How do you know...?" Scallop smiles. "Of course, you would sense their presence, wouldn't you?"

I nod, still frowning.

"We've had many debuggers here in the past," Scallop says. "During the design and early implementation phase." He looks at the medbot. "We're in maintenance mode now, however. Bots are sufficient—"

I shake my head sternly. "There's not a bot pressed that can handle some of this equipment," I say. "And you wouldn't want them to, even if they were spec'd for it. Then there's the Tanzer effect."

Scallop looks puzzled, but he shouldn't be.

"Tanzer in 1727," I say. "He said that the further a machine gets away from the human hand, the more likely it is to lose human effectiveness." Scallop still looks lost, so I continue. "The Designers' Forum? The one where implantation was first suggested?"

He shrugs, shakes his head.

"History, Scallop. You should stream some of it." I feel real fire about the ulama then—about my master, the Imam, the whole controlling hierarchy. That line will get you buzzed good, though, because it is a real easy thing for the implant to dissect—an easy notion to pick up on. So I fight it. Hard.

"Never mind..." I bring a fist to my temple and tap it twice. "Wouldn't it make life easier to have a debugger around? If only to keep the lights on?"

A message pops into my queue. It is sent EI so I lose faith that it is from someone I care about. Easy Impact is the favorite method of stream shills. Part of the reason I frequent GrimJack's is because he doesn't streamshill. Makes him top grade in my book.

I put the message somewhere where I can reach it later. If I find the motivation.

"Perhaps before you finish here..." Scallop says.

I wave him off. "One job, one assignment," I say. "That's the rule. I'd need to talk to my master before there is any reassigning." I tap my head again. "Technically, he funded the implant. Holds the master controller..."

Scallop gets animated, busily shaking his head. "Oh, I'm sure he wouldn't mind. He's an avid supporter of our program. Always has been."

Now that's new information. I wonder if it is accurate. It seems like a right turn from where my master usually travels. He has many properties to maintain and businesses to mind. I know, because I've been to most of them. In fact, I met HardCandy while doing a chore at one of my master's interests.

I guess he isn't all bad.

I slide from the cushioned table to the floor, keeping a hand grip just in case. Steady myself. "Regardless, I would need the certs for it," I say. "I would have to know that it is okay."

Scallop nods. "We will look into it. But again, sending a message directly—"

"Is difficult," I say, frowning. "I understand. But since I know you can pull it off I'll let you figure out how. I have plenty to occupy me already."

Straightening, Scallop brings his hands together to touch at the fingertips—a look of hopeful pleasure. "Yet you are making progress with the bot regardless of the difficulty. I've heard your kind can do miraculous things...that even sleep enhances the process, brings answers to mind."

"*Chute* sleep," I say. "Of which I've had none in two days." I'm reminded of my brain fatigue. It isn't bad yet, but it is worsening. Not helped by the lump on my cranium. I couldn't expect a freehead to understand—especially an Abdul like Scallop. He has his position to maintain and his papers to push. Empathy is not in his programming either.

In point of fact, I'm starting to wonder if his position doesn't depend on me.

Scallop frowns. "Oh, yes," he says. "I forgot to mention. Bringing a chute onboard has proven difficult. They are quite heavy and large. I didn't realize. The weight tariff alone would take a good chunk of our budget. I'm also not certain that it will fit through some of our doors here." He pauses. "It would be better if we could avoid it entirely."

"It isn't some random piece of equipment," I say.

Scallop nods. "I understand," he says. "Still, it is difficult, difficult...but I'll keep trying." Even though I can't stream an Abdul, the look he gives me tells me that he is not going to try. He raises a finger and smiles. "Oh, how could I forget? I do have one piece of good news!"

I can hardly wait. "Yes?"

"The replacement headchip! I have it. It came on the afternoon lift." Reaching into the front pocket of his orange spacesuit, he pulls out an item wrapped in brown paper. "I didn't unwrap it," he says. "I know there is a danger in that."

His fear is a bit of an anachronism—a throwback to the days before the year realignment. Back then, special care had to be taken with nearly all electronic equipment. Those safety concerns are long gone now. Even if the headchip got dropped to the floor and stepped on, it probably wouldn't break, or even mar. And if it did, I could fix it. As long as the headchip's shell remains intact...

I bow and take the package. I don't bother to alleviate Scallop's fear. It is better he doesn't know. Really.

I'm comforted by the feel of the package in my hand. It gives me something I know I can do, and that's a good thing. Validation.

"This *is* something," I say, forcing a smile. "I look forward to implementing it."

AFTER A PROTRACTED MEAL, I return to the servbot's room. The bot sits exactly where I left it, eyes searching forever.

I remove the brown paper from the package Scallop gave me. Inside is a rectangular case formed of clear and unbreakable (nano-enhanced) glass. Within the case I can see a triangular headchip, no larger than a fingernail. I remove the chip and give it a once over. It appears to be the correct model for the bot. Surprisingly, Scallop got it right.

I manually turn the bot's head and, holding the headchip between thumb and forefinger, slide it gently forward. There is an audible *plick* as it is drawn into the cavity and brought into place.

"Are you ready?" I ask. According to the new rules, this is the polite way to address the bot.

Nothing happens.

I attempt to stream to it, but no useful response comes that way either. I *do* sense a soft electronic pulse.

Frowning, I open my pack and find one of the rolled sheets Grim-Jack sold me. Flattening it, I press it tight against the bot's chest. The sheet clears, becoming a window to the inside. I see tiny movements there, but none of the full movements I would expect from a functioning bot. I glimpse only priming rotations and a slight internal illumination. There should be more. The chest cavity should be awash with light, in fact.

I open another sheet and smooth it over the back of the bot's neck, starting at about the midpoint of the back and ending at the base of the skull, right below the injury. Most of the damage is to the skin layer itself. Unimportant. But after a bit of searching I notice a microfiber that has been sheared. I trace that fiber all the way to the end of the sheet. It continues into the bot's trunk.

I touch the stream, bringing up the bot's schematics. Locating that specific fiber is complicated. There are hundreds that wrap through that same area. But after some searching I think I have it. It looks to be important.

I push the examiner stool close to the table and sit down. I take out a rod-shaped device —my tiniest fuser—and a lazburner. The burner looks like a smooth silver pistol, and in some ways it is. I caress the thumbdial, setting the burner to a setting that approximates the fuser's diameter. I burn a small access hole in the bot's back, then insert the fuser.

Touching the sheet, I adjust the magnification. The fuser looks larger than my finger now, the microfiber a glass toothpick beside it. I roll the fuser in my hand gently. Within the bot it transforms, growing two mandibles. I use those to grab the fiber and touch it, starting the fuse operation. I locate the other side then and do the same. I merge them and see a slight glow as they touch.

Success, I think.

Most times it is easier to replace the whole fiber band, especially when there is more than an individual fiber sheared. Properly matching fibers is tricky in any case. I'm commissioned to be as unobtrusive as possible now, though.

Part of the rules.

I check my work again at various magnifications. All seems to be correct, and nothing else appears to be broken. It would be a lot easier if the bot could stream. Or could report to me what went wrong.

"Are you functional?" I ask. "Are you ready?"

"Gurgle, gurgle, plik!" is what I get in return. Better, but not great.

Crichton! What else could be wrong?

This is where a nano-scanner would be useful. I could check all the systems, line by line, bit by bit.

Though it is redundant for me, I find myself watching the archaic clock on the wall again. I feel a little drifty. I've been working on the bot long enough that my efficiency is faltering. I curse Scallop's inability to provide a chute.

How did they get DarkTrench to fly with him in charge? And how did all those high-level debuggers build this thing with no chutes? Rails, it really rails.

I walk over to the wall below the clock. I lean against it and slide to the floor. I close my eyes.

The Abduls have about a half dozen predetermined prayers that might be appropriate for a situation like the one I'm in. It's as if A is this giant version of my crippled bot...requiring the exact combination of instructions and coaxing to make him go. To make him move in the way I see fit, of course.

The verbiage of the prayers speaks about helping me complete my task, or relieving my hardship, fulfilling my needs—and above all else—allowing me to accept my lot if A chooses not to answer. Despite my prodding and preciseness.

I've tried them all, every fixed instruction. Before, when I was younger. I'll try none of them now.

I know he doesn't move.

I AM TWELVE. It has been over a year and a half since the implant. The same skinny man who took me from my parents (whom I later knew as Bamboo, though his real name was an Abdul standard moniker that doesn't bear repeating) now drives me to my new owner.

It may, in fact, be the same black downrider that is taking us there. All I know for certain is that the city is grey today, grey and wet...

As I gaze out over the temples, water beads on the downer's Plexiglas bubble, running down the smooth curve to then dart past my eyes.

"You will be a fine debugger," Bamboo says. "You will keep the world moving."

It is my first time in the City of Temples. The first time I glimpse the dark outline of the TreArc building. Near the top is a silver emblem—three identical loops standing together like a botched letter M or the coiling body of a serpent from the deep. In fact, before my widened eyes the emblem transforms into just that—a serpent clinging to the building's side. I look away.

"We won't be going to his home?" I ask, childishly, foolishly.

"You will not," says Bamboo. "Don't even think of it."

Soon we are inside, awaiting my master's arrival. There are framed degrees and awards on the wall, along with stylized prayers and sacred readings. Already the curtain divides the room. It appears to be made of orange cheese.

"Why is it here?" I ask, nodding.

Bamboo harshly shakes his head. "You have an implant, 63," he says. "Use it."

I feel shame. Information resides at my neurons' edge, always waiting to be touched. I practiced for months, learning to taste the stream, to feed off it—make it my second home. My first home! And now I have forgotten in front of my tutor. I shake my head, silently reprimanding myself, and reaching for the bits, find them.

"To prevent my looking on his personhood in its element," I say. "For I may desire his power."

"Correct," Bamboo says, nodding.

I turn to face Bamboo. "Yet you—"

He tightens his lips, signaling another search is required.

I stream out again. "There is no power in teaching," I say. "Only service. Which is why I'm allowed to see you."

"Correct again."

I turn toward the curtain again. It is a shimmering gold now—no longer made of cheese. But on the floor in front of it to my right is a great dark bird. A buzzard, I believe. It is perched atop the bloodied remains of an animal, which it tears at viciously.

A shadow moves behind the curtain. A door opens and shuts. Eyes appear at the rectangle for the first time. They are dark, of course, and much younger than I expected. "Is he ready?" the man asks.

Bamboo nods. "Low grade, but he is ready. I'm confident he'll be fully competent."

"He is level 11?" says my master. "As we discussed?"

"Both in clearance and in performance."

"And the correction algorithms...may I test them?"

Another nod. "Of course."

My master's eyes leave the rectangle, to be replaced by his left hand. In it, he holds a golden crescent. "Can you see this?" he asks.

"Yes," I say. "It is a hand controller. Model 3-b, range 100 meters, lifecycle 6 years on standalone power..."

"Very good," he says. "And an excellent use of the stream."

I nod proudly. "Thank you, master."

I feel a slight tingle, positioned squarely between my ears.

"Can you feel that?" he asks.

I reply in the affirmative. It wasn't pain I experienced, only slight discomfort, like chewing aluminum foil. On the floor, the bird repositions itself, spreads its wings slightly. I realize then that it is not a buzzard, but a great eagle with a solid white head.

"Also good," he says.

The next thing I feel is searing pain—a brainpan inferno. I fall forward to my knees, and my head somehow touches the floor. I press my forehead to the marble, thankful for its coolness. I try to re-cite a prayer, but pain muddles my thoughts. Destroys everything I know. I might be screaming instead.

Then the burning ends, leaving a well of warm feeling in its place. My hands come to my aid, pushing my head up. I notice a crack in the floor's surface.

"Just the response I was expecting," my master says, addressing Bamboo. "Your results are as dependable as ever."

Bamboo swirls his hand over his face and bows. "You are too kind." They share a laugh.

Meanwhile, I regain my feet. "Very good, DR 63," Bamboo says, bowing my direction. He addresses the curtain. "Would you like to test the inherent stops, as well?"

No, please...

"My time is precious today," my new master says. "I assume the law is fully written within?"

"To the fullest extent possible. He is free to think about anything, of course, but before illicit motivation becomes action, he will be stopped. It is a fine line—to control without hampering. But history has proven our methods."

"I am well aware," my master says. "He is not the only DR in my employ."

Bamboo bows. "May A forgive me, I meant no insult." He bows again. "He has quarters for delivery?"

"Of course." The shadow of my master moves as he stoops to sit at his desk. The opening in the curtain moves as well, as if by magic. It tracks with him, keeping his eyes visible through the hole. "I am sending the address to him now." His eyes search my direction. "You have it?"

I nod. "Ye-yes," I stammer, still a bit disconcerted from the shock I received, the endorphins now having left me completely.

His eyes remain fixed on me. "Is there something wrong, DR?"

I straighten myself, clasping my hands behind my back. "No," I say. "I have the address. I am ready to serve."

My master nods at Bamboo. "Very good."

I grit my teeth, and the eagle screams.

ANOTHER TORTUROUS NIGHT. Partly because of the dream, and partly because of having slept on the floor of the exam room. Never do that again, I remind myself.

I get to my feet, achingly, and approach the examination table. "Are you ready?" I ask, feeling hopeful.

The servbot's eyes move to look at me. "Plick, mibble!" it says, then its eyes begin to rotate in their socket, slowly. First left, then down, then right, then up at me, then left...

I stream the appropriate shutdown codes and the eye movements stop. I can't help but feel that something sinister has happened to it. Even with no one else around, there is something that really tweaks me about the bot's condition.

I again notice the transparent canisters on the counter. They contain the most rudimentary medical supplies: balls of cotton, swabs, tongue depressors. It's not usually bots getting examined in here, after all.

I frown, shake my head. Time for the fine-tooth comb treatment.

The allusion is a little strange for someone without hair, I know, but it works for what I intend. Carefully, I remove the sheet from the bot's neck and—finding it still pliable and adhesive—move it to the bot's left calf. This will take a while.

Twenty minutes later, I find something.

In my initial repairs of the bot's arms, I'd been too anxious, too low level. The arms swivel in their sockets fine, but some of the nanopaths from the chest end at the shoulder sockets. Somehow I managed to crimp one. Confused by the blockage, sensor nanos weren't traveling to the brain correctly. Complicated systems, these bots. It must have caused a partial stall of the bot's processors.

The solution is fairly simple. I stint the path with a lectolater and watch as the nanos begin to move again.

Dance, my children, dance!

The fire of success fills my chest, along with a renewed surge of confidence. Whether the bot is fixed now or not, I've at least made an improvement, and that's saying something.

"Are you ready?" I ask.

There is a long pause. I remember I need to initiate the startup codes again. I stream them and wait for receipt confirmation. Then I repeat the question.

"A is the greatest," the bot says twice, and then: "I am ready to be of service. My model number is RS-19. I was created by the Elipserv Conglomerate. First date of service: Day 33 at 10 pm on 1973 AH. On that day in history: OuterMog was invaded by CenJap, Cerulean Fog won the Derby, and—"

"That's enough," I say, smiling. "Run a full diagnostic, and notify me when you are finished. I am DR 63 Sandfly, and my credentials are..."

The rest I can't repeat for freeheads, sorry. Not because it will bring me any physical pain, mind you. It is merely personal conditioning: I'm against needless boredom.

The bot acknowledges everything I've said with a nod. It then closes its eyes and resumes silence.

It is working. I can't believe it. Finally working.

Still smiling, I leave for the refectory.

THOUGH IT IS EARLY MORNING, I contemplate streaming Scallop to tell him of my success. I haven't solved the riddle of why the bot got destroyed yet, of course, but I'm sure he'll be happy to have a functioning bot again, regardless.

Then I remember the message I received earlier, the EI one. I retrieve it from the implant, let the text stroll through my mind:

I know you're out there, because I received an order from your current employer. The lady tells me you might be in some trouble. Orders are like messages—they only go one way. GJ

I pause midstride, startling a young security guard almost out of his brown outerwear. That's what he gets for navigating the hallway so closely behind me. He drops the communicator he is carrying—creating an awful racket—then quickly stoops to retrieve it. I remain motionless the entire time, even as he walks around me, staring.

I'm used to stares. Doesn't detract one iota from my own surprise.

GrimJack has sent me a message, and a coded one at that. The code was easy for my implant to pick apart, but it was clear that he didn't want everyone looking at it. No random sniff. A government sniff would've deciphered the original message in a heartbeat, though, and that's dangerous.

Still, there isn't much to the message that would really alert someone.

But for GrimJack, any covert interaction with me is questionable. He's the only one I know who has had an implant removed—and not by choice. It was wrenched from him like a bad appendix. Except an appendix operation would've been less painful.

Implants don't come out nearly as easy as they go in, you see. The longer you have it in, the more a part of you it becomes. A clean break isn't possible anymore. That's part of the reason that GrimJack is a shop owner now. He's lost all the highest level stuff, the pure bandwidth that we debuggers travel in.

Compounding the misery is what happens to the status of a decommissioned individual, post-op. Debuggers are considered privileged, with special dispensation, our eternal destiny figured out in advance. Of course, none of us were involved in the negotiations... In the meantime, we're treated like tools—special, elaborately sophisticated tools—but tools nonetheless. Raw power, controlled by a piece of metal in their head, like a horse with a bit.

I've made a joke. Get it: bit/bit? Never mind.

But someone who's lost that usefulness, had it taken away? In the mind of Abduls, someone like that is worse than a prostitute. Worse than a lame mule. All that's left for him is menial labor now and damnation later.

So for GrimJack, getting on the wrong side of the Abbys—making himself a target—is a quick ride to his final destination. Is that why he sent me a message? To reach Hell early?

Except he is the only person I know who seems to have put it all aside, who lives within his lot. He's way more cheerful than he should be. More cheerful than *I* would be.

So why get involved with my mess?

I replay the message, pausing on every word. "The lady" is HardCandy, has to be. And she's clearly stream sniffing on my behalf. Further proof that she cares, I think. In my absence, I'm valuable to her!

It is those final words—the part about orders and messages going only one way—that concerns me.

Is that a warning?

I restart my journey toward the refectory, intent on not stopping again until I reach it.

The message has me wondering, though. Scallop hasn't appeared truly threatening. Pushy and annoying, but not threatening.

Doesn't mean he couldn't be. Every master has a credit boost in one hand and a controller in the other.

I'm only here to do a job, to milk my specialty. And no one wants it finished more than I do!

Plus I'm really tired, and the food could be better...

But Scallop *did* mention decommissioning me, didn't he? And it's clear they're hiding something here. I can tell from all the nasty machines.

Or maybe I'm paranoid. I've heard that lack of sleep can do that to a person.

If that's what I am.

I make the final turn for the refectory, only to spot Scallop coming my way. His face instantly brightens.

"Sandfly!" he says.

I'm a little annoyed by the way he says it—like we're long-lost friends. That could be the sleep thing too. I pause and wait for him to reach me.

"Good news," he says. "I've gotten clearance for you to work on some of our other issues while you're here. You should be getting a confirmation message soon."

He's right. I receive verification from my master almost immediately. It reiterates what Scallop said. That is a bit worrisome too, because even though my master frequently tells me that I'm "not the best," I was certain that he needed me around. I've completed many projects for him. He's got fingers splayed out across the country. Bots working everywhere. He needs his debuggers. And I'm level 13 now, possibly his highest-ranking DR.

"Perhaps you could take a look at that medbot first," Scallop says. "We certainly should have a fully functioning model, don't you think?"

I frown. "I thought you needed to know what happened to the servbot." I feel a twinge of something, a flutter in my connection to the implant. A temporary loss of focus.

"Oh, absolutely, absolutely. That's the top, highest priority. We need to know what happened there so we can send the crew home." Scallop frowns, and I can see the teeth working behind the lips, like he's chewing on the inside. "In fact, they are becoming adamant.

They have lives to return to. And they have powerful families below."

His pauses. More chewing. "Do you know anything new?" he asks. "I can delay them maybe a few days longer. I'm in a hard place—a crew that wants to go home, a mystery that they may help solve."

"I'm making progress," I say. "The bot is operational."

Scallop's face lightens again. "It is? That's wonderful. Wonderful news. So a solution is imminent, then?"

"I don't know..." I feel that lack of focus again. Honest to A, I need a chute. I start a quick diagnostic and let it run in the background. "Regardless, you should probably find someone else to make those fixes, if they are pressing. I need to concentrate on this one thing..."

Scallop looks sad, like I kicked his dog. "Another DR? It would be difficult. Very difficult. Hard to justify."

"But it may be necessary." I shut my eyes, shake my head. "I'm not..." The disconnect again. "It is hard to function at full capacity without chute sleep. I mentioned that before."

Scallop feigns sympathy. "And I'm very sorry for that, Sandfly. But as I told you, bringing a chute up is—"

"Difficult. I get it." I rub my eyes, attempting to emote something he'll understand. "Maybe I can go somewhere else? Someplace that has one?"

Scallop raises an eyebrow. "One of the pleasure craft? Another station? You expect *they* have facilities for—"

Of course not. Of course they wouldn't care about the people who had designed their flying shinys.

"Can't you send me back down, then?" I ask. "Just for a day. Or get someone else. It would be in your best interest to have someone running clean."

I get the sympathetic look again, but with a glint of steel behind the eyes. "Sandfly, I *am* sorry. But we cannot let anyone leave until we know what happened. There is too much risk, too much at stake."

I stare at him silently for a long moment before gesturing with my head, nodding forward. "I'm going to get something to eat," I say, "and then I'll go back to work."

Scallop nods firmly. "Very good," he says. "That's a very good idea. Like the medbot suggested. You need to keep yourself fed to function. Certainly that will help."

I nod. It feels like hundreds of ball bearings all striking the inside of my head. I force a smile and move forward.

"Unfortunately, I have already eaten. Or I would join you."

Yeah, yeah, I would've liked that.

I manage a wave and enable my legs, willing myself away. I have a job to complete, orders to follow.

And orders are like messages...

I GO THROUGH the repast process quickly, interacting with the refectory's servbot as little as possible—and completely ignoring the requisite call to prayer it gives me after delivering my meal. I even hide the table's simulated temple niche with my plate.

If I can touch the stream with my eyes open, why can't I pray with them open too? I'm sure the higher power—be it A or someone else—has the ability to pick up broadcasts in whatever manner they are sent. I'm thinking he doesn't need any particular coding, any particular handshake. He's probably way beyond that.

But just because he can listen doesn't necessarily mean he cares, does it? Maybe we're just sending up his version of Easy Impact, all stale and unsatisfying. Maybe he has other things to do.

Abduls view A as a fierce bean-counter in the heavens, never stooping to our level. But my guess is that, if he exists, he would have to stoop a lot to care about us. About me. Because if he is counting beans, we aren't ever going to have enough.

THE NEXT STOP on my morning tour is my own room. This time I immediately walk to the window. Standing there, arms on either side of the viewport, gripping fast so I don't fall down, I take it all in. I let the little beams from a thousand stars fall right into my eyes, filling my head with light. I feel terrible, but somehow this little exercise seems to help. I drink in the enormity of the universe—all of it rushing into me.

I turn to study DarkTrench. It looks exactly the same—sleek and wonderful—but this time the sight of it almost makes me ill, brings a lump to my stomach and a weakness to my legs. It is like this large metal obelisk obscuring the real beauty beyond it. Hiding something real.

Rails, I need a chute.

Frowning, I push myself away. I grab my clothing at the chest, tug on it. With a little effort I free myself of it completely. I make a halfhearted attempt to get it into the hamper and then stagger into the steamer. I work the controls with my hands, even though I usually stream my preferences to the device.

It accepts streaming, doesn't it? *Doesn't it?*

Shaking my head I engage the knob, push the button. Cold mist buffets me, startles me—almost frightens me. I work the knob again and the steam softens some, becomes a little more palatable. I sigh as my gooseflesh retreats.

Suddenly the steam temperature spikes and my skin rails its discomfort. I'm like a lobster in a pot, awakening to his own demise. Screaming, I bang the knob again.

The steam doesn't stop. Instead, the temperature increases. I pound the knob again, then in desperation stream out to it: *Stop! I order you, stop it now!*

Nothing changes. I push on the steamer door, but it doesn't budge. Finally, I put my full weight against it. The door gives way and I fall out, crashing hard to the floor. *Tha-dummp!*

I pull my legs free of the scalding vapor and lie there a moment, infantile, shaking—fearful. The horror of the event only now starting to register.

What has happened to me? I couldn't control the steamer—not by hand, not by stream. In fact, it went beyond my commands being ignored, they were actually being inverted—toyed with. The steamer was working with maniacal intent to first freeze and then roast me. It was almost like it came alive.

Most machines are alive in some respect, though. Little nanos dancing…

"Overreacting," I say with a hiss. "Lack of sleep affecting your responses. There is a coherent reason."

The steamer abruptly ceases operation. Only a wispy tendril of steam now proves it had ever been on.

I push away from the floor and stand up. There's nothing available to dry myself with. It isn't usually necessary. So I pull one of the sheets from my bed and use that. I grab the clothing from where I left it, still unclean, and put it on again. I then ease down onto the bed, slide back toward the wall, and pull my knees up.

I need to think…

I stream out for some music. Something light and soft, something to sooth me. I'm grateful when I hear it start in my mind. I do a quick diagnostic again on the implant. Everything appears normal. Still.

I check for messages. Finding nothing new, I review everything I've received in the last few days. I linger especially long on Hard-Candy's message. Even with the urgency it exudes, it is comforting to me. I study Hard's facial features, finding them nearly perfect.

Most women in my world are forced to hide themselves, shroud themselves from head to toe. I found the practice completely normal until years after implantation. Now I find it presumptive.

If a higher power constructed the face, gave it symmetry, made it beautiful to behold to lovers and friends alike, should man hide it? Wouldn't that be like putting a bag over a flower?

Yet the eyes are never hidden, I think, watching Hard's eyes as she talks.

I frown, shake my head impulsively. I know from my meetings with my master, and the ones *he* calls "master," that the eyes are the most dangerous part. Always the eyes are dangerous. Why not cover what is most dangerous?

Like the nasty machines.

I realize I'm breathing fast, and I will myself toward calm. There is something wrong with me, there has to be.

"We can't fix you here." Scallop's voice from earlier.

I can't be fixed.

"...have to decommission you..." Scallop says again.

Messages only go one way.

"...like that LED..."

Singing!

"What's important is your state of reference..." Handler that time.

The insides of my cheeks ache. I grit my teeth, trying to force the feeling away. I shake my head rapidly. I'm relieved when it begins to subside.

Singing! Something about singing.

I know what you are wondering, freehead. You wonder how HardCandy can go around with her face uncovered in such a restrictive society. The answer is simple: she isn't considered a woman. Just like I'm no longer considered a man. She can't lead a man to evil because there is no evil for them to be led to. She is a *mahram*, an unmarriageable and unapproachable relative—to everyone.

Plus, HardCandy's head is shaved. And no good Abdul wants a bald woman, especially one who isn't really a woman, who couldn't respond like a woman. Who isn't allowed to!

And that's talking about good Abduls. There are many. Some are kind. Generous. But there are bad Abduls out there too. Plenty of them. Like those I saved HardCandy from. Like the man on the lift. Except they all *think* they're good, and anyone who acts as judge is likely to agree with them. A man's voice counts for more, you see.

I'm distracting myself, I know. I need to get back to the work. Back to my keep.

Maybe after some sleep...

IN MY PERSONAL DARKNESS, the shadows call me.

I receive an urgent message, and even though it isn't Full Impact, I can almost feel the emotion. I'm wanted by the pool.

I'm in a master's house—whether it is my current master or not, I'm unsure. I just need to get to the pool right away. I stream out for the map, because regardless of whose house this really is I don't know the way to the pool. It is a big place with lots of stone. Stone in the walls, stone in the floors, stone as decoration. Everywhere stone. Multicolored, stunning, and expensive.

Maybe the stone is affecting the stream, because even though I receive the summons I can't seem to figure out where I am. I'm lost for the first time. Inside! I stagger around searching, at times reaching out to drag my hands along the cold marble walls.

I initiate a labyrinth algorithm to figure my way to the pool. I keep making right turns until a dead end stops me, then return to the last turn and try again. Turn after turn I wander; I find lots of closets and locked doors.

A badger parachutes from a chandelier above me. I stop and watch as he floats downward. He smiles and, with a flourish, hands me a folded piece of paper. I don't respond other than to take the paper, but he still manages a head bow as he drifts by. When he lands he begins to scurry about, looking lost himself, before finally disappearing around a corner.

I unfold the paper and find a map. Every room is labeled. Even the positions of bots and people are drawn into place. A useful map! There's a large blue rectangle that signifies the pool. After locating my current position, I note the turns required to reach my destination. I'm needed there. Urgently!

The badger's map proves accurate, for in little time I find the actual pool. Beside it is a small band of people. They are standing over a prone body. I hurriedly join them.

A great smelly man looks at me. "You are here, DR," he says. "Finally!"

I'm a little annoyed that he addressed me as "DR," but, feeling a warning buzz, I ignore my annoyance.

On the ground is a girl, approximately twelve years old, with dark hair and a face that is very, very blue. She looks dead to me. The other odd thing is the string of radishes around her neck.

"You can fix her," the man says. I notice his hands are stained black, the same color as the girl's dress.

I look at the girl. She still appears quite dead. "She seems to have been drowned," I say to the man. "Did you do it?"

"Yes," the man says. "She disobeyed the law. It was the proper thing to do." He indicates two men swathed in brown. "The mutaween are here, and they approved." He smiles. "But you can fix her."

I feel bad—awful—but also confident that I can't do a blinking thing. I try to stream anyway. I'm surprised when the act of streaming seems to make the girl's arms tremble. I get no response from anything approaching mechanics inside her, mind you, but her limbs still move. It is troubling, but so is the badger that, having returned, is now biting the man's ankle. The man doesn't seem to mind.

"I saved a woman once," I say. "But that was different. She had bad nanos in her heart. There are no nanos here."

The badger pauses in his biting. "I guess we don't need you on DarkTrench," he says. "We already have enough tenors."

Tenors? For some reason, that statement really rails me, so I stream out to the girl again, trying, desperately trying...

Her eyes open.

And so do mine.

ON THE WAY to the examination room, I decide to check my streaming abilities. I call out for the status of random machines as I walk by, turning off and on lights that are stream aware, mentally molesting two servbots on their way to their appointments—anything to see how well things are working.

In general, things respond as I expect. They seem to be stable, seem to be good. But occasionally there is a mystery. Like when I asked a drinkbot for juice and it shot coffee at me.

Hazard in the air, Sand. Much about this job isn't right.

I've received three messages from the outside, and two of them—excluding the trivial confirmation message from my master—were warnings. Both seemed to indicate danger, anyway.

HardCandy's was more subtle. Only the two of us know that the LED hangs overhead beneath the bridge. If I am that LED, then that means *I'm* overhead, doesn't it? Or am I simply hanged? And she really emphasized the word "care." Care, careful, I get it. She knows I'm up here and wants me to be careful.

Grim's message was worse, because it suggested my trip to the station was only one way. Since I doubt that notion is free for the streaming, it suggests one thing: Grim and Hard have been heavy sniffing on my behalf. Dancing real close to disaster.

How many hours has Hard spent touching the OuterMog, smelling salt water? Is she safe still? Is GrimJack?

Regardless, my prospects look slim. Only way to know for sure, though, is to finish the job. I would like to do that, but not if it means I'd later be taking a walk in space, sans suit. I'm not high on space, as you already know. Seeing it all brilliant and airless? No thanks.

It could be all paranoia. The rumblings of a distracted, hampered mind...

I don't trust Scallop, though. Never have. He's too relaxed for an Abdul.

Abduls breathe control—control the temples, control the streets, control the women, control the bots. Tweak them, beat them, make them stop!

Then there's the transmission I heard on DarkTrench. I remember it fully now. I know it sounds whacked, but I really thought I heard singing. Couldn't tell what kind. It wasn't any Abdul singing, I know that. Nor any bot. It was more symphonic, glorified. Blinking strange!

No real sleep. That's the main problem.

Which very well might be. Lack of chute sleep is certifiably problematic. Could it account for all of my problems? Explain all the weirdness? My problem with the shower? My having passed out on the ship?

Signs point to *No*, Sand. This job is just wrong.

The best thing I can do is to get out and be done with it. Let the ship flip wherever it wants. I have a few tricks in my head yet. Maybe I can dodge whatever it is that Grim is worried about.

I reach the examination room and stream open the door. That works without a hitch, thankfully. I stumble inside and tell the door to shut behind me, which it gleefully does. I stop in my steps.

My friendly servbot is no longer sitting on the table where I left it. In fact, he doesn't seem to be in the room at all.

The room isn't that big, but I search it anyway. Frantically. Where the...?

I close my eyes and try to remember the last thing I told it—my last command. I'm fairly certain it was to run a diagnostic on itself. That was it, wasn't it?

Yes, it was. I know it was.

Just like you told the steamer to maintain a comfortable temperature. How did that work out?

I tug on my jumpsuit, begging it to rip a little. Now what?

Regardless of his ultimate intentions toward me, there is no way I'm telling Scallop that my job got up and left.

Frustrated, I decide to go looking for the bot. Maybe someone moved it. I attempt to stream open the door, but get no movement. I walk to the door and lay my hand on the manual pressure-plate—the same plate any Abdul would use. The same plate Tall-Spot used only yesterday.

Again, nothing.

I bang my fist on the door, but all I get is the dull *thunk* of flesh on steel. I smash the pressure plate again, still nothing.

Shout! Need to yell!

Instead I try streaming again. The door merely chirps back at me. It is receiving the message, but ignoring it. A wave of panic hits me. Next comes exhaustion—my legs feeling wobbly.

No. Rails, no. I'm not passing out again.

I start a mental test on myself, recalling memories from child-hood, thinking of HardCandy's face—anything to keep me active. I touch the stream again, looking for schematics, latent manuals, something that can help me get the blinking door open. Surprisingly, I'm still banging on the door as well. I might also be shout-ing.

The door slides open to reveal Scallop. He is right there. Stand-ing just outside the door.

I quickly move to block his view.

"Are you all right, 63?" he asks, brow rumpled.

I feel moisture on my temple. Surprised, I reach up to dab it. My hand is slick with sweat. Got to get into spec here...

I straighten myself, and try to widen myself too. "Fine," I say. "Functioning fine."

Scallop's eyebrows rise almost imperceptibly, but I notice. His neck cranes a bit too, bringing his head up past my left shoulder.

But I don't allow it. I straighten more while willing my shoulder to grow, hoping it becomes a mountain in Scallop's line of sight.

His eyebrows lower, as does his neck. "The condition of the bot...?"

"Close to functional," I say. "That headchip you brought me helped a lot. I could use a few more things, though." I do my best to sound serious, in control. "In fact, I may take you up on that offer to send a handwritten note. Have any paper with you?"

It is a good thing Scallop is short, because I'm not really a big guy—most debuggers aren't—and if he were bigger, and even a tad more belligerent, he'd be in the room already. Instead, he takes a step back. "Paper? No...back in my office..."

"Would you mind getting it for me?" I ask. "Only a few more items. I'm so close." I force a grin. "Unless you want to open the stream for me?"

"You know I can't..." Scallop stops and wags a finger at me. "Playing with me, Sandfly. I see."

I shrug. "Sometimes I have to. Keeps the neurons limber." I smile. "Anyway, about that paper..."

"Would it be possible for me to see the bot?" he asks. "I would like to see your progress. I'm sure you've made some, of course, but I have superiors to deal with. The crew—"

"I was just going to talk to them," I say. "I need to use the facilities, and then off to see the crew. I'll tell them what I've done."

That gets his attention. "You would do that?" he asks. "I mean, I know you are able. But you're kind aren't known for, um, interpersonal skills. I would hate for you to be misunderstood..."

This is taking way longer than I expect. "How far is your office?" I ask, stretching my head into the hall.

Scallop looks down the hall nervously. "It is...some distance...why?"

My mind races, secretly searching for some way to distract Scallop without bringing the wrath of correction on me. It is a hard cliff to climb. Finally, I think I have something.

The gold com device on Scallop's chest begins to flash. With a look of annoyance, he reaches down and yanks the thing free. It makes a slight sucking sound as it disengages. He lays the device in one palm, where it quickly elongates to fill the available space—which means, not a lot. An image stares up at him. I can't see what it is exactly, but I have a good idea.

Scallop's face registers surprise. "It appears that there is an issue I should address," he says, slapping the com back to his chest. "If you will excuse me?"

"You'll bring some paper, then?"

Scallop is backing down the hall already. "Of course... yes...I will."

I wait until he turns a corner, then step into the hall and manually pull the door shut. I stream to it and, finding it responsive now, instruct it to remain locked until I return. To be certain, I take out my probe and burn a small hole in the control. It isn't big enough to see, but it shears enough of the mechanism to keep the door shut.

Until I fix it, of course.

In fact, unless they get another DR soon I'll probably have to also fix the maintenance bot that Scallop is going to see—the one that has somehow mistaken the cracks around the refectory door for hull breaches and is now dutifully sealing them.

Not sure how it got to that part of the station, but with its faulty optical circuit, it was bound to miss a few turns...

I run down the hall, smiling, streaming wide.

FROM EARTH, THE STATION is doubtless a speck, but having been on it, having spent over an hour searching for a renegade bot, I can honestly say the place is honking big. Over three kilometers around—which, using conventional mathematics, means it is better than a third of that across. In the simplest terms, it is large enough to make finding the bot difficult.

"You're a debugger," you say. "It should be easy, shouldn't it? You have that fancy implant in your head—doesn't that get you anything?"

Normally it would, that's right. Normally I would stream out, get myself a map—mostly so I don't bump into any walls or wander into a restricted area—and use the stream to find the location the bot is logging itself. That would be the easy way.

There is a big problem with that method, though: the bot isn't reporting its location *at all*. Or if it is, I'm looking for the wrong bot. You see, I think I have the right ident for the servbot stored in my head. I mean, that information was one of the last things it gave me. But I'm becoming a little suspicious of that. Did I get the number right? Because if I did, the bot is nowhere to be found.

Or the reporting mechanism is broken. I thought I went over everything, but maybe I missed something.

All that is left to me is a concentrated and frantic search. Like in my dream, I'm forced to use labyrinth techniques. I take each hall as I come to it, open each door, peek in cautiously—even call out for the bot in the stream—then move on. Further complicating my hunt is the incredible number of bots on this station. Hundreds!

I enter another unfamiliar hallway. By the dimness of the lights it appears to be rarely used. The lights don't notice my presence, however—they stay dim. That's odd, but there is still enough illumination to see by.

Near the far end of the hall is a bottle-shaped servbot, colored green and running on four wheels. Its primary function is to keep the glass clean, or so the stream tells me. Otherwise, the hall is vacant.

There are four doors ahead. I make my way to the first on the left and attempt to stream it open. No-go. I frown and work the touchpad. The door slides away. I look in and find an empty room. I work the touchpad again, but the door doesn't close. I shake my head.

This station needs some maintenance...

The servbot has now closed half the prior distance between us. It has an appendage extended, the end of which is a narrow rubber wiper, held at an angle. I glance back the way I came. I don't see any windows there. Frowning, I cross the hall to the next room. This one streams open fine. The lights don't come on, though, so I work the manual switch.

This room appears to be for bot storage. There are three servbots—older hominoid models—lined against the opposite wall, completely void of life. None is mine. There is a storage rack filled with rectangular containers. All clearly marked. They contain replacement parts. "Cricket legs," one container reads. "Serv hands," reads another.

Lying in a bundle to my left are a handful of long metallic bots, representatives of the exploration snakes I noticed when first entering the station. They appear lifeless as well.

I return to the hall. The cleaning bot—having passed my position—now turns to look at me. Orange lights blink across its chest. I take a few more steps, watching. The bot aims my direction, and lurches into motion. The wiper appendage rises to eye level, straightens.

I stream at it, telling it to stop. Which it does.

Crazy bot.

I move to the next room. The door there snaps open without asking. As I stick my head within, the lights come on. Nice. I hear a clicking sound from above and turn back into the hall. On the ceiling—maybe a meter back—are two fist-sized cricket bots, standing immobile on six legs, excepting the antennas on their heads. Those vacillate slowly back and forth. As I watch them, a third exits the air duct and takes a position next to his brothers.

"What are you doing here?" I stream.

The bots report only that they are functioning normally. I somehow doubt that. Is every bot in this station blitzed?

A small maintenance bot skids around the corner behind the halted window cleaner. He slows his pace, draws even with the cleaner, and stops. The five of them—including the crickets—just stand there, blinking and clicking.

Now I'm a little freaked.

With another glance into the room, I determine it is empty. I don't bother closing the door. I cross to the last one, glancing back as I go. The bots move forward, keeping pace with me—the window cleaner included.

It isn't listening anymore.

I hear a rustling *clonk* from the storage room I searched. Soon a humanoid model appears, pausing at the door. One of the snakebots slinks out to curl around the serv's feet. Then another snake comes out. Then another.

I decide I don't care about this last room that much.

I quicken my pace, heading for the next hallway. "Stay there," I stream to all the bots behind. "Just stay there."

I hear the clicks and clanks of movement.

I reach the corner, turn into the hall. The lights here begin to flicker on and off.

I break into a run.

At about the hall's midpoint, an alarm begins to sound. It is muted—clearly a test tone—but it still annoys. I stream to it, see if I can stop it. It only increases in volume.

Another turn, I need another turn. Get away from this craziness.

I enter another hall. Glancing back, I feel relief to see no bots have followed. I slow my pace and contemplate continuing my search. Spying a door ahead, I move that direction.

Another alarm begins: *twee-looo, twee-looo, twee-looo.* The lights turn red and start to flash.

I hear footsteps. Someone coming on the run.

Guards?

I hurry to the next hall, enter it, and start walking casually. A few minutes later two brown-suited Abduls rush toward me.

I see a look of recognition—a glint of surprise—then they raise their heads and move past. I only bow as they *thump-thump* by.

I release my breath. Hurry on.

What is wrong here? What is going on?

ANOTHER THIRTY MINUTES of searching brings me to where I had first entered the restricted area, my current prison. Ahead are the same large double doors I'd walked through only a few days prior. Barely twenty meters separate me from freedom: from the lift and then real ground beneath my feet. I almost collapse at the thought of it.

I find myself blindly walking toward those doors, hand outstretched, grasping for a return to normalcy.

I become aware of the security measures then; the nasty machines I'd sensed on the way in. Those devices are watching me now, doubtless recording me. I sense their glassy eyes following my every step. A little further and an alarm will sound, I'm sure.

I feel a tingle in my head, the beginnings of something bad. Above, ceiling plates slide open. Two arms extend, at the end of which are mechanical fingers that curve inward like claws. In the center of each palm is a purple crystal.

I know what those machines do, and it isn't nice. They're called sonic inhibitors. Not deadly—I assume *those* machines come later on—but these machines will give you an earache that will floor you. Continued exposure will render you deaf.

Could you fix it, Sand? Make them so they won't harm you?

I can't believe I'm thinking it. Even more, I can't believe I haven't felt my own internal checks come into play yet. The implant isn't working like it used to. Clearly! Even thinking about disabling government equipment is tweak-worthy. It has to be.

And yet, no tweak!

Could I get free? Walk away from this whole mess? Sleep right again?

I look at the spots where the cameras and loudspeakers are hidden.

Shouldn't an alarm be sounding? Those guards pounding the halls?

But still no alarm. Nothing to indicate that I'm doing anything wrong. Well, except for the purple crystal claws.

Things are *not* right here.

I look at the sonic inhibitors again, one above to my right, the other to my left, both standing poised and ready.

Sound travels in longitudinal waves, freehead. If you send an equal and opposite wave from one source to another, they'll cancel each other out. At least, that's the theory.

I stream out to the claws and hear a chitter of response. Good, very good. I pull out their code bundle, make a fair guess at what I'm seeing, tweak it, and send it back. I instruct each to turn toward the other.

I watch in disbelief as they obey. This can't possibly work.

I take a slow step forward.

Nothing happens. I detect no sound whatsoever.

Another couple steps. Something happens, because I see the claws vibrating, but the sound is barely audible. I shrug and, with a glance behind me, continue forward.

I hear something more then. Sonic leakage. My programming couldn't be completely accurate, I know that. I'd guessed based on what I thought might work. I *feel* something in my ears now too—a mouse-like scratching. If the mouse were the size of an elephant.

"Couldn't you turn them off?" you ask.

The answer is no. Nasty machines like these never turn off. They're vigilant watchdogs. That's why they're nasty.

I stream out to the rightmost inhibiter, telling it to adjust its frequency a tad. It complies, but the adjustment doesn't help my head. Makes things worse, in fact. I'm forced to cover my ears...

"Back," I stream. "Adjust back."

Finally, I remove my hands. The cancellation is precise enough now that I can continue forward, which I do.

Still no alarm, no tweak.

I reach the point where I'm under the inhibitors. I'm still ten meters from the door at the end of this hallway. Over a dozen steps. The sonic claws are now screaming at each other silently. But more ceiling panels open ahead. This time the mechanisms that descend are cylindrical. Long emerald tubes.

What are these?

I hit the stream, looking for an answer. Before I locate anything though, I see silver bubbles form at the ends of the tubes. They grow to about the size of a human head, then disconnect from the tubes and fall to the floor. They remain stationary just ahead of me. One bubble to my right, another to my left.

The stream is hushed on silver bubbles. Of course, it's Scallop's stream...

Curious, I take another step. Nothing happens for a moment, then I detect a bit of movement in the leftmost ball. It presses downward slightly, flattening, and expands upward, elongating, reaching for the sky. After a few slow repetitions, it begins to bounce in place steadily. The right ball soon follows suit.

I stand there for a full minute, watching the two silver sentinels bouncing before me. They are balls composed of nanos, they have to be. I could think of no other way for them to work.

If they are nano-powered, I should be able to touch them...

I stream out, giving them a poke, trying the most likely channels. I sense nothing initially, but after a few seconds I detect a faint, high-pitched shriek. I magnify it, listen closely. The pitch seems to change as the balls contact the floor, right before they push off.

Got them. Has to be their communication.

I think I can...

Nervously, I take another step forward. The balls' bounce pattern increases, as do the pitch changes. The balls also begin to converge toward me, without moving forward.

I don't like this game.

I can discern code information for individual nanos now. That brings a smile. It is going to be okay, I think.

I rearrange some parameters, adjust some values, and stream it back to the balls.

Now instead of bouncing once every two seconds they bounce

once every three. Easier than I thought! I can control their motion fully—I'm sure of it!

Confidently, I stride forward, moving between them and then past. I reach a spot maybe three paces beyond. Only four meters to go now.

I hear a pitch change behind me. It isn't coming from the balls, though.

The inhibitors!

Looking back, I see the claws swinging away from each other. Toward me.

Crichton!

I reverse myself, walking toward the inhibitors again, streaming commands as I go.

A buffet of sound hits me full in the face. I grit my teeth and quickly cover my ears. What is going wrong? I continue to stream, but it is like I'm locked out.

The implant is failing me again. That has to be it. Nothing else would explain—

From the corner of my eye, I see a shadow descending.

I drop to the floor and roll, just as a silver ball plows past my left side. It hits the floor hard enough to make a dent. Not good.

There would've been a nasty sound too, if it weren't for—

The inhibitors' resonance increases, becoming a screeching wail. I regain my feet, but am forced to duck as the other ball swoops by my head. I hit the floor again, somersaulting, rolling, anything I can do to keep ahead of the silver stallers.

That's what they have to be, I realize. Some method of keeping a wanderer stuck in place until the guards arrive. Like an ant in glue.

I can't imagine being caught will be a pleasant experience. Abduls are rarely civil in their punishment. An image passes through my mind—me with both legs glued to the floor, struggling to free myself, before my hips finally collapse. I fall...

Not pretty.

I continue my retreat, the balls dogging me, matching my stride. They start to work in concert, trying to head me off as I scamper down the hall. Meanwhile my hands are plastered to my ears. The noise is so intense now that my eyes well up. Water droplets slide down my cheeks...

"*Stop it!*" I stream out. "Leave me alone!"

It is like speaking to the wind. Like praying. Nothing changes.

The balls almost have me. One hurdles over my head to get in front of me. Almost. It lands about five paces in front and two to the right. The other leapfrogs that one, landing toward the center of my path, but farther up. There is no way out.

I tickle every frequency I know, sing to everything that matters—willing the implant to work *just this once...*

Suddenly everything stops. The inhibitors' screaming comes to an end. The balls drop to the floor like sacks of nails. They press downward into perfectly round nano-puddles.

*A familiar sound returns: twee-looo, twee-looo, twee-looo...*I contemplate making a fresh run for the exit doors. But the puddles still percolate like molten mercury, so I decide against it. I race the many steps to the moving walkway, and then past it to the far end of the hall. To my corporal prison. No guards at all.

Regardless of the state of the inhibitors and the silver bubbles, I still had many steps to go before I reached the double doors and freedom.

And A knows what would've come next.

I TURN THE NEXT CORNER and take only ten paces before nearly colliding with TallSpot as he exits an adjoining room.

He instantly recognizes me, smiling through his head bubble. "Sandfly!" he says, his voice amplified by the suit. "I didn't know you were still here."

"I am." My heart is pounding from fleeing the nasty machines, so my response is a bit clipped. I hope he doesn't notice. "You're here too, so…"

"Right, of course," he says, chuckling. "We aren't going anywhere until you sign off." As much as I hate to admit it, aside from being handsome, Tall is exceedingly likable. It is no surprise he's made it as far as he has.

Actually, he's probably made it farther than anyone now, huh?

"Are you feeling all right, Sand?" he asks. "You seem a little out of breath."

"I'm fine." Though, of course, I am not.

He pats my shoulder with a gloved hand. "Might want to get some exercise. We're actually a touch lower grav here than down below." A brotherly smile. "You'll feel it when you get back."

"Thanks." I consider trouncing his rep on the stream, then decide against it. He is trying to be friendly, I think.

I still have a bot to find, so I take a step forward. Intending to walk away.

"Your path?" he asks. "Where does it lead?"

Going to be hard to shake.

"No place in particular," I say, smiling a bit. "Just taking a walk."

"Mind if I join you?"

Suppressing a frown, I nod and start walking again.

Tall strides up beside me. "Have you gotten back to the neighborhood recently?"

I should mention that because of FI transmissions, because of the way we debuggers normally communicate with each another, the benefits of chitchat for us are slim. The slow reveal of someone's background and emotions is redundant and often unnecessary. In fact, if I wanted to make the effort, I could easily find out if TallSpot himself has made it back to the neighborhood lately, so why ask?

"I haven't," I say. "After implantation, visiting our roots is discouraged." Plus, my parents sent me away, remember? I smile. "And we're kept busy."

TallSpot laughs. "Of course, you would be." He draws silent as a rectangular maintenance bot approaches and moves past. Perfectly behaved. "It is too bad, what they did to you," he says. "Too bad you got taken away." He glances at me through the bubble. "It was a good place to grow up. I made many fond memories there."

Bullies normally remember their hunting grounds that way...

"Um-hmm" is what I say.

"I have regrets too, of course." He frowns. "There were times I didn't treat others like I should have. Times I didn't stick up for those in need."

TallSpot stares down the hall now, so misses the long look I give the side of his face. For a moment, I suspect he's been implanted—his statement being a little too close to what I was thinking. Not that I could see an implant if he had one, of course. Or that an implant makes you a mind reader.

We reach a corner with a large viewport. The Earth is shining brightly through it. Instinctively, I shudder and turn away.

TallSpot approaches the window and looks out. "Time is important." He reaches out to lay a gloved hand on the glass. "So much is wasted on things of little lasting value."

Avoiding the corner, I take a slow step up the next hall. Amazing how each hall looks exactly like the other—stark white and lonely. "Like going to the stars?" I ask.

Tall draws up beside me again. "Oh, there's value in that," he says.

"Perhaps not what the Imam expects, but real value all the same."

Aside from when they're passing edicts on what tech I can or cannot use, I actively ignore the government. It is difficult, though. There are "Ministries" for every conceivable part of life, the most notable being that for the "Promotion of Virtue and Prevention of Vice." It is to that ministry that the mutaween from my dream belong. Their chief goal is to control thoughts without the benefit of an implant. Ironically, that means they are partially responsible for the relative free thought the implant allows.

Without it: no tech, no solutions.

I've seen glimpses of history—the unfiltered kind from the OuterMog—that talk about past governments. There were some that were truly free, where people could say and do nearly anything they pleased.

But somehow, inexplicably, those who claimed to fear government were the ones who increased the power of it. And in defense of rights, they somehow managed to surrender theirs, blindly, to the worst of those they sought to defend.

The trick is to know what is worth defending. If you can't find that, the Abduls have you.

A debugger's life is simple, though: think whatever you want, but only do what we say.

TallSpot is restricted too, of course. Living in his streamless world, he couldn't fathom the information I have available, nor the ways in which I can use it. But communications are much more dangerous for him, even through limited means. His last statement, in fact, was borderline treason.

"Why do you say that?" I ask.

Tall shakes his head slowly. "The Imam seeks to prove himself the mahdi," he says. "A savior to unite the world."

No surprise there. Every imam since the date change has sought lasting appeal—constructed statues, commissioned paintings—only to have the next guy tear them all down. It is an obsession with these people.

"And shouldn't he?" I ask.

Tall is the freest speaker I've met in a long time, so anything he says now is interesting. Slow or not.

He sighs. "It is his right, of course. Certainly, something is needed to stop the wars. Certainly, they should've stopped by now..."

Part of me agrees. The other part thinks that Abduls wouldn't know what to do if they weren't fighting someone. If not unbelievers, then those who don't believe enough. Another "state of reference" thing, I guess.

There are debuggers involved in war too, of course. Usually only those considered communal property by a group of investors: DRs past their prime or those found to be troublesome. Government owns some, as well, but those are usually wellprotected. No one wants an implant falling into the wrong hands.

We pass another viewport and this time I venture a look that way. The band of the Milky Way sprawls out, filling nearly the whole port. Billions of stars moving in symphony. The mass of it seems to push in at me, filling my head with invisible matter.

"How?" I ask. "How does he intend to prove that he is the mahdi?"

TallSpot sniffs noticeably. "He seeks the birthplace of Black-Rock."

BlackRock?

Since the beginning of our time, Abduls have paid homage, virtually worshiped, a rock in the city of M. It is thought to be a meteorite that fell to Earth shortly after the creation of the world. An altar said to have fallen from A's own hand.

There has been very little testing allowed on it. It could be a lump of coal for all we know.

"And the logical place to look is Bait al-Jauza?" I ask, doing my best not to scoff. Scoffing can be tweak-worthy.

Tall shrugs. "There are other possibilities, of course, but there were many issues involved in the choice of our first trip. The meaning of the name was certainly a factor."

"Armpit of the central one?" I say, and this time I laugh out loud. I can't help it.

He smiles and shakes his head. "Not *that* meaning," he says, "the other one. The hand—*hand* of the central one."

Absently, I pull for messages on the stream. I have none.

"So you went searching for...what?" I ask. "Jannah? Paradise?"

Tall's face grows serious. "We were searching for anything to appease the Imam. And to keep the more radical elements happy. An asteroid with similar properties as BlackRock would work. But again, there are many objectives on any such journey."

"I'm still not finding the logic," I say.

BlackRock was originally thought to have been white in color, but the sins it has absorbed over the past two thousand years have turned it black. Is the rock now full? Wouldn't BlackRock, if they found it, be white? And would the world accept as genuine a white BlackRock?

"Since when has logic had any bearing in our world?" TallSpot asks.

Again, I'm amazed by his transparency. I agree with his insights, but they are risky to openly discuss. Especially when speaking to someone who could release your discussion to the stream in a moment's time. He must either trust me or have absolutely no fear of my implant. I'm not sure what option intrigues me more. It stirs another question.

"Why are there no debuggers on this station?" I ask. "Or on DarkTrench?"

TallSpot is quiet for many steps down the hallway, so many that I'm sure I've reached the end of his frankness—the point where he finally retreats within his Abdul shell. Then he touches my shoulder again. "The bot you fixed, what did you discover?"

Oh, yeah. That.

"I haven't fixed it yet, completely," I say. "Getting close, but not yet."

TallSpot turns to look at me, surprise evident on his face. "That is odd."

"What is?"

He shakes his head, a fairly efficient way to communicate, all things considered. Less so when one's head is within a bubble. Then it is borderline strange. "I could swear I saw that bot only a few moments ago."

"That hardly seems possible," I say. "I'm still working on it."

A sniff of puzzlement. "Now that is odd. I've seen that particular bot so often, I could've sworn that was it. It is like seeing my brother's face." Another head-bubble shake. "No matter. That wasn't the point in my asking."

It would be nice if he told me where that bot was going... "What *was* your point in asking?"

"They have been experimenting with the bots up here," Tall says. "You should look closely at them while you can."

"I cannot," I say. "At least, not as closely as I might like." I tap my scalp. "New rules."

"How recent?"

I shrug. "Since my last real sleep. A few days ago."

"But they could've been set earlier?"

Another shrug feels necessary. "Of course."

"The bots in this station are intended to be maintenance-free," TallSpot says. "Works in theory. Not so often in practice."

"That would be my experience," I say, glancing back to be sure a horde of bots isn't shadowing us. "Many things here need adjusting."

"I expect that was part of the problem with our bot, as well," he says. "They've bitten off more than they can swallow with their innovations. The masters. I fear their intentions may not be wholly admirable, Sand."

You see, this is the reason we debuggers hate normal communication. So much lead time to get to the point. Do you know how many things I could've gotten done in that time, freehead? Any idea?

"Meaning, what?" I say.

"Meaning...I think they mean to replace you, replace your kind. That's why there were none on the mission, no debuggers on the station. It is all proof-of-concept stuff up here. They want to see if they need you at all."

For a moment I'm speechless. "We're completely controlled," I say. "We can't be a threat to them. To anyone."

"I'm not saying I agree with the idea," he says. "But I think that's the plan." He pauses, looks me in the eyes. "As long as you've been implanted, has there ever been a mechanism that hasn't been superseded, hasn't been retired?"

"No."

"Then what makes you think you're any different?"

We've walked some distance now, and I have little to show for the calories burned—at least, as far as my original search is concerned. Even now, the job tugs at me. I've been unable to look into any of the countless doors we've passed. Consequently, I shrug again, giving TallSpot the feeling that I don't care about the current subject matter. Which may be accurate.

"It makes no difference to you, does it?" he says.

"At some level it does, of course. Who wants to be decommissioned? Who wants to be rendered useless?"

"But, in general, the idea doesn't bother you." Tall shakes his head. "Amazing. They really know what they're doing with those implants."

I feel fatigued again. An unwelcome reminder that nothing is really as it seems with me. One way or the other, I need to have this job behind me. I need things normal. Whether that means decommissioning or not.

"When you saw that bot," I say, "the one you thought was mine, which direction was it going?"

TallSpot studies me silently for a long moment.

"I may need it as a reference bot," I say. A lame explanation, but Tall wouldn't know.

Tall shakes his head. "You're really not human, are you?"

Silly question. "Of course not."

Ahead of us is an intersection, he points to the right. "Back that way. Planetary north. My guess is it was heading for one of the prep labs. That's where it used to work, anyway. Before."

"Thank you," I say. I leave TallSpot behind.

Like every Abdul.

I DRIVE TALLSPOT'S THEORIES from my mind. It does me no good to hear them. Not unless he can do something to change things. *No good.* In fact, it only diverts me from the chore at hand. Food is a diversion, sleep is a diversion. Fear is definitely a diversion.

If you fix the bot and they decommission you—or even eject you—what happens next? Do you trust their words that all is gold for you then? Are you sure you're on the right path?

Diversions. My life is full of them. Because even though I'm a little more than human, I'm definitely not a machine. My mind can go all kinds of where.

To the right, Sand, the lab was to the right.

I give my head a shake, forcing it to clear, then stream out for the station map to verify. The lab is to the right, as is DarkTrench. All the more reason to go there. I turn that direction and hurriedly make my way.

I begin to plot what I'll say to anyone who happens to be in the lab. They'll probably wonder why I'm there searching for a bot. It might be difficult. I might need to get creative.

Scallop said I had free rein, didn't he?

Finally, I see a door ahead and to the right. The door itself is outlined in yellow, and above it are large letters that say "LAB." Beyond the door, the wall is transparent for many meters. Slowing, I approach the clear portion and peer in.

Within the lab, I see that the wall color is grey, with all the upper cabinet faces being primary colors, forming a little rainbow around the room. That could be for some bot's benefit, a helpful indicator where to find things, or someone's strange idea of "cheeriness." In the center of the room is a slab of black granite. A work table. And there are matching countertops around the perimeter. There is no sign of any Abduls, but across the room is another closed door. No sign of my bot, either.

Curious, I touch the outer door's pressure plate and, relieved, hear the door crack open.

Inside, I give only a passing glance to the articles on the table and countertop. Much of it appears to be chemistry-related. There is the usual assortment of clear mixing and storage devices—test tubes, beakers and the like—along with sinks and warming mechanisms.

Placed in one corner is a refrigeration device, about shoulder height. I resist the urge to look inside that. Scared that someone might be storing a new disease in an unsecured manner. Not that I couldn't create a miniswarm of nanos to combat anything they could devise. It is the hassle of the thing. Abduls can be careless.

I walk to the inner door and activate the plate, but nothing happens.

I touch the door in the stream, find that it has a three-decimal locking code, and smirk. Such a mechanism would stop most Abduls cold, of course, but no DR worth his bits would stall on it for long. I give it a quick turnaround, let the implant work the numbers, and hear the lock break free.

Need to raise the bar a little higher there, Abbys!

The door slides away. Beyond it is a large, dimly lit room. The floor is the color of onyx and splits before me into separate paths around a central, glass-enclosed section. Through the glass I can see motion on the far side of the room. There are large vidcreens along the wall there, but there is also a moving figure.

I take the left path around the enclosed center. As I walk, I examine what is inside. There are a dozen large canisters, each about a half meter across and four or five meters high. All are set on end, like great columns. Their surface is reflective—a glossy black material, excepting a small transparent circle in front. There is a steady stream of information being projected onto the transparent portion, making them glow slightly.

Display cases? Holding tanks?

The whole room has the feeling of activity, of important information, flowing knowledge and power.

Moving closer to the glass, I realize that a portion of each canister is filled with liquid. The portion near the top, because whatever is inside is being magnified by the medium. The whole thing looks quite advanced, more advanced than anything I've seen on the station yet, excluding DarkTrench.

Access to this inner chamber is on the other side, so I move ahead quickly. Soon I reach the far end of the room, where the vids are. The figure I saw is not a human but a bot. It stands there, hands playing over the desk in front of him. Above him, images change, move...modify.

He is completely naked.

Sensing motion, he turns to look at me. His face is bland, like the faces of all servbots, with a mouth incapable of opening or closing. The visage is changeless, yet somehow it produces emotion in me. My adrenaline has increased, sparked by a mixture of relief and fear. The cause of my relief seems obvious. My fear...I'm not sure.

"Peace be to you," he says. "You require service?"

I test the bot's rudimentary communications link, querying for his identification. The link works perfectly. He responds with all the pertinent information. He is my bot, the lost one.

"Why are you here?" I ask—aloud, for some reason.

"I am performing my duties admirably, DR," he says.

"I am DR 63," I say. "And I instructed you to run a diagnostic after I woke you. Do you remember that?"

"Of course. My systems are performing as per the last updated spec."

"Then why are you here?"

"You instructed me to run a diagnostic, DR 63. Rudimentary was completed in 46 minutes, 23.1 seconds. Systems were found to be working within optimum parameters. Flow: at acceptable levels, biofeeds: at full pull, patents: protected, headchip: empty, remedial instructions: uploaded from TC, encryption uncompromised..."

"But you got up from the table and left," I say. "Why?"

"Rudimentary was complete. Optimal performance dictates a return to service. When DarkTrench is at dock, this is where I serve."

Bots are nothing if not structured. Completely loyal to their programming. "And what is it you do here?" I ask, glancing back at the tanks.

"That information is protected, DR," he says. "Only the station administrator can give permission for me to discuss it." He pauses, tips his head. "Is there another way I can help you?"

I feel a little railed. First, because the bot up and left, and second, because it thinks it is now okay to go on with life as usual. I'm not finished with you yet!

Not that I should expect anything different. Knowing the rules is one thing. Rules are easy to formulate into code. Understanding the nuances of human interaction is something else. That's really hard to get right. Things like politeness and manners. Things that require intuition.

Like waiting to see if the debugger who repaired you is finished with you or not.

Actually, there are humans who still have problems with those things as well.

Something else is bothering me, though. "How do you know that?" I ask, still aloud. It feels right.

"How do I know what?" he asks, unblinkingly. Face as bland as ever.

Rails me. *Really.* "How do you know any of that? How do you understand permissions or protections, or..." I look up at the screens. One is displaying the code that allows motion in a particular class of nanobots. I point a finger at it. "Any of this? Standard uploads wouldn't give you this knowledge. It is way beyond spec."

He turns to look at the screen, then back at me. "It is part of my programming, DR."

At this point I wish I had my supply bag with me. I would pull out a sheet and give the bot another going over. I missed something. Something important.

I look at the center section again with its black pillars. One of the canisters is close enough that I can almost see the object within the liquid. It is very tiny—in actuality, probably smaller than a fingertip. But the outline is extremely familiar.

Teardrop-shaped.

An image bursts into my mind. A slice of my life...

Bamboo, my tutor, is dressed in white, standing beside a giant black chair. Hanging from the ceiling is a silver machine: a large metal spider. A dozen arms end in a dozen different appliances, some looking dangerous and shocking, others appearing quite harmless. Bamboo brings out a vial filled with liquid. Floating inside is a tiny object—a speck of dark within a pool of amber.

"This is it," he says. "So tiny. So very wonderful."

I'm a genuine child, not even eleven years old, yet I'm attempting to be strong. "My implant?" I ask.

His smile broadens. "Your connection to the world. A memory backup, a communication device...an integrated conscience. All should be so fortunate."

"And it won't hurt?" I ask, as somber as I can manage. I try not to stare at the metal spider overhead, but it is difficult.

"You'll be awake throughout the entire procedure," Bamboo says. "And yet you won't feel a thing. In one of A's wonderful omissions: the brain has no nerve endings whatsoever. As if it were made for implantation." Another smile, followed by an awkward pat on my already smooth head. "See how He cares for you?"

Bamboo steps away, gestures toward a mounted vidscreen. "You'll be able to watch whatever you like during the procedure. I really think you will enjoy it..." He places the vial on a nearby counter. The motion causes the implant to swivel in the solution like a bug in a whirlpool. "And when this is over,"

he adds, "you will be a level 10 debugger. A connected man. A valued possession. One of a chosen brotherhood."

I force myself to stay in the moment, to listen to everything Bamboo is telling me. Because it is important, it is proper...it is the *right* thing to do. I have been chosen!

But I can't fully pull it off. All I want is to be back home with my parents. All I think about is the metal spider descending onto my brain as I attempt to watch vids, its arms articulating over me, boring into my skull to insert a metal tick within.

I scream!

Returning to the present, I find the door, push my way into the central enclosure, and stand before one of the cylinders. The object inside it is an implant, it has to be. The surrounding fluid would make sense: it would help maintain the connections, keep it functional.

"Why are there implants here?" I ask.

"I do not know the why, DR. It is not part of my programming."

"But what *is* this?" I ask, pointing at the cylinders in succession.

"Exceptional immersion fluid," he says, moving up to join me. "Able to simulate a biological host within a margin of error of less than .00043 percent."

I wish I was sure of the exact numbers, but by mere speculation I'm sure I can get close. Each implant is stamped with a number, you see—cataloged—and those numbers are all known to someone in government. They are like rare coins, except they don't trade on the open market, or any other kind of market. They are the chief of controlled substances. I have never seen even two together at once. There is only one way the station has so many in one place.

"These are the DarkTrench designers, aren't they?"

The bot stares at me silently.

"Their extracted implants, I mean."

Penchant pauses aren't normally a part of bot personality specs. Finally, he nods. "That is correct, DR."

I move slowly from one canister to another, like a preschooler studying fish at an aquarium. I'm both frightened and awed by what's inside. The warnings were true—none of the debuggers got off the station with their implant intact. I suspect none of them got off, period. That insight has great significance for me.

Just as significant, however, is the other part—the awe part. I can't believe what these implants (inside the DRs, of course) were able to accomplish. DarkTrench is a work of art.

"And why have they been preserved like this?" But before the bot can respond, I say, "No, let me guess." I stare at the information flowing across the nearest cylinder. "To preserve the technology in its basest form. To have the source recorded for later access so they can get to it all again if they need to. When they make the next one."

The bot drops its head. "That is beyond my knowledge, DR."

I stride past the bot to exit the glassed chamber. I stop at the workstation, the vid panels pulsing with activity above me. "You're maintaining the catalog of information, aren't you? Making sure it is available at an instant's notice." I pause. "Does this console connect to the outside stream?"

"It does not," the bot says. "That would be against isolation rules."

I frown. "And would mean the investors aren't much for sharing information. Probably don't want other DarkTrenches flying around." I watch the information flowing above me. "Who knows what someone from the OuterMog would do with the tech?"

Or whoever our current enemies are.

Fatalism runs through Abdul teaching. One of the first things they teach us—even before debuggers are chosen—is to accept our lot in life. If you are given an implant, you are a tool of your master, a tool of the state. That is the way it is destined to be. True hope is stripped from us long before implantation. Essentially, we are all bots—Scallop, Tall-Spot, GrimJack—all of us. Cogs. Nanos swarming on a speck of dust we call Earth.

I've been conditioned to accept that. I *do* accept that. But I don't always like it.

I wish for the chance to be back at HardCandy's spot beneath the bridge. The place where the edges blur.

Ironically, as I'm thinking that, I receive a message from her. It was sent Full Impact, so I know I will enjoy it. Sometimes I need to touch humanity—feel the emotions. They *are* a distraction, but right now I think I need them. Especially hers. I know the bot won't mind.

I close my eyes to the flickering vids overhead. I want to embrace whatever's coming.

HardCandy's figure appears, but this time there is no toughness apparent. I get the usual spine-tingle from her presence, but have little time to bask in it. Her emotions are all over the place, vacillating between highs and lows. Her arms are straight in front of her, twined together at the hands. Her fingers are knitting together and releasing. Nervousness in action.

She looks beautiful.

"I don't know if you're still out there, Sand. I think you are...hope you are." She pauses, swings her arms up slightly. "Anyway, I got a call today from the proverbial We. You know—MasterChief—and he said they need someone out there. Soon. So I got it, Sand. Me...I'm taking the lift...coming up there... to you!"

Her eyes play the ground in front of her, only rising briefly to the space where my face would be if I were actually standing in front of her. Then I feel a drop in her emotions: from a nervous happiness to a bitter low. "I come up tomorrow." As she turns her head, I see an indication of purple on the side of her face.

Shock and anger fill me.

"I still haven't forgotten," she continues, her eyes staying forward for a long moment. "He didn't want to send me, but I *really* pushed him." A pause where she looks at the floor. "Maybe a little too much." A forced chuckle. "You know how I can be, sometimes, right? That's why they call me Hard."

Another twined arm swing. "Anyway, if you're still there, if you're still streaming, and you don't have your head up the sphincter of a trash reducer or something, I'll see you." Another pause and a smile. "Soon."

The message ends. Another few seconds of HardCandy's brain connecting to mine. Still not enough. Plus, any joy I might have from the transmission is suppressed by the thought of the canisters that stand behind me. I wonder: somewhere on station, is there a canister with my name on it? Or now maybe two?

She's coming here. Clarke and crichton. I've got to stop that somehow, don't I? I mean, I want to see her, but not *here*... not if it means she'll lose her implant. Or her head.

I turn to the bot, who is standing exactly where I left him. "I need to see you again," I say. "Soon. I need to check you again."

The bot mimics a shrug. "I am performing at full capacity. The diagnostics ensure that—"

"I don't care a rick about diagnostics." I blast into the stream, for emphasis. "I am the DR assigned to you and I want to check you again. That's my prerogative."

"Yes," he says, bowing. "May A give you a good reward."

A returning bow is expected, but not given. "I seem to have a problem finding you on the stream," I say. "Why are you masked from me?"

Another shrug. "It could be this room. I'm told it can interfere—"

"If that's the case, then I want you to come to me at a precise time. Does that register?"

"Absolutely, DR 63. Your word is mine to follow."

"That is correct," I say. "It is."

"All praise be to A, with whose benevolence the good things lead to perfection."

I give him a specific time, something that should be easy to remember. He confirms verbally and, after I dismiss his attention, he immediately returns to the console and his cataloging.

This job is a can of wombats.

I have no idea what that term means, exactly, but it's something I got from GrimJack, and it seems to apply.

"One last thing, servbot," I say.

He turns my way again and bows. "Yes?"

"Put some clothes on!"

With a final glance at the glowing canisters, I leave the room.

I HURRY DOWN THE HALL, checking side passages for groups of rogue bots just to be sure. None at the moment.

I haven't given much thought to my implant and how it *has* been behaving over the last few hours—probably because it has been behaving, at least as far as I can determine. During my whole conversation with TallSpot, and my time with the bot, everything seemed to play normally. Ever since my foolish run on freedom and my battle with the nasty machines, I've been generally okay.

Was it all the result of sleep deprivation? A disconnect brought on by the chemicals that are present when a mind is tired? Lingering lactic acid or something?

I *am* tired, have been for days. Thinking about that, I contemplate slipping back to my quarters for another nap. It couldn't hurt.

I need to keep HardCandy from boarding the station, though. It is the least I can do. No sense both of us getting decommissioned. No sense abandoning my protectorate role now. Maybe that's love, I don't know. I'm not supposed to know! I simply know it is what I should do. And since apparently there is nothing tweak-worthy about that impulse, I'm going to do it.

Checking the station map, I locate Scallop's office. It is planetary west—the direction I'm already traveling, which is helpful. I EE his personal servbot to see if he's available. The bot is hesitant with a response, which is a trifle annoying. There is no reason for a bot to hesitate, ever. When it finally speaks, though, it says Scallop isn't in. Says he's still at lunch. Another trifle annoyance. Means a course change. Refectory, it is!

I get maybe four turns into my journey before I recognize Scallop coming my way. He smiles when he sees me. The guy rails me beyond belief.

"Sand, Sand," he says. "I have wonderful news for you!"

I'm pretty sure I already know what it is, but I don't want him to know that. Whether they say so or not, most Abduls are uncomfortable with the information we debuggers know. They would be even more uncomfortable if they knew what we *really* know.

"What do you have?" I ask.

"Another of your kind is coming aboard. In fact, he'll be here early tomorrow."

"Why?" I ask, forcing annoyance.

Scallop looks nonplussed—eyebrows wide, forehead heavily wrinkled. "You yourself suggested it. You said we needed someone to take care of all these issues you found. I didn't think they'd allow it, but they have. You should be happy."

"Well, they shouldn't have," I say. "All I need is another DR here messing things up, looking over my shoulder..."

"Is that really a problem?" Scallop says. "I've never seen debuggers in conflict before. I would think that your implants keep such behavior to a minimum..."

I shake my head. "You might have noticed debuggers working together and *thought* there were no fights." I tap my head. "But you couldn't imagine the real conflicts that are going on."

The reverse is most often true, of course. Though conflicts arise between debuggers, they are quite rare. In fact, multiple debuggers working in harmony are a thing of beauty. Like geese traveling north.

"Oh," Scallop says. "I see." A pause. "I'm sorry to hear that."

"Well, there's no helping it now," I say, frowning. "But it could certainly slow things down..."

"I'll do my best to keep him out of your way." Scallop frowns and scratches his chin. "Perhaps he can work on the medbot?"

I deepen my frown. "What level are we talking here?" I say. "Another thirteen?"

"I believe he is a twelve."

Another head shake, for effect. "Not sure I'd let him work on the meds first, then. I'd let him try something a little less complicated.

Maybe the servbots in the refectory. Or maybe the walkway..." I make a show of thinking. "A twelve may not be qualified for anything here, actually."

Scallop bounces with agitation. "Well, we can't afford to promote another," he says. "The lost expenditure on you..."

I hear a clicking sound. I glance at the ceiling, locate the nearest airduct. There is nothing there. No watchful crickets. Thankfully.

"I have the servbot working," I say. "Fully functional."

Scallop claps his hands. From winter to spring. "That's wonderful," he says. ""So you know what stopped it?"

"I should know that by the end of the day."

"That *is* good news. The crew will be ecstatic. And the ulama—not to mention the Imam himself—will be very pleased."

"Yes, that's important to me," I say, then pause. "About the additional debugger..."

"Yes?"

"Does he have a name? Perhaps I know his rep."

Scallop pulls loose his communication device and brings it up to look at the screen, squinting. "Yes, I think I have it." More squinting. "Ah yes, yes, *here* it is. DR 79, also known as HardCandy."

"*79*," I say, refusing to use her name because of the emotion it might bring. Instead I think of the worst DR I ever knew—a guy by the name of BluTroll. He definitely shouldn't have been implanted. He never got past the base level, level 10, because he didn't have the logic for it. He once locked himself in a stream-proof room.

"You know him?" Scallop asks.

"Of course," I say. "But it isn't a him."

Again Scallop looks shocked. "A woman?"

"As far as I can tell," I say. "With all the inherent disadvantages."

"A woman," he says, "on this station?" Scallop continues to stare at his com screen, as if it will suddenly confirm what I say. He isn't doing anything to manipulate it, though. He is frozen in place. "I'm not sure the regulations allow... Is she covered?"

"As covered as I am," I say. "Of course, you're more casual here than below."

Scallop's hand finds his forehead and slides slowly backward, smoothing the few strands of hair he has left. "That is true, of course... But an uncovered woman...here? We have men who have been gone a long time."

I shake my head sympathetically. "They're bound to be tempted."

Scallop touches his communicator screen quickly, sporadically. I doubt he is doing anything yet. "It may be too late to stop her," he says. "I think she's already on her way."

I nod. "You'll do what you can. I'm sure you'll find a way."

"Yes, you can be sure of that." Scallop returns his communicator to his side. ""You'll report as soon as you are finished? I will need to clear you from the station."

"Of course," I say. Clear me how? Through a garbage chute?

Scallop nods, still looking worried. "I will see you soon, DR."

He walks around me to head in the exact opposite direction from the one he was originally traveling. Which seems about right to me, overall.

I'M PREPARED WHEN THE BOT enters the examination room. Clothed in the traditional green robe.

I'm sitting on the exam stool, a sheet in one hand and the light probe capsule in the other. "Up on the table, please," I say.

"Certainly." The servbot—this Elipserv model that only days ago seemed hopeless and irreparable—hops onto the table as if he'd never been injured. I glance at the wallvid behind him. It registers his weight at a bit over seventy grams. Higher than spec.

His eyes lock on a point below my gaze, which is proper and expected, but he remains quiet. Eternally patient. I touch the stream, check his emissions into it. Nothing seems unusual.

"How did you know to return to your duties?" I ask.

"It is part of my primary instructions," he says. "If a diagnostic succeeds, I should return to my current duties. When we are docked on the station, my duties are in the catalog room."

"That may be," I say. "But I installed a blank head chip in you. Your previous one was missing. Completely destroyed. The sort of instructions you describe—primary command instructions, your tasks while on the station—these would be burned onto the headchip later, correct?"

A slow head bow. "That is correct, DR."

"But I installed a new one—a blank one. So where did those instructions come from?"

There is an odd and penchant pause. "Ah," he says then. "I understand what you require. Standard procedure—when a headchip reads empty, remedial instructions are loaded from the TC."

"The TC?"

"The vernacular term is 'tailchip,' DR 63."

"*Tailchip?*" I stream out for the bot's schematics again. The process is a bit slow since I'm attempting to touch the Elipserv domain. I should've kept a local copy, but so much of what is in a typical bot is second nature to me. Call it pride.

Finally, I've got the bot's diagram. I rotate it in my mind—feel along the outline, flip the thing over. "Where exactly is this chip located?" I see nothing that looks like a secondary chip socket.

The bot places a hand at the pit of his back. "I believe it is right here," he says, then pauses. "I have never seen it, of course."

I stand and walk behind him. Parting his green robe, I find the place where he touched. It feels exactly like it should. There is no indication, either visually or tactilely, that anything has been added there. "I want to apply a sheet here." It isn't necessary for me to ask, but such interaction is encouraged by the new rules. "Is that all right with you?" I unroll the sheet expectantly.

"It is fine, DR," he says. "May A give you a good reward."

I apply the sheet to his back, gently smoothing out the bubbles. The lumbar portion of a bot's anatomy is very complicated, as one might expect. Many pathways cross through there, as does all the bundling for both the top of the legs and the base of the spine. Circulatory fluid, plasti-sinews, nanocoils—there is a lot going on. It would be a strange place to position a chip, actually.

Nothing pops out at me initially, so I increase the mag and slide the image. A sinew bundle is directly in front of me, and those are fairly resistant to viewing—with a sheet, anyway. "Where is it on the z-axis?" I ask. "Is it nearer your front or back?"

"I am sorry. I do not know."

I didn't expect him to, but sometimes asking questions aloud helps me. Slows down the processing a bit. "I'd like to try a light probe now."

"That too is fine. May A give—"

"Thanks."

I find the tiny access hole I'd burned in the bot's back earlier. It should be large enough for the light probe. I press the bronze probe capsule against the hole and squeeze it. Another—near microscopic—capsule is ejected into the hole and begins moving, reporting to the one in my hand, which then relays the messages to me via the stream.

The information is rudimentary—quick system analysis of the components it passes, measurements of nano flow, charges over hard circuits. Nothing like what I'd get from a nano scanner. The probe *does* provide an inside visual, though, and that's something new. Slowly it winds its way down to a spot between the bot's hips.

Finally, I see something unusual. It is teardrop shaped, not unlike an implant but not entirely the same either. It is large enough for a chip, regardless. "I think I see it," I say.

"That is comforting," the bot says.

Funny guy.

I study the tailchip for ten seconds longer, reviewing everything the probe gives me. Most of what I'm getting is visual images alone. Not much. Not nearly enough to be certain. I'm tempted to bring out a burner or a slicer, cut the thing out, and look at it.

As much as it looks like an implant, it isn't transmitting into the stream separate from the bot's main unit. I'm getting only one emission point from him. The tailchip must be hardwired straight to the head. Not exactly imaginative, but a solid way to devise a backup unit. Did Abduls do this?

I command the probe to return to the entry point. Wait for it to return. "How much does it hold?" I ask the bot.

"I do not know the precise specs, DR."

"Let me ask it another way: do you remember your time on the DarkTrench?"

The bot pauses and I'm sure that if I strapped a sheet to his cranium right now I'd see nanos dancing like crazy. "The answer bears qualification. Standard impact memories begin at 2000 AH, Day 39, 6:30:52 a.m., aside from resident creation date memories."

I frown. The date he gave is today, of course. The precise time I inserted the new headchip. "But nothing before that?"

"As I stated, the answer bears qualification. Standard Impact memories begin at 2000 AH, Day 39—"

"You said that already."

"Yes, but if you'll let me continue, there are earlier data references that have been stored in Easy Impact. Plus a small amount of data in Extended Easy."

I get a bubble of hope. "Stored where?" I ask. "In the TC?"

"If the scenario you have given me is accurate, that my headchip was destroyed, then there can be no other location for permanent storage, DR. Each movement this model makes is recorded in EE for later playback if necessary. Movement is crucial to my function, of course."

"Of course." The idea of stepping through millions of movement notes does nothing to raise my spirits, however. Even implant-enhanced, there are some functions that border on monotony. How many movements would you say you make in a day, freehead?

Still, it is something. More than I thought I had. A small window into the past.

"Can you go back to the last entry you have prior to my reawakening you?"

"I am able," the bot says. "High velocity strike. Head to metal tubing."

"And before that?"

"High velocity strike. Head to metal tubing."

"And before that?"

"The instruction loops for many iterations, DR. Would you like me to play through them all?"

"How many iterations?"

"Ninety-eight."

I sigh. Ninety-eight head bangs ought to do it. Headchips aren't as fragile as an Abdul may think, but they can't withstand that kind of punishment. Ninety-eight times? I'm surprised it lasted through fifty.

I check the analog clock on the wall. Still ticking. HardCandy could be here any minute.

"Alright," I say, "Before those iterations, what do you have?"

"Single leg hop. Distance: two meters."

So the leg was missing by then. "And before that?"

"Another hop. Distance: one meter. Stabilization difficult. Obstacle found."

"Were your visual receptors working at this point?"

"Absolutely, DR, that is how the obstacle was found."

"But you have no visual storage from that moment."

"I can tell you verbally what the visual receptors logged. Images were not stored."

I can't help but frown. "All right, what did they log?"

"They are the dimensions of the object." The bot reiterates the dimensions in exhaustive detail. It is something fairly long and thin.

"Wait a minute," I say. "Is that one of your arms?"

The robot raises both hands. "I am not certain. The dimensions would fit, within a few millimeters."

A wave of fatigue hits me. I desperately need a nap, not to mention the fact that there is something inherently depressing about hearing a robot describe how he tore himself apart.

"What's the last entry from your arm receptors?"

"Which arm?"

"Either."

"Extend arm over phase disruptor."

He stuck his arm over a disruptor? "And then?"

"There is nothing more from that arm receptor, DR."

No, there wouldn't be, would there? "What is the next movement from *any* receptor?"

"Pivot trunk, bringing arm over disruptor—"

"All right," I say, extending a hand. "I've heard enough."

"I apologize."

I shake my head. "That is all right. Hold tight for now. Let me think."

"I await your instruction."

It is clear, finally, that the bot destroyed himself. One mystery solved. That's not the answer to the real question, of course. Not by a long shot.

Returning to the circular stool, I sigh at the expression of relief I get from my feet and legs. I must have been tensing without realizing it. The feeling is like the last time the downriders were shut down for a day. I walked for kilometers.

"I need you to go back further," I say. "Possibly thousands of movements."

Another nod. "Of course," he says. "Do you have a particular go-to stretch in mind?"

It would be easier if I could skim the mass of movement instructions stream-wise—do a visual check. Do I trust this bot to get everything to me correctly, though? His behavior hasn't exactly been what I would call predictable. Plus, what about the new rules?

I access the rule list on my implant, but find nothing specific about streaming movement instructions. They haven't taken away all my options. *Yet.* "Can you package the entire list of movements from where we are in your record now to, say, a thousand movements back and stream it to me?" I ask.

"You don't wish me to speak audibly?"

"It is a bit slow," I say. "I'd like to internalize it. See what sticks out."

"Easy Impact?"

"Whatever is quickest."

He goes vacant, processing and bundling. While I wait, I roll closer to the blue planet picture and study it closely. There is more than just banding on the surface, there is a large spot—an obvious circular pattern on the lower hemisphere. I know a storm when I see one.

"Are you prepared for transmit?" the bot asks.

I nod.

"Transmitting now."

It is a fairly small package. I grab it from the stream and swallow, place it in a primo spot where I can get all my internal gear around it. I see the instructions we went through, the head-banging, the dismemberment.

I move back a few hundred instructions. Many of the movements are meaningless to the investigation: status reports from various internal mechanisms. I see the main nano-pump registering an increase in flow, the transverse sinews noting the increased load necessary to balance, sans arm.

I reach the spot where the first arm was dislocated in a manner similar to its twin. If set correctly, phase disrupters can be a real bear on connection ligaments. If nothing else, the bot really knew how to take himself apart. They design them to have a measure of creativity, though. And I have a feeling that this bot is more creative than most.

I move back further, searching for the spot where the chaos began.

Thinking back to my visit to DarkTrench, I can remember now that this bot had been holding something in its hand, something that crashed to the floor. That particular section of movement should be easy to find. Both hands releasing!

I locate that spot and search back a few instructions more. There has to be something there that is out of the ordinary. Something that started this mess.

After more searching, I frown. Nothing sticks out at me. All I see is the bot's nondescript movements around the room. Nothing fragmentary or haphazard. No stalling, no bursts of speed—no balancing responses to ship movement. It is like he was skating on glass. All smooth and beautiful.

"This is everything?" I ask. "You've withheld nothing?"

"That is all the movement information you asked for," the bot says.

"What about eye and audile receptors?" I ask. "I don't see anything from them."

A pause. "I am sorry, DR. I misunderstood you. Normally such information isn't considered movements. Would you like me to send another package including all information from every receptor?"

I shake my head. "No, I'd like to give you a position to start from and you can talk me through from there."

"That will be fine. The timecode for your particular instruction?"

I zero in on the most likely instruction, the one where the bot releases with both hands.

"Confirm. Release object, both hands?"

"That is correct."

"Eye receptors register color black. Possible sensor overflow."

So...the bot blacked out. Odd. "All right," I say. "And the audio?"

"Broad bandwidth reception from unknown source."

Broad...what? "Unknown source? Quantify."

"*Unknown* is the quantification, DR. The source is unknown."

I lean forward on my stool, bringing my full attention to the bot. "Not from the ship?"

The bot shakes his head. "DarkTrench emanations are well known to me. Clearly marked."

I smile. I agree with that observation: there is no mistaking Dark-Trench. An angel of the deep.

"Something the crew was working on then?" I ask.

"I would not know," he says. "But I doubt it."

"Why is that?"

"Because it emanates from outside the ship," he says, "and the stream is beyond human range. It is multifaceted. Superlative. Why produce something they cannot perceive?"

I stare silently at the bot. Humans frequently produce transmissions that they cannot perceive. These are produced not through natural means, but through mechanisms. In the past it wasn't uncommon to control systems through ultraviolet or infrared, or even radio. Such systems are long outdated now, of course.

I have a feeling the bot is trying to describe something else, though. I detected a distinct hitch in his voice. His system is still affected, whether he claims to be performing normally or not.

"You used the word 'stream,'" I say. "Was that intentional?"

Another pause. "There is no other way to describe it. 'Stream' is the word that translates best."

Interesting. Except streams don't easily cross the bounds of space. And they certainly don't travel through the kind of shielding that DarkTrench is supposed to have. Did an errant stream somehow reach Betelgeuse from Earth while they were there? "What do you think it is, then?" I ask. "What is its purpose?"

"I believe it to be aimed at the human crew, regardless of their ability to perceive it."

"Aimed at the crew?" I say, doubting. "An alien transmission? A call from another world?" I glance at the framed picture and dip into the stream. "There are no planets around Betelgeuse," I say, reading aloud. "And it is doubtful there ever were. The star is large—many times larger than our sun. If it were placed in the same location as our sun it would swallow all the planets out to Mars."

"That is correct," the bot says. "There are no planets there."

I continue checking, frowning at what I find. "It is thought to be in danger of going supernova," I say. "Isn't that a dangerous first choice for a trip?"

"I would not know that."

I recall that there was a certain time element involved with Dark-Trench. Back to go forward? Could that be insurance for the crew against a supernova? Arriving at a time you know to be safe?

"Would you like to hear the transmission?" the bot says.

"Hear it? I thought you had no audio or visual memories."

"Incorrect. I said there are some EE memories. This happens to be one of those sections."

I feel a tinge of excitement, a feeling not unlike what I get when HardCandy is around. I tell the bot yes, but a few moments later I regret the request.

I hear singing.

THERE IS A RINGING in my head. I awake, finding myself on the floor. I reach for the stool and pull myself onto it. It rattles and clanks, attempts to roll away.

The bot is still perched on the table. As if nothing happened.

"How long was I out?" I ask.

"Five point zero six minutes, DR."

I shake my head. What is wrong with me? The implant feels fine, seems fine. Please let it be fine. "And you didn't call anyone?"

"There appeared to be no danger. Your implant produced no warnings."

I almost laugh. "That's not necessarily a good sign." I gently smooth the back of my head. I think I have another bump! I pull myself onto the stool. "That transmission," I say, "that... song. It didn't affect you."

"I took the liberty of shielding myself this time," the bot says, head bowing. "May A have mercy on me. I didn't know it would affect you."

I can almost hear the sound in my head, even now. A chorus with every voice part engaged. A roaring symphony. The essence of every melody ever sung.

Was it possible that the human crew was somehow affected too? Neither Handler nor TallSpot mentioned anything remotely like this. And yet the bot seems to think the transmission was meant for them.

And how was the transmission delivered? Especially with the way DarkTrench is shielded, no part of electromagnetic spectrum—from radio to gamma waves—should've been able to get through to the inside. "Why do you say it was aimed at the crew?" I ask.

He pauses, and for an instant I hear Bamboo scolding me for not streaming. "Because it is a form of programming, DR 63," he says. "With an audible component, yes, but programming just the same. You are stream-aware—I am surprised you did not notice."

Programming? Someone beamed code to the human crew while they were in orbit around a star four hundred and twenty-seven light-years away? Who? How?

"And what was this programming?" I ask. "What was it about?"

"It was a change of instructions, DR."

I blink. A change? What kind of change? Something sent from Earth? But how could anyone orchestrate that? Have it arrive when DarkTrench was there? And is the bot more prescient than me now? Able to detect incoming code that I cannot? Or is my implant still failing?

"All I heard was a song," I say. "Where was the code in that? This 'instruction change'—where did you find it?"

"There are two methods of determining whether instruction changes have been received," the bot says. "The first is by observing the instructions themselves."

That point is obvious. It is the core of my existence. I send and receive programming instructions all the time in my work with bots. "And you can perceive actual instructions in that transmission?"

"I cannot," the bot says. "I lack the required mechanisms, if such mechanisms exist. However, the second method of determining that an instruction change has been received is easier to perceive."

"What is that?" I ask. And where is he getting this information?

"The second method of determining an instruction change, DR, is through observed behavior. If the observed behavior of the object being programmed has changed, then, at some level, so has its programming."

I lean back in the stool, cross my arms. Another good point. A surprisingly astute point. There is something different about this bot. Something...enhanced. It's almost as if I'm speaking with another human—another DR, in fact. Do bots really have souls now?

I don't believe that, but I do recall TallSpot's theory about the Abdul experiments. That they're attempting to replace debuggers.

But what does this have to do with the transmission they received? If the programming change was intended for the crew, what behavior changes could he have possibly observed? And how could he have observed anything while tearing his arms off and banging his head against a pipe ninety-eight times? "All right..."

The bot's head tilts slightly, as if I missed something obvious. Again I'm reminded of Bamboo. "The behavior of the crew has changed dramatically since we left, DR."

This is incredible. "How so?"

"Many, many things."

"But you've hardly been exposed to the crew since you returned." I pause, trying to think. "Have you even seen them?"

"Absolutely," he says. "I saw both TallSpot and Grackle on my way to the catalog room. Both exhibited changed behavior."

There still must be something wrong with this bot. His perception and reasoning abilities are way above spec. Is this part of the adjustments TallSpot warned about—the Abdul's bot experiments?

"I understand that the crew was given a full physical when they returned," I say. "If there were any inconsistencies I'm sure they would've been noticed, logged as cause for concern."

The bot approximates a shrug. "Normally, that's true," he says. "Yes."

"Then what makes *your* observations correct?"

Servbots have no emotion, per se. In more complex models, though, some thought has been given to the suggestion of emotion. It is a tricky feature to design when most of the facial constructs remain eternally frozen. There are some emotional cues, though...if you know where to look. Immediately following my question I witness one of these inherent emotional cues: the bot lowered his head, like a pet that has forgotten to go outside.

"I am designed for observation," he says. "That is my primary purpose."

So I've insulted his design. Bots can be sensitive to that.

I stretch my legs, study the off-white tile beneath my feet. "I understand," I say. "And what have your observations shown you?"

"I have observed that humans are more prone to recognize differences when they are considered a negative. Especially when it pertains to the types of measurements that would turn up during a physical examination."

Above spec. Way above. "But the changes you've observed are positive?"

"Such value judgments are difficult for me where it relates to humans, DR. I've noticed differences in the crew, though. And, from my observations of humans, I doubt they would be seen as negatives."

"Such as?"

"Lowered standard blood pressure, for instance."

"Meaning they are, what, more relaxed?"

"Again, I wouldn't know. I simply have observed lowered blood pressure in both crewmembers I encountered."

I frown. "That's hardly definitive."

"I am only reporting what I've observed. There are other elements."

Talking is tedious, time-consuming. "Can you stream me a list?"

"Certainly. Give me a moment to compose." The bot grows quiet and outwardly motionless. Within is a different story, I know. "I am ready," he says finally.

"Transmit."

I receive the list. It is relatively short—perhaps a hundred items. On it are things like respiration rate, heartbeats per minute, facial muscle movements, eye dilation patterns. "Are you charting the crewmembers' moods here?" I ask. "Because that's what it seems like."

"I am only listing what I have observed. Conclusions are yours to formulate."

I skim the list again, skeptical. "You realize this could all be meaningless?" I'm explaining it to him, but really I'm explaining it to myself. Little of what I say is going to matter to the bot at all. "You only saw the crewmembers for, what, a few minutes in passing? I doubt a heightened mood is uncommon after returning from a long journey. It is called 'happy to be home.'"

A feeling I would like to experience again, as it happens. But an image of the canisters pops into my mind, reminding me that, perhaps, I will never feel that way again.

"If my time sensors are functioning correctly, the crew has been home for many days now," the bot says. "Wouldn't the state you mention have diminished by now?"

I have to give him that one. In fact, the way Scallop tells it, the crew should be feeling worse right now—angry even—for having been delayed. I haven't felt that from either TallSpot or Handler, though.

"I knew them before," I say aloud.

Another head tilt. "What is that?" the bot asks.

I shake my head. "I knew both TallSpot and Handler before. When we were younger."

"So do they seem different to you now?"

"I wouldn't know," I say, smiling. "It has been too long—over a decade. People change regardless of having been away. Especially over that length of time."

"I have observed that form of change as well," the bot says. "This is not the same."

I stare at the wallvid, where the bot's weight is still displayed in large, brilliant characters. Deep inside I realize that TallSpot and Handler *are* different. Both of them. Or they would be intolerable to me now. Wouldn't they? My former tormentors...?

I mull the situation. TallSpot was the first Abdul I saw after my encounter with the base's security machines. Little nasties. Was that meeting a coincidence? Did he stop them? Start them?

Weariness enters my eyes, fills my forehead with pain. Rails, why can't I have a chute? Soon, complex thought will be almost impossible. Much time has passed since I last slept even outside a chute—hours—and the intermediary seconds have been filled with lots of heavy thinking. Maybe it is time for a break.

"I need to leave you," I say. "I need time to think."

The bot nods. "All time is for thinking," he says. "But more is certainly better."

Ah, a philosopher now too, I see. "You don't need to stay here," I say, "but will you remain somewhere where I can reach you?"

The bot tips his head, doglike. "My task while on station—"

"Is in the catalog room," I say. "I know. Is there something else you can do? Something stream-reachable?"

He gives a full version of a bot shrug—a noisy up and down of his shoulders. "I have secondary chores, yes."

I stand. "Do some of them then." I turn for the door. "Anything that puts you where I can reach you. All right?"

The bot nods. "I will do that," he says. "Unto A I commend your faith, your trust, and the consequence of your work."

COMPLAINING TO SCALLOP about not having a chute to sleep in hardly seems useful anymore. The fact remains though; it is really messing with my head. And my nerves.

I return to my quarters. Everything operates as it should. I climb onto the bed, fully clothed, thinking that HardCandy is coming here soon and there's nothing I can do to stop it.

My napping dream is about TallSpot and DarkTrench. They circle a large storm-laced planet. Tall tells me how wonderful it is in space with thorn-tipped arias slicing through your thorax. "Songs can hurt!" he says. "Look at my neck!" I see an image of the Imam with a large rock stuck up his nose. I think he has rocks for eyes, as well.

I wake, only slightly less fatigued than when I fell asleep. My chronometer tells me I have slept less than an hour.

My next step is important. My fear resurfaces—my fear that there is a problem I can't solve. I think this might be it.

If I tell Scallop that I'm finished with the bot—or, worse yet, tell him everything I know—I can mark my task as done. Muddle my way through a causal explanation. The bot shielded himself from the song this last time. I can use whatever shielding it's using to suggest a remedy for protecting bots on future flights.

That won't do anything good for the crew, though, and I suspect it won't do much good for me either. I don't know that any debugger has ever truly left the station, do I? Not in the sense of going back to Earth, alive and whole. I may be ejected as soon as Scallop is through debriefing me. Cleared from the station, right?

The other option is to try to glean more information from the crew. Can I learn anything new by talking to them? I'm not sure. I certainly can't slap a sheet on their head and look around or stick a light probe in their ears. As much as I might like to.

That course would be a bit of a stall, but I stave off my eventual "departure" for awhile longer that way. And their departure as well. Maybe.

But not for too long. My biggest problem is the implant, you see. Outright deception will never fly with it. It doesn't care that I've been deprived of chute sleep. The longer I go without filing an End of Task Report (EoTR), the closer I get to falsehood. The implant can sense that stuff. It may take awhile, but that grand tweak will come, and it will be at a time not of my own choosing.

There is no clear path out...

Still in bed in my quarters, I look across the room. Even though I can't see the Earth, it feels like it is present there anyway. Like it's a large and hungry mole lurking beneath the surface, burrowing under an unsuspecting earthworm. Waiting with mouth open. Until suddenly...

I look away. Focus on the translucent walls of the steamer.

I receive an EE message—from Scallop, of all people. Closing my eyes, I unhinge it, unfold it, flip it up where I can see it. Scallop's voice reads loud in my mind.

"I am unable to prevent the female DR from coming. She is already on the lift. No turning those around, unfortunately. I guess we'll have to make do."

My heart lifts...and sinks. Another variable has entered my code. I can't let her come here. Not if it means death for debuggers. I can't.

Would it be possible to keep HardCandy from entering this part of the station? Could I at least convince Scallop to do that? Keep her out with the tourists? Out of harm's way?

I should go see Scallop again. Somehow convince him.

There is something you need to do first, Sand. Something you are missing. If you don't get that, you'll never get anything. And it will all be meaningless.

Panic strikes me. I can sense my heart pounding—heat draining from my face. What now? What am I forgetting?

HardCandy is coming. I need to go!

The bot, DR. You haven't solved anything yet.

I have! As much as I can, anyway. He got zagged by some sort of interstellar symphony, something that could get through the Dark-Trench shields and mess with his head. But he's working now—at least, as far as any Abdul could tell—and he seems to pose no risk to our great society. Plus, he now has a way of shielding himself.

It occurs to me that the same signal that struck the bot may have also messed with the crew. But that quandary I don't need to solve. Maybe it would be better if I *didn't* solve it, actually.

I leap from my bed. Start pacing nervously.

There is something more, isn't there?

I want to scream, but I don't. Instead I hit the stream, reach for an answer. Standard Impact.

Bot, bot, where are you?

Quick as electrons spin, he answers. "Peace be to you, DR 63. What do you require? I am performing menial labors, just as you commanded."

"And to you be peace together with A's mercy," I say. "I have a question for you, bot."

"One moment, please." I get the image of him descending a ladder. Above him is hanging fruit. Oranges, I think.

Crichton, this bot is versatile. Or am I still dreaming?

"I am waiting for your question," he says finally.

"Good," I say, forcing a smile. Nerves still in full bloom. "I can't believe we didn't discuss this before. I mean I realize it doesn't matter to you, really, but it is a major oversight on my part." Evidence I haven't been sleeping well.

The bot's posture doesn't change one iota. "Yes?"

"The stream we talked about. The programming beamed to the crew. Why did it cause you to disassemble yourself?" And just as importantly, why does it affect my implant?

The bot's head tilts, as if all the nanos inside have leapt to one side in surprise. It is a long minute before he speaks. "I do not know, DR."

Now he loses prescience? "Why did you shield yourself then?" I ask. "How did you know to do so? Or what to shield against?"

Long pause. "It was obvious that there was something in the

stream that affected me," he says, "so I disabled all receptors. However, if I might surmise..."

"Yes?" Such prodding is unlike me. It's borderline rude. But sometimes even stream-speed is too slow.

"I would surmise that a primary rule has been shown to be invalid."

A primary rule? Primary rules were those laid in at the base level when the bot was first created. Most important are those rules for rudimentary functions: movement, hearing, and speech. But there are some that deal with societal conventions. The things the bot would need to be aware of at all times in Abdul culture.

"What rule?" I ask. "And how has it been shown to be invalid? You mean that something in the programming message contained an argument against a primary rule?" Crazy.

The bot shakes its head. "I would not know. If you like, I can do a full bitwise search. That would take some time. My chores would be delayed."

Picking oranges?

"Do the search," I say. "And inform me of anything you notice."

The bot nods. "I will do so now," he says. "Unto *A-not-A cubed*, I commend your faith, your trust, and the consequence of your work."

The bot attempts to terminate the communication, but I stop him, wrench him back. "Wait, what was that?" I ask.

If he were able to blink, I'm sure he would have. "What is what, DR?"

"Your parting phrase. What was it?" Unwilling to wait, I retrieve the dialog bundle, zero in on exactly what he said. "A-not-A cubed," I say. "Is that a formula? An algebraic expression? $A \sim A^3$?"

The bot shakes his head. "I apologize. I seem to have had a bit of a fillip in my conversation coding. Would you like to examine me personally?"

Instinctively, I shake my head. "No, not now," I say. "Just do the search I requested." I've seen enough bot internals already.

The bot bows respectfully.

MY CONNECTION TO THE BOT closes and my mind returns to my quarters, to my principle dilemma, and perhaps my primary failing.

What do I do now?

My eyes travel the room, again noting the subtle color changes from floor to ceiling, the steamer that almost scorched me, the simulated-wood desk. Eventually my gaze rests on the white sajada tube. The prayer rug container is standing as it was when I arrived. Untouched and unopened. Would that help? Could I figure out where to point it?

The door slides open. Before I can even rise from my bed, TallSpot and Handler enter. Both are still ensconced in their protective gear. Are they here to rough me up, like the old days? Sign off so we can go home, or else.

TallSpot moves to take a seat by the window, effectively eclipsing the stars. Handler leans against the wall, very near the door. Neither looks particularly intimidating, but they don't necessarily look cordial either.

"We think it is time we talked," TallSpot says.

"I'm easy to reach on the stream," I say. "No need to come here in person." I pause, manage a smile. "I *do* have a task to finish."

Handler looks at TallSpot and then at me. "We don't think so," he says. "TallSpot saw the bot functioning. Saw it twice, actually: once on station and once on the ship."

"Are you sure it was the same bot?" I say. "There are quite a few of those models on board."

TallSpot smiles, but shakes his head. "I know that bot, Sand. I saw it every day for weeks."

"Unusual," I say. "So you're saying the bot left the examination room?" I stream to the door, checking to see if it is locked. It isn't. Yet. "It appears my task is almost finished then. Perhaps you should inform Scallop."

"You know that won't do us any good, Sand," TallSpot says. "None of us leaves the station until you sign off. That's why you were brought here."

Handler nods his bubble-covered head. "And we think it is time you do that. We've been patient, but we need to get back. If the bot is done, we should be free, right?"

I have a sudden flash of memory...

I'm ten years old and in the boy's locker room at school. More specifically, I'm *inside* one of the lockers. Handler has my head wedged in and is instructing me to figure out why the interior plasmalight is out. "You can fix it, right?" he says mockingly. There are at least four other boys standing with him, laughing. "Come on, Sand. Fix it!" My shoulders are pressed against the locker sides and are hurting. A sharp metal edge has cut one deeply. The laughter echoes off the metal interior.

The irony is that in a few short years I would be able to fix the lights—without even opening the door.

"It isn't up to me to free you," I say. "That would be up to the station administrator."

I contemplate sending a distress call to enforcement. Bring some of those brown suits to my rescue for a change. Normally, I have little to do with them. But this might be a situation where I should make an exception. Of course, they might also be the ones to toss me off station later. After cutting off my head.

"What else needs to be done with the bot?" TallSpot says. "You know Scallop is going to be asking soon. If it is fixed, why hesitate?"

I glance at Handler, who is now bouncing against the wall slightly.

What can I say?

There is silence for some time before TallSpot sighs—a sound hideously amplified by the suit. Like falling water. "Does this have to do with what I said earlier?" he asks. "About the studies to re-place DRs?" He waves a hand. "It is just suspicion. Clearly, some of the bots up here are advanced."

"I've seen the room," I blurt out. "The room where implants are stored—after they're removed from DRs."

They exchange looks, a show of surprise. It has to be simply that, a show. Handler does stop bouncing, however.

"Where is this room?" Tall asks.

"One of the forward labs," I say. "Where the bot works."

More troubled looks.

"We wouldn't know anything about that," Handler says. "We've never been there." He draws quiet, thoughtful. "Are you saying the debuggers who worked here...on DarkTrench...?"

I nod slowly, then turn to sit on the edge of the bed.

Silence fills the room, lingering an abnormally long time. "So, do you think you'll be decommissioned when you finish?" TallSpot asks. "Your implant enshrined in that room?"

My emotions are fluctuating again—a tornado ripping through my synapses. "It doesn't matter," I say. "I'm only a tool. I live to serve."

I could stop the breathing mechanism on both visitors' suits, I realize. Give myself time to get free. The thought alone is danger-ous, however, because willful endangerment of others is forbidden. If a master ordered me to, that would be different. But acting on my own impulse...

"Listen," Handler says. "We didn't come here to threaten you. You know that, right? But we need to get going." He taps his bubble. "This suit is chafing me."

TallSpot stands and begins pacing. "There's more to it than that. The trip opened our eyes to a lot of things. Things we never expec-ted. Things that need to change." He pauses and looks at me, eyes probing deep. "I'm curious what you have learned, Sand. Why did the bot malfunction?"

There is one instance in which my implant allows outright de-ception. If dishonesty will protect a master's secret, then it is ac-ceptable. Otherwise how could DRs operate? How could something like DarkTrench be built covertly? It all stems from an ancient precept: deception is allowed if it furthers the cause of our society's beliefs.

The question that never gets asked, though, is whether a society built on deception is worth furthering.

"A design flaw, TallSpot," I say. "The effect of time-space travel on nanopaths was never fully accounted for." I shrug. "How could it be?"

Handler frowns. "So you've found something that none of the DRs who worked on DarkTrench did?" he asks, sounding skeptical. "They spent weeks preparing that bot. They ran lots of tests..."

"And they were high-level debuggers," TallSpot adds. "Fourteens and fifteens. Isn't it unlikely they would miss something like that? A design flaw?"

I shrug. "Everyone has flaws," I say. "Even DRs."

"But you've fixed the problem?" Tall watches me closely. Looking for traces of falsehood.

What he doesn't know is that I've been monitoring him too. Logging readings from his suit. Searching for anything that seems inhuman. Changed instructions.

"It won't happen again," I say, nodding.

"Amazing," he says, "outstanding." Pausing in his pacing, Tall brings a hand up as if to rest on his chin. Finding the chin covered, the hand flummoxes a bit before returning to his side. "The problem of the implant room still remains, though, doesn't it? It poses a real danger to you. I can see why you hesitate..."

HardCandy is drawing closer by the nanosecond, and I have to find a way to protect her. To keep her from harm. I really need to leave!

My implant tweaks, surprising me. I try to keep my eyes open, but it is difficult. My hand rushes to my head.

"...perhaps we can help." TallSpot says, but then stops. "What is wrong, Sandfly? Did you get disciplined again?"

I can barely respond for the pain, which has now increased exponentially. I think I am on the floor. For what? Then, a message.

"DR 63, I need to see you right away. I've learned the bot is fixed—has been fixed for some time. Status reports show it performing station duties. Why haven't you told me?"

I get a picture of Scallop holding a controller. Suddenly, the "casual" executive doesn't seem so casual anymore. He's like every other master I've known: please me, or else!

I manage to stand. "I need to go," I say, suppressing a wince. "My services are needed elsewhere."

"Is it Scallop?" Tall asks, looking concerned. "Is he calling you?"

I massage my temples. It gets me no relief. To TallSpot, I nod.

"Handler," he says. "Get the door for him."

Reacting as someone who still knows his place in the pecking order, Handler spins and slaps the touchpad. The door slides open. Only then does he step into the opening, partially blocking my way. "Tall," he says, frowning deeply, "is this right? Should we let him go without...?"

TallSpot stands, straightens. Me, I'm still bent nearly double and staggering toward the Handler-eclipsed door, aiming for the rectangle of freedom I can see.

"Of course it is right," Tall says behind me. "Let him through!"

Handler repositions himself, obscuring my escape. "Maybe we should think about this. If he goes to Scallop he'll tell everything he knows, right?"

"That's the only way we're free, Handler. Have you forgotten?"

Handler pauses, shuffles his suit-covered feet. "No. That's obvious. But it isn't only about us anymore, is it?"

Pain is ever-present, but not quite to blinding again yet. Not so strong that I can't understand what is going on.

The bot wasn't completely wrong in his guesses about the crew changing behavior. In fact, it may have been precisely right.

"Altered..." I whisper, then stop myself. Why would I speak? Why would I ever speak first?

TallSpot notices. "What did you say, Sand?"

I cover my eyes with my hands, shake my head. "Nothing. I didn't say anything. I hate to talk. I'm a debugger." I take another step toward the door, hoping that with my eyes closed, Handler won't see me.

He does. He grips my shoulder. "Wait. Tall asked you a question."

A new message from Scallop: "DR 63, where are you? If you don't answer this instant, I'm calling security!"

"I'm coming!" I stream—and also say. I turn to look at TallSpot, who is staring into me, his face a mask. A mask in a bubble.

"You know something more than what you're saying," Tall says. "I can see that."

Handler grabs both my shoulders now. Not forcefully, not like back in school, but firmly nonetheless. "So maybe we should keep him," he says. "I mean, if he knows too much, we're goners."

The headbuzz increases and I sort of fall into him so that he's actually supporting me. Thankfully, he *does* support me.

TallSpot clucks his tongue thoughtfully. "Is that really what we want, Handler? Does it seem right to you?" He moves close and draws his bubble even closer, searching my eyes. "There is truth, Sand, do you understand? Listen to me. They have A all wrong. He isn't at all like what they've taught us. He's not even just A. He's beyond A."

"A-not-A cubed?" It comes out automatically, with no thought behind it. A simple regurgitation of data.

I get another buzz, and it is crazy bad. Like my brain will detonate.

Scallop: "Sandfly, I have someone here with me. Security, yes. They're here. But I have one of your people with me, as well. Contrary to what you said, she's actually quite stunning. We really need to talk. I have no doubt she can be useful here. No doubt."

I have to go! This time I don't say it aloud. They are still blocking me.

I stream out to the room lights, bringing them to a brightness level approaching the sun. Handler grunts, and at that instant I lunge against him with all my slight body strength. I'm rewarded: his hands release me.

Nanoseconds later I stream out to the hall lights, commanding them to darken completely. Normally they wouldn't do that, but I tell them I'm running a test, which they seem to be okay with. I stagger into that darkness.

Another head buzz! Now that he's discovered it, Scallop loves that tweaker. Loves it.

It is difficult to pull up the station map, plot a route to his office. Or am I trying to find the swimming pool? Somehow—between throbs of brain lightning—I manage to find the map. I have to move fast. The altered TallSpot and Handler will be right behind me.

Ahead is an intersection where three halls meet. I run a test on those lights too. Now I have five escape routes I can use, all sufficiently darkened.

"Wait!" I hear Handler cry out. "Come on, Tall, we've got to stop him."

I don't hear TallSpot's response, but I don't need to. I beat it to the intersection and dip into the leftmost corridor.

Darkness isn't necessarily my friend now either. To solidify that point I fall over a knee-high maintenance bot. The thing screeches and scurries away, leaving me in a disoriented heap. Where's a band of rogue robots when you need them?

I hear running footsteps behind me, and turn to look toward the intersection.

I can see little. There is a dim ambient light, but nothing my eyes can actually use. Panicked, I roll over against the wall and lay there. The footsteps seem to be getting louder.

Maybe it is only the pounding in my ears—

ZAM! The headbuzz returns.

"I'm on my way!" I stream out. Give me a crichton break!

Gripping the wall, I regain my feet. I listen hard, but it appears I was wrong about the footsteps getting closer. They've taken a wrong turn!

I use the opportunity to run to the next intersection and turn down it. Just in time, because as I turn the corner, the hall lights come back up.

I've escaped.

Sort of.

I REACH SCALLOP'S OFFICE and, little surprise, there are two brown-robed security men posted outside. I don't want to go in there, I really don't. But I have to. Plus there's HardCandy. So I'm stuck.

And the fact that the security guys have already seen me.

"You are DR 63?" one says. He's a large Abdul, not that dissimilar from the one in wife-beater's employ on the lift. Big and burly. His mate is a touch smaller, but meaner looking—with a hook-shaped nose and a ragged scar across his brow. Ugly.

Neither deserves the effort of words, so I simply nod. Their presence is unnecessary. Scallop clearly has a controller.

"Go in," the larger one says. "He's waiting."

Really?

The pressure plate is pushed, the door opens, and I walk through.

The first room is the secretary's domicile and so has a bit of refinement to it. It is painted a deep red, and there is plastiwood paneling here as well. Lots of projected pictures on the wall. Most are of temples in Central City.

But those come standard. And since Scallop's secretary is a bot, the more personality-defining niceties aren't present. No family picture on the desk, no plant in the corner...

The bot streams at me as soon as she sees me. How do I know it is a she? The burqa. Her streamings are all identity checks, which my implant quickly clears up. Within seconds, an interior door to my right begins to open. As the air between the rooms mixes, I catch a vaguely familiar scent. HardCandy...

Are you here, Sand? What is going on?

I try to assemble all I know into an EE for her. But can I trust the station stream enough to send it?

And do I dare tell her everything? Wouldn't that be increasing her danger?

I walk into Scallop's office. I can't see him, for a shimmering nano-curtain has been erected. The rest of the office is dimly lit and deplorable. Bookshelves crammed with tomes at odd angles, a countertop filled with papers and blueprints. A DarkTrench model shares a table with empty drink containers, like drink can asteroids.

Hard isn't here now. She has been before, I'm sure of that—and she's clearly somewhere on the station. But where? Surely not with Scallop on the other side of the curtain.

I sense another familiar being in the room, as well. It stands in the shadows near the back of the room. Subservient. Patiently waiting.

"Ah, DR 63," Scallops says from behind the curtain. I almost smile because the viewing rectangle is noticeably lower in the curtain than it is when my own master uses it. Like I'm serving a child.

"Should I call you master now?" I ask.

"You've been hiding things from me." It doesn't sound like he's smiling. The casualness is all gone now.

"That is a near impossibility," I say, "for an implanted debugger."

"Ah..." His raised forefinger obscures his eyes. "But you are a resourceful one now, aren't you?"

I bow my head. "We're trained to be resourceful."

"Of course," he says. "This position is not one that is comfortable for me. I hope you realize that."

"There is no way for me to know your comfort level, Scallop," I say. "Unless you are implanted and full impact it to me."

Scallop snorts loudly. "That aside, I do not like these trappings. I do not like the wall. But sometimes the stick works where candy does not."

Interesting choice of words. "What do you require?"

Scallop's eyes lower. "Do you recognize that bot there?"

Of course. I recognized it as soon as I walked in. "That is a model RS-19," I say. "The same unit that flew on DarkTrench." Without looking, I stream to the bot, requesting a list of everything he has told Scallop so far. After a brief perusal, I remain hopeful.

"That is correct," Scallop says. "And it tells me it is fully functioning. Why didn't you inform me?"

"I believe I did," I say. "I told you this morning that I had it operational."

"Operational, yes. But this bot claims to be ready to serve. If that is correct, then your mission is complete. It is time for your End of Task Report."

Another head bow. "If the EoTR is all you require," I say, "then of course. I will compose it." I close my eyes, retrieve the necessary form from implant storage, flatten it out so I can see the whole thing. I give as brief a summary of the bot's reconstruction as I can, and send it away. Straight to the other side of the nano-curtain.

"Ah, I'm receiving it now." Scallop's eyes leave the opening as he presumably turns to his vidscreen. I can glimpse the tip of his left ear and the hairline there. What's left of it. I hear a stream of vocalizations, the kind of humming that men do when they're mulling something over. Then comes a final, commanding harrumph.

"There is nothing here!" he exclaims.

"That is not true," I say. "I have adequately explained everyth—"

"You've explained nothing. Nothing! Why did the bot malfunction, DR? That's why you were brought here. That is the salient mystery! Have you been wasting our time your entire visit?"

"The bot is functional," I say, waving a hand in the bot's direction. "It stands before you now. It is you who has said my task is complete."

Scallop's eyes show heat. "But why did it malfunction in the first place? You don't specify anything about that."

Another bow to hide my eyes. "Which is why I hadn't sent the report. I am...unsure."

"The bot claims that the problem is corrected."

I stream a scowl to the bot. "That may seem to be the case," I say. "But the headchip was destroyed."

"I know it was destroyed," Scallop says. "I brought you a new one!"

He's railing me again. It is all I can do to contain it. "That chip was a blank slate," I say. "It only allowed me to make the bot operational. The information it held was lost."

"And you learned nothing new?" Scallop asks. "*Nothing* that gave you pause?"

Here's where it gets difficult, freeheads, because now I've been asked a direct question. I've resisted my suspicions, because I don't know that they amount to much. I'm not a medical expert, and I can't take the bot's word for what he senses—because he isn't a medical expert, either. Even a medbot wouldn't know, I would guess. Certainly not the one on this station, anyway.

And so I have finally found it: the problem I don't know how to solve.

If I describe the bot's hypothesis, if I tell Scallop that I think the crew has been altered in some way, by a set of instruction changes from deep space, I'll have assured their deaths. There is no way the current Imam, the current consensus of masters, would ever take the chance of letting the crewmembers live. If they won't allow me to communicate freely for fear of infection, imagine if they knew what I suspect about the crew?

"But didn't Tall and Handler abuse you when you were little?" you ask. "Wouldn't you be glad to see them suffer? Weren't they just chasing you?"

True. Not to mention Scallop and his abuse to me now. I'm a slave without chains. The implant is my whip. Little has changed.

The other alternative is completely unknown. If I let the crewmembers walk, if I somehow manage to get through this interview without revealing anything incriminating...well, what am I allowing? Reprogrammed humans running amok? An invasion by proxy? Some alien intelligence giving "changed instructions" to humans and sending them back to Earth, perhaps to be triggered later and controlled remotely?

For a midlevel debugger, that is a pretty big weight to shoulder.

But what does it matter? My fate is sealed, regardless.

Then there's the fact that—

I get a mild tweak, enough for me to return to the outside world.

"Are you paying attention to me, Sandfly? What did you learn from your investigation?"

Weariness hits me. Not that it ever left me, but this time it is like the dome of a temple falling onto my head. "My apologies," I say. "I'm actually quite tired." I initiate a smile for good measure. "No chute sleep."

"You will sleep soon enough," Scallop says. "After we get through this."

Yes, sleep in a decaying Earth orbit, sans suit. But if I lie, he'll know.

The implant will tweak me in the middle of the deceit and there's no way I can remain motionless when it happens. That's the way it works.

Plus, his controller will tell him.

Which way to go? Save Handler and TallSpot or save the status quo? And what of the bot's superlative stream, the star curiously singing?

I feel a weight in my pocket. Remembering the coin, I think of the word "Liberty" stamped upon it. What does that mean precisely? I stream it up, let the essence fill my head.

The freedom to act or believe without being stopped.

A noble idea, but it doesn't help me. Not here. If ever I needed A to stoop for me, to strike me with inspiration, this is it.

Then something comes to me. A fresh line of reasoning.

"I suspect the bot has been modified," I say. True, all very true. So no head buzz.

Scallop's eyes widen. "Modified? " he says. "In what way?"

"For one, his capacity has been altered. He has abilities way beyond original specs."

There is quiet for many seconds. "That may be true," Scallop says finally. "Some modifications were made for the trip."

"It is beyond that," I say. "More than subtle enhancement. Though I don't know who would be performing the kind of things I've seen, it is almost as if these modifications are aimed at enhancing the bot to near DR level. I would like to stream out to other DRs for comment, but because of your restrictions I have not done so."

More humming vocalizations. Scallop in a bind. "That's interesting, Sandfly," he says. "I will look into it. No need to share it yet."

"I see," I say, bowing at the waist.

More quiet from beyond the curtain. "How does this affect your conclusion on what happened to the bot?"

I feel the weight of the bot's eyes on me. "I believe these alterations—done, I presume, by your scientists?—made the bot...susceptible...to conditions it experienced during the trip," I say. "Therefore it was these modifications that are the root cause of the bot's disturbance and subsequent destruction."

"I see," Scallop echoes. "That is quite interesting. So, you would see no problem with a servbot going on such a mission again?"

I bow again. "The problems he experienced have been accounted for. If you don't believe me, you can ask him." I indicate the bot for good measure.

In point of fact, I don't want Scallop to ask the bot anything, because bots are even worse at lying than I am. For safety's sake I stream the bot, telling him to be as precise in his answers as possible. The same instruction a lawyer might give a client in an earlier world. Back when truth mattered more than who holds the controller.

I think I am almost in the clear now. I have given an answer that implicates neither me nor the crew. TallSpot and Handler and the others can go home. And there shouldn't be much need for HardCandy here now. Have I done it? Saved everyone?

Everyone but me.

Scallop ignores the bot. "That won't be necessary. I know you have stops in place."

I nod. "That is correct."

"So the mission can be called at an end then." Scallop's bluster seems to have fled. As if to accentuate the point, he lets out a noticeable sigh. "Well done, DR. I am sorry I doubted you."

I nod again. Another wave of weariness passes through me. I really need to sleep. "Am I free to go now?"

"Yes," Scallop says. "I will pass your report along to my superiors." The curtain drops and Scallop is revealed at his desk. A small man in an orange suit, surrounded by heavy lacquer and wood grain. He stands and approaches me. "I will have Security show you the way out." Again, he touches my elbow to guide me.

The impulse to pull away returns, but I suppress it. "Before I go," I say, "I would like to meet the new debugger. She may have questions for me."

Scallop opens the door. "The stream protections will be reduced after you leave the restricted area. You will be free to communicate with her then."

He should know better than that. I'm a debugger. Stream communication is second nature. I'm not waiting to leave the restricted area before contacting HardCandy. I'll do it as soon as I can.

Internally I work up a warning for HardCandy. I suspect Scallop has some sort of tap on the stream here, but I won't leave without telling her something. A glimpse of the implant storage room, at least.

I encrypt it all for good measure, scramble it three ways, and prepare to send it.

The implant hits me hard. A big tweak.

For what?

The implant room is apparently a master's secret. Can't be sending that.

The look on Scallop's face is unreadable. Not necessarily happy, though. "You are a good servant," he says. "I will brief your master on your performance. You will be richly rewarded."

Emotion hits me. It may be lack of sleep, but I feel both happy and sad. Moisture builds in my eyes. To cover, I turn to look at the bot.

He is standing incredibly still, yet seems active. A block of ice in a desert. "I have something," he says suddenly. And streams at me: "A~A³!"

It is good that Scallop can't see my face, because I'm breathing heat now. "What is it?" I stream. "Speak only to me."

"The heavens declare the glory," the bot streams. "The skies proclaim the work of His hands. Day after day they pour forth speech. Night after night they display knowledge. There is no speech or language where their voice isn't heard."

"What?" The cadence and tone sounds like something from one of the Abdul's religious writings. But it isn't anything I've heard, and I've heard quite a lot. I glance at Scallop, who looks baffled.

"What does the bot want?" he asks.

I shake my head. "I'm really not sure." No head buzz there, because that's the honest-to-A truth. I stream to the bot, shouting for an explanation.

I was almost out of here, bot! The crew was safe!

"Can you bind the beautiful Pleiades?" he asks. "Can you loose the cords of Orion? Do you know the laws of the heavens? Can you set up A-not-A cubed's dominion over the Earth?"

I'm thankful the bot is still streaming silently, but I'm also freaked because he is clearly *not* fixed. I hate on-the-fly debugging, hate it. Hate trying to catch the pieces as they fly around the room.

But I have to try. "Are you ready?" I ask, meaning, *Clear yourself and prepare to be checked again.*

To no avail.

"You are streaming to it!" Scallop exclaims with anger. "What is it saying?"

I do my best to ignore him. Something the bot has said strikes me. *Orion.* It is a familiar name. I go streamwide, looking for the reference. Bingo, I find a correlation.

The star DarkTrench visited, Bait al-Jauza, is a member of the constellation Orion. In fact, that's where the hand (or armpit) meaning came from. Orion represented the figure of a hunter in the sky. Bait al-Jauza could be the hand. Right or left, depending on the way the hunter is drawn.

The bot is still rolling. "He seals off the light of the stars. He alone stretches out the heavens. He is the maker of the Bear and Orion. He performs wonders that cannot be fathomed, miracles that cannot be counted."

"You are speaking to each other," Scallop says with added emphasis. "I order you to speak with me now as well."

Unfortunately, the bot is more than ready to comply, and there's nothing I can do to stop him. He looks Scallop squarely in the eye.

"Instead," he says aloud, "you have set yourself up against the Lord of heaven. You had the goblets from His temple brought to you, and you and your nobles, your wives and your concubines drank wine from them. You praised the gods of silver and gold, of bronze, iron, wood, and stone, which cannot see or hear or understand. But you did not honor the one who holds in his hand your life and all your ways."

Scallop is as stunned as I'd ever seen him. Freaked. After a long moment of silence, he finds his tongue. "Is that one of the corrupted books it is quoting?"

I shrug. "I wouldn't know."

Color fills his face again. "It is clearly not working properly," he says. "It is not fixed. You have been wasting our time."

I shake my head. "No, he checked out. He was fully—"

"A is not A," the bot says. "He is superlative, true—yet He stoops. He *stoops!*"

That stalls me. Has he affirmed something I've sarcastically thought?

I hear Scallop calling the guards, which can't be good. He has no reason to blame *me* for this, though. No reason. Not that it will stop him.

I stream to the bot again: Please, for both our sakes, be quiet!

"I tell you," he says, "if they keep quiet, the stones will cry out."

Clarke and crichton, we're lost.

"The stones of the wall will cry out: Woe to him who builds a city with bloodshed and establishes a town by crime."

I try streaming the shutdown codes to him for the fiftysecond time. Nothing.

"Take from my hand this cup filled with the wine of my wrath and make all the nations—"

I hear a thunderous clapping sound. The bot is lifted into the air, as if by an invisible hand, and flung backward into the wall. Both arms and legs separate from his trunk and clatter to the floor within feet of his body.

I turn to look at Scallop, who is now bookended by BigUgly's brother and HookNose—the two guards. The latter is holding a long black stick against his waist. A nanopounder, I assume.

The bot is dead.

SCALLOP AND THE GUARDS snap into action as if trained for such an emergency. Scallop recovers the controller from the desk and grasps it tightly. Meanwhile, the guards abandon their positions around him and assume new positions around me. The nanopounder is raised to my head.

Silently and swiftly they hustle me into the hall. It isn't until we have walked twenty meters before Scallop—probably because he is wired that way—begins to speak.

"It was dangerous," he says. "The bot. Clearly infected. We couldn't allow it to continue. Now the danger for us is what else has been exposed to him since he became active. It is a good thing we have stream protections in place."

I say nothing, stream nothing, as we round a corner. Ordered to remain silent and ineffective, what else can I do? I'm worried for myself, sure, but I'm also worried for HardCandy—and the crew, surprisingly. Worried much for the crew.

"I'm concerned that we'll have to call this whole experiment a loss," Scallop continues. "How could we possibly do otherwise? The Iman will not be happy. The body of investors will be livid. Much has been lost. Much." He looks at me, his forehead glistening. "And then there is *you*, DR 63. You are a huge disappointment. This certainly adds fuel to the controversy, now, did you know that? Some are saying that free thought at any level can be dangerous. Even harnessed free thought."

Which explains why they're wanting to get rid of the DRs.

We reach another hallway, one that is crawling with hidden nasty machines. Security devices so deadly they make the path into the station look like a downride to the beach. At the end is a large red door marked "CAUTION." There are doors lining the hall as well. I'm taken to the last of these on the left. I notice it has stream-free mechanical locks on the outside.

I think I know where the DarkTrench designers stayed.

The door is open, and I'm pushed inside. The room is stark white, with only a dark rug on the floor and an exposed wasteunit. There are no windows, and the ceiling is only a foot above my head. Stream out for the word "bleak," freehead, and this is the picture you'll receive.

Scallop's sweaty face appears at the doorway. "Regardless, the bot's performance sheds a new light on *your* behavior, DR. I haven't forgotten your blackout, the way you ran me in circles while you 'fixed' our bot." He looks at the floor, shakes his head. "Unfortunately, this means we can't take a risk on another DR, either. I will consult with the ulama before doing anything rash, of course, but I'm fairly certain how things will proceed from here." Another head shake. "The crew is lost, I fear."

Thanks a lot, servbot. You had to flip a breaker right then, didn't you? Clarke and crichton.

The guards surround him in the hall, and for the first time I notice the similarity between their attire and that of the mutaween in my dream. Maybe they really *are* trained for this...

Scallop turns the switch. The door draws shut quietly, but in my head it sounds like a slam. Immediately I feel the stream lessen, grow more opaque. I try to reach out for HardCandy again, try to warn her. But I get nothing. It is like scales have been placed over my eyes. I'm fumbling in the dark.

I am alone.

I NEED TO SLEEP, but I can't—won't. I'm afraid of what I might see.

GrimJack is one of those people who puts value in what he sees while he sleeps. He's always boring me with the infinitesimal details of his nightly imaginings—asking me what they mean, wondering if his waking life will play out similarly.

I'm the one always having to smack him with reality. Bring him back in-stream. "Dreams are just a mechanism," I tell him. "A way of moving internal information along. They help us process, but the images themselves usually have no meaning."

In no way do I believe in the content of dreams. How could I, considering? Have a maladjusted chute one night and you'll find yourself swimming in a lava lake with a calarabi and a two-headed bat named Sam. What's the significance of that? Where's the usefulness?

And yet, of all the dreams I've had lately, the one with the drowning girl feels the most real to me. Except I'm not her savior; I'm the girl. I've been held underwater too long, forced to drink everything that flowed my way, and it was my own parents keeping me there. The people who created me. The Imam, my master, and everyone like them.

You're broken, Sand. You're bit-blasted broken. Walk this wall any further and you'll lose your mind forever.

I begin to wonder about this "corrupted book" the bot was quoting so freely. I push out to the stream for information, but, freehead, it is real hard. The stream isn't completely closed off here, but it is like trying to pull a log through mud. Thick, hard-packed mud.

How did the DarkTrench DRs work this way? They didn't. They couldn't have.

Things were better for them, I imagine. Right up until the end.

I do get some information, finally. From a backwater domain where I can almost hear the crickets chirping.

It seems these corrupted works predate the writings the Abduls find most important, sometimes by thousands of years. In fact, at one time the person most vital to our faith found these same books laudable, informative, and valuable. Even used them to justify his own writings, his own importance. Yet now they are forbidden.

It all seems inconsistent somehow.

Which brings me back to the bot, to the circumstance that caused his breakdown. Since bots spend so much of their time with Abduls, they are made to be fully agreeable, compliant, to Abdul beliefs and rituals. That is the focus of their primary rules. They ensure that the bot will never offend, either through action or inaction. Never offend.

Every human, Abdul and debugger alike, knows the central tenets of our religion. They are printed everywhere, spoken in places both public and private, whispered into the ears of children as they sleep, repeated over and over throughout the day. So of course I know them. Whether I believe them or not, I know them.

And so I certainly know what the most important tenet is.

It is this: there is no other god but A.

Yet both the bot and TallSpot bore witness to another conviction following their encounter with the "superlative stream" at Betelgeuse. "They have A all wrong," Tall had said. "He isn't at all like what they've taught us." A is not A. In fact, the bot went on to substitute a different naming convention altogether: $A \sim A^3$

Whether the bot's formula is an accurate algorithmic representation of the being they encountered or not, it certainly suggests one thing: whatever was out there was not A as the Abduls know it. Consequently, to the bot's mind, a proven inconsistency was presented. Internal consistency errors to a bot psyche are catastrophic, meaning almost anything can happen. The tower of eggs has cracked and splattered.

The house of cards is falling.

Doesn't explain the ad hoc oration the bot gave, necessarily, but it doesn't preclude that behavior, either. Destroy yourself one day, become a powerful speaker the next. The bot should've been a politician.

It also doesn't explain my blackouts. Per spec, the implant isn't supposed to have any primary rules of thought. Not like a servbot. I have rules of behavior, sure, but rules of abstract reflection go against Tanzer's original principle.

If I *had* such regulations—unknown to every DR but deep within the implant's programming—a blackout might happen when confronted with something that violated them. Is that what happened to me when I heard the singing?

And what about that singing? Is the song I heard an audible side effect of the stream's presence, like the wake following an ocean liner? And if it *is*, what must the full stream be like?

But would a door refuse to open for me? A steamer try to scald me? A window-washing bot try to skewer me?

I can't imagine it. Can't believe it.

You're broken, Sand. Seriously.

Debugger, debug yourself.

THE DOOR RATTLES and clanks. Squinting, I watch as it begins to open. I expect to see one of Scallop's goons charge in, nanopounder in hand, but I'm surprised. Greatly.

Another human is pushed in beside me—rolled inside, really. I approach the mound of flesh slowly, respectfully, and hover over it.

In the door's diminishing opening I see the outline of Scallop. The hall behind him seems dimmer now than it had before. The door snaps shut then, but only a short time later an eye-level rectangle in the door appears. Eye-level for most people, but not for Scallop. From my spot on the floor, I can see only the top of his balding head.

"You wanted to meet her," he says. "Out of mercy for you both, I've granted that request." The semicircle of his head shifts a little. "I've done some research. You two have more of history together than you admitted, Sandfly. Is it normal for DRs to talk so derogatorily toward another of your brotherhood? Even if, as in this case, it is a sister? Arguably." He chuckles. "Be assured, I've given her all the information you gave me. I wanted her to be fully informed, despite how you treated me."

I say nothing. I continue watching that talking rectangle. So like what I'm used to. The rectangle of power.

"Sorry to say, but it appears the ulama is reaching a consensus with the Imam on her fate, and possibly on the fate of your kind." Scallop sighs. "However, your case, 63, is wholly unique. I'm afraid we'll have to go to greater lengths. We'll have to remove that implant of yours to see what went wrong. To see if something can be done to prevent such a thing from happening again. It is unfortunate, but necessary."

The top of his head turns slightly, so I assume he's looking toward the door I saw on my way in. "Thankfully, we have the facilities to perform such an operation right here. Right through that red door there, actually. They're fully functional. We've used them many times before."

Another Scallop sigh. "I'll leave you two alone. I am confident that her behavior will be controlled by her implant. That much, at least, appears to be functioning correctly."

And with that, the rectangle closes.

Impulsively, I reach out for HardCandy's shoulder. Before I can touch her, though, she rolls over into a sitting position. She backs tight against the wall, directly opposite me. Head bowed low.

I whisper a greeting into the stream. Her arms cross defensively. Her face is camouflaged, unreadable. The only thing I have left to use now is my smile. Not sure how much that will help, but I try it anyway.

I notice a line of bruises on her face and head. Puffiness around one eye.

"What did they do to you?" I ask.

She shakes her head. "Nothing that concerns you."

Of course it does. Of course it concerns me. "Why would you say that? Was it Scallop, or one of his guards...or someone else?"

She jerks her head once quickly. "Don't fret it, DR 63."

"Sandfly," I say. "I still like Sandfly."

She looks away from me, toward the door. "Rails, Sand," she says. "What is this place? What is going on here?"

Frowning, I shake my head. "I made you an FI of everything I know. Sending..."

Hard looks down, then shuts her eyes as the message hits her—triple encrypted and specially tuned for her frequency. I can see her emotion as she views it. The creases on her forehead deepen and her arms tighten. Her head shakes on more than one occasion. What will she think about A-not-A cubed? Finally, her eyes open again.

"That was intense," she says. "Bright orange intense."

At least she doesn't seem mad at me anymore. "Like a movie?" I say, unsure what the reference means precisely.

She stares at me a moment. "You got that from Grim," she says.

"He's so backward." She looks toward her right hip, as if remembering the DR pack that usually rides there. "He sent stuff, btw." A frown. "Of course, they took it all."

"I doubt we'll need it," I say, shrugging.

Her arms uncross, but only so she can pull her legs up and cross *them*. "Did you really thump all twelves to that Scallop Abby? Because that's bad play, Sand. Way out of spec. Twelves are fully capable. We can handle the hoppers, the dirges. Rails, we can even handle the servs after the nineties."

Her eyes are heating me. "A, I thought you were unique—distinct, even. But maybe I was wrong. Thirteen now and you're high heaven. A real big pounder." She looks at the door again. "I don't know if I can vid you, I certainly don't want you mucking up my stream."

I shake my head, incredulous. You'd think after sharing terabytes of data with someone through various jobs, after countless messages—full impact messages, mind you—I'd be able to understand her, just a little. But I really, really don't.

I'm a bit frightened by her, actually. "I was trying to save you," I stream, letting my emotion flow right along.

She's still staring at the door. Not even moving her head. And her arms are crossed again now too. A genuine body double cross. She might even be blocking my messages.

"You're looped," I say aloud, because I know she can't block that. "Endless, single-entry, zero-exit looped." The unhurt side of her face is toward me now, and I can detect the hint of a quiver in her mouth's corner. She isn't *all* stone to me. Not really.

"Did you say I was inherently disadvantaged?" she asks.

I look at the floor, searching for a bit of light in the pattern of the rug there. I'm not finding it. "I said whatever I had to," I say. "Anything to keep him from bringing you here."

She gives me a sideways glance. "Am I *that* bad of company?"

Crickets on the beltway! "No! Of course not."

I get a full look now. "But you do think I'm disadvantaged. Inherently."

"Again, I was trying to keep you away. Keep you safe." Like on the driftbarge, remember?

"But you said what you really thought," she says. "Because you have to. It is what you believe. I have stops built in too, Sand. I know what I can say and what I can't. You couldn't outright lie to him."

Well, she has me there. I bet you don't have this problem, do you, freehead?

"It was a generalization based on *his* societal expectations," I say, "not mine." I feel a flash of heat now regardless. "But I gotta say, considering how hard it is to convince you of something, the generalization is starting to make sense to me."

Big. Glare. "What does *that* mean?"

I'm in a circle spinning helplessly. Pieces are starting to fly apart. Gotta correct with passion. "It means nothing," I say. I notice a stray thread on the floor rug, and I pull it free. "I was railed. I haven't chute slept in nearly five days. Scallop is like most other Abbys: he thinks women are bots with lipstick. But I don't. I never have. Especially not you. You might be the most productive woman I've ever met. Certainly the bravest."

Her eyebrows arch. "The most productive woman? You're a real Bogart, Sand."

I shake my head. "The most productive anything anywhere, does that help?"

"It is better," she says. "Not great. But better." The beginnings of a smile. A luscious, glorious smile. She looks at the door again. "So, being so productive, I gotta ask if you've thought of a way out of this for us."

I study the iron rivets of the door, still visible beneath the enameled covering. "Mechanical locks," I say. "Completely stream free. We're like two BluTrolls."

Hard's smile widens. "Yeah, he was missing parity wasn't he? BluTroll..." The smile diminishes then.

I'm forced to notice her bruising again. It hurts me. Tentatively, I creep in her direction.

"What are you doing?" she asks.

I frown. "I'm just..." I reach out a hand. She watches it the whole way, looking frightened, but somehow doesn't stop me as I cup the left side of her face and move it so I can see the right. My gut aches at the sight. "I wish I could do something," I say. "If it was synthskin..."

She shakes her head, disengaging from me somewhat. "Don't bother with it. Don't worry about it. Thing about yourself. He's taking your implant out, Sand. He's going to cut you."

I'm distracted, still studying her injuries...and the curve of her chin. "Like a sheep before shearers," I say.

She squints, looks at me hard. "What?"

"Nothing."

She brings her hand up to push mine away. Somehow, our hands become twined. I look at them. They still are. The touch sends fuel to the blaze inside me. It is a fire with an ice pick at its center, though, because I know Scallop is coming back. I also know that this is as far as it goes between HardCandy and me, with our stops in place, and all.

That's okay. I'm a debugger. I'm a tool.

And right now, I'm working.

LITTLE TIME PASSES. Very little. I figure because Scallop doesn't want to miss one moment of his own precious sleeping time. Regardless, the door clanks and squeaks again, and there he is, with HookNose and BigUgly 2.0 right behind him. He has the silver, banana-shaped controller in his hand, and he's griping it so hard his knuckles are white.

"It is unfortunate we have to do this, DR 63. Unfortunate to remove your implant," he says. "But it is time. Please get up and come with me."

There is little else I can do. I push away from the floor, achieve a standing position.

HardCandy, in a newfound burst of emotion, reaches out to grasp the back of my calf.

The feeling is shocking, confusing—like a tweak beginning at the point of contact and radiating outward. She slides her hand down to just above my plastiformed footwear and rests it there. That touch messes with my brain too. But it is not painful at all. Warm. Rails lotta warm.

Scallop thumbs the top of his device. Hard immediately releases her grip, brings her hands to her head.

"Please release him," Scallop says. "That is only a warning."

I grit my teeth. "That wasn't necessary."

The guards storm in to support him, pounders at the ready. HookNose grabs my shirt, nearly taking me from my feet, and pulls me toward them. Slight frame, freehead, remember? I wasn't planning on a struggle anyway.

I know what you're thinking. You're thinking that maybe after my implant is removed I'll have a chance. Maybe I can get away, go home. I don't put much hope in that, though. I doubt the Dark-Trench designers left after their implants were removed. And I seriously doubt they're still moving around, or selling parts somewhere like GrimJack. Grim never worked on anything this important. Grim never was a *real* thorn.

I hear a soft whimpering sound from HardCandy behind me, but resist the urge to look at her. It won't help, and would only give those holding us the satisfaction that they hurt us. Instead, I whisper to her in the stream: "Sweet Candy, I'll miss you."

She replies, saying the same, and more. It is enough.

They yank me into the hallway and the door slams shut again. I feel a sudden burst of streamflow. I'm amazed by how comforting that is, even now. Fill me up, stream. One last time.

We take the two dozen steps to the red caution door. This one has a mechanical component as well—the turn of a starshaped wheel followed by the pull of a handle. It *thunks* free and I can almost feel the pressure change as it opens. The mass of the door is great, moving air as it swings. Beyond it, I can see only a reflection of the hallway lights and our dark profiles in the doorway. The odor within is stale and sweet. Scallop enters and HookNose pulls me along. BigUgly brings up the rear.

The lights are dim, but increase in brightness following Scallop's touch on a switch. To my right is a curved metal control desk, maybe fifteen meters in length. Behind it are three black chairs, all empty. In the center of the room, concealed within glass, is another, larger chair that faces away from the desk. It too is colored black and has a glossy shine to its surface.

Above it hangs a machine both familiar and foreign. Not precisely the spider of my youth, but with similar articulated arms and daunting appliances. The notable difference here is that *this* machine has one arm that is thicker and longer than the others. If the machine were an animal, this bigger appendage would be its tail.

It isn't a spider this time—it is a scorpion.

Scallop moves to stand behind the desk, at the same time directing the guards, with hand motions and curt commands, on where to take me. Soon I'm within the glass, strapped to the big black chair at both hands and feet. The guards move beyond the glass.

As much as I can, I turn to look Scallop's direction. He stands behind the control desk, activating monitors and mechanisms. "The last time I did this," I say, "there was video to watch." There are no vidscreens in this room anywhere. At least, not that I can see. The walls are white and completely blank.

Scallop chuckles. "I am sorry. There will be no cartoons this time." A pause as he checks something on the console before him. "And no anesthesia, either." He nods to the two guards. "You may wait outside. I am perfectly safe here now." HookNose and BigUgly silently obey. The door booms closed behind them.

"I am told that you were implanted by the notable Bamboo over a decade ago," Scallop says. "I heard him speak once. He is a bit of a pioneer himself, actually. Did you know that?"

"One man's pioneer is another man's slave trader."

Scallop sniffs loudly. "Come now," he says, "you don't mean that. I'm sure he treated you admirably, as he did all his pupils. Even those clearly at the bottom of the pool."

My irritation with Scallop has now graduated to full loathing. "I wouldn't know," I say. Snappy comebacks seem a little juvenile at this point.

If I could spit on him, though...well...

"And now to begin." Scallop takes a seat, looking like a keyboard player before a restless audience, awaiting them to grow silent. Vidscreens built into the desk reflect back onto his face, giving it a yellowish cast. His hands move, and I hear the machine above me begin to hum. Nano-formed tendrils grow from my headrest, drawing themselves firmly across my forehead and chin, securing my head in place.

"I don't know if you are aware," Scallop says, "but implant removal is never a clean process. The longer an implant is inside, the more it bonds with the cells of the brain. That is why older implantees tend to be so much more efficient than new ones. Normally you think of brain functions being reduced as time goes on, but not so with debuggers. The longer the implantation, the better."

I test the headrest tendrils, wrenching my head both left and right. No give whatsoever.

"Unfortunately for you," Scallop says, "many years with an implant makes *this* procedure worse. After so much time, your implant will have become quite seated." An exaggerated sigh. "I hope there aren't too many memories that you are fond of."

The machine above me is in motion now: talon-like hands clasping and unclasping, circular tools spinning and turning, arms swinging and articulating. Scallop is putting everything through its paces, demonstrating his power.

The one I'm worried most about is the big appendage. The tail. It contains the extractor, and it looks large enough to scoop out my whole skull.

"Aren't you at least going to deaden my skin?" I ask. "Or do you want me to scream?"

"I can deaden it if you prefer," Scallop says. "Though I doubt it will prevent every scream."

A needle descends and, with little warning, buries itself into my scalp. Immediately my left temple goes numb.

"You once told me to stream some history, 63," Scallop says. "I found that remark humorous, actually, and since you're apparently such a student of the past yourself, perhaps I should tell you some things you've probably never streamed before. From back before implants and bots. Back before your illustrious Tanzer."

I hear mechanical shrieks and squeals from above. The sounds of nightmares.

"Since the early AH," Scallop says, "we have been fighting. Fighting the people of the corrupted books, fighting the encroachment of godless beliefs, and, yes, sometimes fighting even within our own family. We were patient, knowing that through all this turmoil A's will would someday be realized. We struck and then we hid. We talked peace while planning destruction. We used our own brothers' suffering as fuel against those who were more sympathetic of such things.

We sowed discontent. And we encouraging the growth of large families for A. We bided our time..."

I pretend to be strong, but I am not. No more than when I received the implant as a child. I'm a quivering mess. My pulse is racing, made worse by the beep-beep echo I hear from one of Scallop's monitoring devices, even through the glass separating us. I can feel a tingling in my hands and feet as well—symptoms of my overall nervousness. Or the tightness of my restraints...

"Around 1550 AH," Scallop continues, "we realized that with all our planning, with all our many soldiers, with all our patience and deception, we were still losing nearly every battle we entered. The reason for this was simple, 63: technology. With the proper technology even the smallest army can conquer. In fact, they could do so without putting soldiers onto the battlefield! They could sit in the comfort of their homes and watch our children die on vidscreens, and *still* win.

"So, finally, our leaders of that day realized their errors. They left behind the old ways of scimitar and dagger, and embraced technology as the excellent tool that A had provided. They put that tool in the hands of their children, who wielded it mightily—and improved it. That was how we finally won."

I think of my parents, wonder if this is what they expected from their son. Wonder if they ever had other children. I hope they did. I also think of HardCandy, of course, and Grim. The crew makes an appearance in my thoughts as well. Even the two I have yet to meet.

"However, after A's army redeemed the nations," Scallop says, "after we brought down the infidels and dispelled their laws based on greed and idols, there were many who again wanted to dispose of all technology. 'Why do we need such things anymore?' they asked. 'Certainly now that our laws are in place, we should return to the life that our founder lived.'"

The scorpion above makes a turn, swiveling so the back half is directly overhead. I see a device that looks like the cutter—a thin razor—separate from the other arms and begin to descend. I close my eyes and reach out to the stream for distraction.

"A strong faction of that mindset still exists, Sandfly. If you descend to the streets, you will see many of their number. They were wrong, DR—they still are wrong. Technology is the only thing that will keep our society alive, allow it to expand to the heavens. So we must have nothing to lend credence to their beliefs. Not a malfunctioning bot nor an infected debugger. All must believe that our technology is infallible."

I get a contact request in the stream—Full Impact. I suspect it is from Hard, so I grab it, turn it, mentally rip it open. No better way to free my mind from what's coming.

Instead, I get an image of a servbot, armless, lying flat amidst a pile of refuse. And it appears to be sliding backwards. "DR 63, are you available?" the bot asks.

My mind is officially distracted. "Model RS-19?"

"Correct, DR."

"Where are you?"

"I am on a refuse slider, soon to be ejected into space."

"How—" The shadow above me shifts again. I hear a renewed whirring sound. "How are you still functioning?"

"I believe it is the TC again, though it appears my reanimation may be short-lived this time." The bot's voice is considerably slower than I remember. He's functioning, but barely. His nanos have to be in a complete scramble.

"I'm sorry I can't help you," I stream.

"No need," he says. "I had to reach you one last time. I have information to share."

The knife is centimeters from my face now. "I doubt it will matter, bot."

"Regardless, I have a message. New information about the superlative stream I encountered."

The knife reaches me. I feel the pressure at my temple. "Yes?"

"The message—I said it was directed at the crew, and I still believe that to be true. At least, in part."

I grimace uncontrollably. "You said you thought they were reprogrammed, that their functions were changed..."

"That is correct. They were. They are. But just as much so, possibly more so, there was another message riding the stream. One specifically encoded for you, DR 63."

The knife cuts me. Blood must be flowing, because another arm descends with a sponge.

"For me?"

"Or someone very much like you. If you remember, you *did* pass out."

"Yes, but I ran a check. The implant is perfect."

I see the bot drop into a crate, that crate moving toward a door. He takes some time in responding. Milliseconds, even. "I would expect it is better than perfect," he says. "Regardless, here is the message, are you ready?"

I glance up and see the scorpion swivel again. A serrated blade moves into position—the skull saw. "Yes!" I stream scream.

There is a pause, enough to make me wonder if I'll ever hear from the bot again.

"Humble yourself under the mighty hand of A~A^3," the bot says finally, "that He may lift you up in due time."

"*What?*" He is completely whacked—he has to be. But I'm a bleeding man, about to be thrown to the sharks. I'll listen to anything.

I see the bot's crate approaching an open door, entering a small white chamber, and the door closing behind him. Another door begins to slide. The rushing of wind.

"Remember, DR, it is for you," he says. "Personally."

And the connection ends.

THE SPONGE TOUCHES ME AGAIN and then ascends, glistening the color of cherry. The skull saw begins to spin, its sound a cicada at dusk.

Humble myself? Who is more humble than a debugger?

We spend our whole lives bending knee to whatever master holds a controller, and to the whims of whatever imam sits in power. We are tools with emotion. Children of both man and machine. Unable to sleep properly unless we entomb ourselves like a pharaoh. Captive minds swimming in a sea of ether...

"Now comes the difficult part," Scallop says, his voice so loud it startles me. "Expect extreme pressure."

Again I'm moved to tears. I'm finished. Done. An orange peel in a waste unit.

The bot's words echo—pinball—through my mind. Humble yourself. A message for you. Personally!

That last seems so unlike the A the Abduls describe. A personal god? Sending *me* a message?

He stoops!

Where has he been all this time? Why did he let all this happen?

In due time.

I barely gave it a thought previously. I spent billions of cycles on everything from nano songs to puppy rebellions, and never spent time to wonder, to research. To hope!

You praised...silver...stone...which cannot see. But you did not honor...

Not me! That was them—Scallop, Master, Bamboo—but not me!

There is no speech or language where their voice isn't heard.

The saw is so close now I can feel the breeze it makes. I shut my eyes.

It is your personal state...that is important.

There is someone out there. Real. Personal. Searching.

Yes, of course. You know it to be true.

And he is not A. To him I must be no more than a nano dancing in the stream. And yet he stooped to send me a message. Me. The stars scream his name. I can do nothing beyond his sight. Speak nothing beyond his ears. Anything that happens now is entirely up to him.

And, to my surprise, I find I'm wide open to that.

I feel the saw's pressure. I jerk back, into the headrest. Struggle—

"*Get back!*" I stream. "*Stop!*"

THERE IS COMPLETE SILENCE for a thousand nanoseconds. Then I hear Scallop swear loudly, and the repeated beeps of his hands on the control pad.

"There seems to be a problem," he mumbles. "The machine appears to be stalled."

I'm speechless, eyes wide and staring at the skull saw now eight meters above my head. Retracted and dangling like a broken limb. "Oh," I say with difficulty, "do you want me to fix that for you?"

Scallop doesn't miss a beat. "Is that possible?"

Are you blinking joking, Abdul?

A notion streaks into my mind. "Wait a moment," I say. "Let me try..." I stream out, searching for the signature of the scorpion above. I find it: hulking, barbaric, nanos marching to a warrior's tune—all snare drums and heavy brass. I do a query. Try to find their reason for stopping...

It is what I suspected: because I told them to.

Now that's interesting, you see, because if the machine is listening to me, that means it recognizes my authority. But all DR authority is derivative. Given by our master, or by the rules we follow. Explicit or implied, our behavior is controlled.

Another experiment is in order. I mentally pat the scorpion's head and tell it to dance for me.

The machine begins to spin—arms extend and retract, swivel and bounce. Intrigued, I let the salsa continue. A smile plays across my lips.

"So you *can* fix it?" Scallop says. There is wariness in his voice. A cautious but disbelieving ignorance. "Can you stop that now, please?"

I let the scorpion continue to spin. I add something new, however, making the tail appendage pump up and down like a porpoise in the water.

"Okay, DR 63, you've had your fun," Scallop says. "Now I order you to stop." I hear the clink of metal on metal, as if he's retrieved something from the desk.

The controller, of course. Knew it wouldn't be long...

But the scorpion doesn't stop, and why should it? I haven't told it to.

And yet, no head buzz. I disobeyed a direct order. No buzz.

The stops...are they off? Could they be?

That's supposed to be impossible. An implant without stops? Impossible. Dangerously impossible.

I reach out to the nanos holding my head. "Be gone," I say.

They obey, snaking back into the chair. My head now free, I turn to look at Scallop.

His face is completely white—an amazing look for a guy who's normally brown. "I'm going to use the controller, now," he says. "I don't want to do this."

The threat is humorous, because his hand is already molesting the controller. Nothing is happening there, Abby. No stops. No buzz. No controllers.

Interesting.

Scallop is desperately pushing buttons now, both on the controller and the scorpion board.

I tell the scorpion to stop, realign itself on the chair, and bring the scalpel down for my bonds. Swivel, hum, *slick, slick, slick*—Sandfly is free.

I rise to my feet.

Scallop mashes the controller down and flees the desk, heading straight for the door.

I look around. I'm still encased within the glass. What to do about that?

Scorpion!

The tail flicks upward, momentum bringing the skull saw around and up. In seconds it carves a large circle in the glass canopy overhead.

That will do.

I put up a hand. *Let's go, barbarians.* One of the more docile appendages reaches out and takes my hand. Lifts me up into the opening.

Scallop reaches the door and begins to pound on it.

I'm well aware that whatever has happened to me may be only temporary. For whatever reason, I'm suddenly strong. I have authority. I also know that if Scallop gets the word out, the purge against all debuggers on Earth might come sooner than anyone expected. I certainly don't want that.

So now what?

Let's put the fear of A into them.

No, the fear of A~A^3!

Lights out!

The room plunges into darkness. Scallop's pounding is recognized, though, because the door begins to clank and open. I walk toward him. No need to rush.

"I'm here, Scallop," I say. "Ready to serve."

"You'll die, debugger," he screams. "I'll pull out your implant with my bare hands!"

Brave words. Stupid, brave words.

Scallop manages to get the door open. On the other side are HookNose and BigUgly, looking lost. Scallop wrenches a nanopounder from HookNose's hands, turns it back toward the room. The darkened room I'm still standing in.

Now he's annoying me.

I sing out to the lights in the hall. Down they go.

I hear a curse, and the sounds of bodies colliding. "He's free!" Scallop yells. "'Without stops!" More curses from different voices.

I stream out to HardCandy. Tell her to stay put and be good. No matter what she hears.

There's the clamor of footsteps running. Beyond this hallway, the station is lit, of course, and the three men are heading for that light. I've forgotten something.

Oh, yes. The nasty machines. They don't care about the dark now, do they?

Everybody, it is time to show yourselves!

I feed the machines pictures of their targets. Nano bubbles drop from the ceiling. Sonic inhibitors begin to blare. Another nasty something that causes random flashes of light also comes to play.

During one of those bright moments I see Scallop and the guards at the far end of the hall. Their pounders long abandoned, they have their hands over their ears. Round, grey companions follow.

How many guards are on this station? How many occupants?

First in, first out. I feed information to the station stream. Tell it there are fires on all levels. Recommend an immediate evacuation. The station manager is also berserk, I report. Handle with caution. Stop him at all costs.

I remember the crew. Where are they? Are they alive?

They are.

And the station is mine.

I HALT THE ALARMS in the hallway, return the lights there to their full illumination, and step free of the darkness.

In the distance, and on the stream, I still hear a claxon—the result of my evacuation alert. I stream access to the views from various station cameras. They show pulsing lights and the occasional scurrying Abdul. Those Abbys have a problem, however. This portion of the station is completely locked down now. No one is going anywhere.

A smile erupts on my face. I'm free—absolutely and completely. I can do anything I want! Anything. Suddenly I'm nine again and master of my destiny.

But what next? What next?

I take the handful of steps to HardCandy's cell. I work the mechanical locks. Pull the heavy door open. She sits on the floor with bowed head. She looks up at me, surprised.

"What is happening, Sand? There's all kinds of crazy music on the local stream. Is the station on fire?"

I shrug. "In a manner of speaking." I smile.

"So, where is Scallop?" she asks. "The guards?"

I check the cameras again, pull the nano-bubbles for status. A mere three hallways away, one of the guards is stuck. Firmly affixed to the wall by a bubble, with only hands, forehead, and nose visible. HookNose, clearly. He's done for the day.

I find the other guard—who must be fleeter of foot—hiding in a lab farther on, with a nano-bubble bouncing expectantly in the hallway outside.

Of Scallop there is no sign. I do one more check. "He's smart," I say aloud. "Ditched his communicator."

"Who's smart?" Hard asks. She's standing now, but she still appears weakened to me. The bruises on her face don't help. In fact, they rail me, stoke my fire. *I owe Scallop for those...*

"You're hurt!" she exclaims.

In the excitement of driving Scallop away, I had all but forgotten the incision on my head. "Am I bleeding?" I touch my temple near the spot and wince.

"No," she says. "Not now." She wrinkles her nose. "It doesn't look deep..."

"It's not," I say. "His operation wasn't successful."

HardCandy squints, looks confused. "Then what happened? How did you get free?"

"I'll send you a report later." I force a smile. "Nothing that concerns you."

She looks momentarily upset, then frowns and clutches my elbow. "It *does* concern me," she says. "I mean, it should, shouldn't it...?"

I frown, unsure of what to say. Of course I want her to care. I need someone to care. Now...everything has changed. And with freedom comes uncertainty.

"Where's the crew?" she asks.

"They haven't been executed, I know that." I hold up a finger and, diving into my head, focus my search. I find the detention center—a place of blank walls and bolted doors—and start flipping through the visuals. Empty cell, empty cell... wait!

I see a small room, the entrance of which is blocked by a shimmering gold nano-curtain, similar to those used by masters to separate themselves from others. To separate themselves from me. Any guards that had been there have long since gone. Not surprisingly, they chose to save themselves first, leaving their charges to whatever fate awaited them.

Which, if they believe the stream warnings I planted, meant to be burnt, asphyxiated, or flushed into space. Possibly all three.

I like to be thorough.

I stream up the station files and start furiously paging through them. It is the crew's cell I've found. And I know where it is located on the station. I stream the information to Hard.

"I don't know why Scallop didn't execute them immediately," I say. "Like he did with the bot."

I feel a wave of fatigue, the culmination of days of improper sleep.

"Should we free them?" she asks. "Can we?"

I nod. "Yes," I say, "We can. But not yet...."

"Then what?" she asks. "We need to get out of here, right? Escape while we can?"

I see a report flash across the stream—in a secured thread that only guards are supposed to be able to access. Scallop managed to elude the bubbles and is back in charge, regrouped. He's beginning to gather guards. Assemble them. He knows I have to be stopped. Here. Kept from riding the lift down, carrying my little revolution to Earth. His fear is an elixir, a fuel for dangerous action.

He's trying to reach the ground. Call for help.

I slam the communications grid down. Bind anything outgoing. "If I can't call out," I say, "neither can he."

"What?" Hard says.

I smile. "You want to walk with me? Watch me have some fun?"

She shakes her head, eyes wide. "What happened to you?" she asks. "What fun?"

I tap my head. "Stops are gone. Completely." I raise my hand, close it into a fist. "I'm a blinking freehead, HardCandy. Can you believe it?"

"How is that possible?"

"A-not-A cubed," I say. "And the servbot. The song did something to my implant." I shake my head, still unable to believe it. "He stoops!"

Another long look from HardCandy. "He what? What are you talking about?"

"I don't know," I say. "But whatever or whoever he is, he made me special. Incredible. And I have to plan for that. Use this gift somehow. Make some noise."

"How?" she asks. "Do what?"

"Get back at them," I say. "The masters. Make them pay for

robbing our childhood, our lives. For binding our heads. For controlling what people think and do."

The stream has lots of chatter now. Nanopounders are being gathered. Lines are being formed. I check on the prisoners again: still okay. I contemplate releasing them from here, but decide against it. Not until I know they'll be safe. They're too important now.

"Sandfly, I know you're listening." Scallop's voice, unmistakable in my implant.

I smile. Stream back: "What do you want, pig?"

There is a long pause. Been a long time since Scallop has been disrespected, I would guess. When he EEs me again, his voice is decidedly less bold, less demanding.

"Whether you realize it or not, 63, you are dangerous. Infected. I hope you understand that we can't let you survive. It is unfortunate. Your reputation was stellar."

I scowl and see HardCandy's eyes widen as a result.

"I'm better than I've ever been," I stream. "Why would you want to destroy that?"

I hear a chuckle, but the resulting text string is meaningless. "I have to admit," Scallop streams, "you are entertaining." A pause. "Is HardCandy there with you?"

"You can't tell?" I ask. To whatever stream device Scallop is using, our whole area of the station would appear to be filled with implants. That's what I want him to feel. That we're an army.

Another chuckle. "I'll assume she is. Are you looking at her now?"

I *am* looking at HardCandy. At this point, where else would I look? Her face, even bruised, seems flawless to me. Her almond eyes, the even texture of her skin...

HardCandy wrinkles her forehead, shuts her eyes, and brings a hand up. "Aahhh!"

"So a controller still works on her," Scallop streams. "That's comforting. I was told these were virtually uninterruptible."

Scallop has another controller. Little surprise with as many debuggers as they once had here.

Hard is doubled over now, one hand on her knees, the other still at her forehead. She's holding back a scream, I can tell—fighting against another outburst. I don't like feeling helpless. Not today.

"I won't try to persuade her to clash with you," Scallop streams. "Even though she might make a good showing. I only need to get your attention. I want you here where we can contain you. That is all." A long pause. "So, DR 63, will you come to me? Bring yourself out?"

Hard eases to the floor, resumes her seated position. Her head still aches, even if the buzz isn't persistent. I know how it feels.

"Stay here," I whisper.

I step into the hall again and close the door. But I don't lock it. I never want to see her imprisoned again.

"I'm coming, Scallop," I stream. "Just wait."

MILITARY LEADERS NORMALLY have months to prepare for battle. Time to disciple, to coordinate, to recognize weaknesses and strengths, to build fortifications, to practice for any eventuality and the brutality of war ahead. A time to mold the many into the one—to hone completeness.

In that respect Scallop has the advantage. There is no denying it. I have no team, no tactical knowledge, and no training.

But I do have something: the power of the unexpected. The situation that no Abdul could ever prepare for. Even Scallop. Even my master. Even the Imam.

And I have the stream.

A dozen turns ahead of me, not far from his office, Scallop has arranged a blockade of twenty men with the orders to nano-pound me into obsolescence. I know this because I've watched them on cameras, heard their orders over their supposedly protected stream.

I'm not okay with their plans. I can do whatever I want now. Say whatever.

"Idiot masters!" I yell, simply to show I can. "Stupid Scallop!"

To my right, at the juncture where this hallway dead ends into another, is a small alcove—a bright spot with a large window for viewing the earth below. It isn't for any potential sightseer, though. The whole alcove is dedicated to prayer. There's a shining mechanism for "purifying" one's hands, one's feet, one's arms, the inside of one's nose and ear canals.

There is a meter-high servbot standing to one side. Square head atop square body, all colored blue. It is charged with keeping the place perpetually clean—especially the rectangle on the floor before the window. There, among the otherwise colorless tile, is an intricate design that points toward the Earth and wherever M is located. It is the place where Abduls kneel.

"Abdul," as I should've told you before, means "servant." It works as an inside joke for us debuggers. Our way of snickering at those who force us to serve. But looking at the alcove, I am reminded of a fact: everyone on Earth serves someone. Everyone has to bow. Everyone has a master. Everyone needs to be free.

He stoops!

What does stooping mean in regards to the eternal, though? In regards to this $A \sim A^3$? Does it mean He might get in the dirt? Might actually get His own hands dirty? Might find them filled with bot guts, or barge grease, or whatever? Like I have most my life?

And if He is not A, then who is He?

After the suffering of his soul, he will see the light of life and be satisfied; by his knowledge my righteous servant will justify many, and he will bear their iniquities.

What is that? I squint, search the hall around me. Words in my head, but coming from nowhere. Without the implant's help. The bot never said that. I never read it. Where is it coming from?

"Sandfly, are you coming?" This time it is Scallop's voice. Smug. Prepared.

I smile. Stream back: "On my way."

Luckily for Scallop and his band, they are positioned a good distance from any of the nasty machines on the station. A testimony to their training. I would've liked to have used those against them. Pity.

There are plenty of other mechanicals around I can use, though. I look down at the blue cleaning bot.

"Are you ready?" I ask him.

"A is the greatest," the bot says. "I am ready to be of service. My model number is BT-53. I was created by SynTactical Corporation on—"

I hold up a hand. "That's enough." I scan the alcove again, shake my head. I compose and feed instructions to the bot to make the coming transition easier. ""You aren't needed here anymore," I say. "Come with me."

I walk the halls slowly, feet firmly in my path. From every hall I pass, from every circulation duct, lab, kitchen, cleaning facility, and med center, a silent army builds. They roll on tripods, they shuffle on feet, they click-clank-click along the ceiling tiles above and brikety-brack over the walls. They close around me, protecting me. Because of what I am.

Both their master and their servant.

I HIT THE STREAM, page through the cameras until I find the one closest to Scallop's band of huddled men. All are dressed in brown and have nanopounders at the ready. Scallop is nowhere to be seen.

"He's tweaking me again," Hard streams softly. "Sand...it hurts so bad..."

I grit my teeth. Force myself to wait. I'm vastly empowered now, but still the controller's signal is uninterruptible.

The blue bot rounds the corner and meekly approaches the band of huddled men. They stare at it speechless for a full twenty seconds as it rolls toward them.

"What is that doing here?" one says finally.

They really should stop communicating via the stream...

"It is a ceremonial bot," another says, "from one of the prayer alcoves."

I feed the bot something directly. Command it to speak.

"In the beginning A~A³ created the heavens and the earth," it says. Text originating from the same corrupted books that the RS-19 quoted. A fragment I gleaned during my detention cell research. Somehow it feels appropriate.

The boxy bot continues toward the group. They have made no move to stop it yet.

"Orders?" one of the guards says. "Do we have orders?"

"The Earth was formless and empty," the bot continues as it rolls forward. "Darkness was over the surface of the deep. And the spirit of A~A³ hovered over the waters..."

Still no movement from the guards. They're completely baffled.

The bot is within two meters of them now. Apart from its wheels, it makes no overt moves. Finally, it stops and grows silent.

"There's no way it is armed, right?" a dark-skinned guard asks. "Or wired with explosives?"

"There are no explosives on this station," another guard—with a beard thick enough to hide his face—says. "Don't be a fool."

The bot's trunk splits open, and from a speaker hidden within, blares the standard call to prayer.

The guards exchange confused looks. Some put hands to their ears. Others look as if they intend on honoring the bot's call. Eyes search the floor, the guns relax.

"Now!" I stream. "Go!"

"What is going on there?" A question from Commander Scallop, somewhere out of sight. "You imbeciles!" he yells. "Shoot it!"

I walk forward, bot companions packed like a wall in front of me. The cricket-like scratchers that maintain the station's ductwork travel along the ceiling. The meter-long snakes used for exploring tight spaces slither along the walls.

We turn the corner and finally face the blockade. The guards raise their weapons. The first shot rings out, shattering the ceremonial bot into pieces. I wince, but press the bots onward.

Confused curses mingle with random nanopounder shots. The bots I've assembled behind their blockade have arrived, the sounds of their movement having been masked by the ceremonial bot's ministrations. A welcome surprise. The guards turn this way and that in confusion.

Meanwhile, I check on Hard. She's suffering, but still hanging in there. I search the stream for information on controllers, try to determine if there is any way I can help her. So far, nothing.

"Crichton..." she whispers. "He's nailing it again..."

I growl in disgust, in righteous indignation. We're closing on the men, but I've lost a dozen bots to nanopounder shots already. The guards are using the highest setting, so every bot that is struck is thrown—wildly, appendages spinning—into those behind them. This disrupts our steady forward progress, but thankfully, there are many of us. Dozens. And, thankfully, the bots feel no pain.

Crickets! You need to get there!

These littlest bots—distant cousins of the hoppers that maintain our downrider strings—are incredibly nimble, fitted with the best obstacle avoidance software. As the frightened men fire, they leap from ceiling panel to ceiling panel, skitter over lighting surfaces and structures. Only two from my personal escort are lost before they reach the lead men.

As the crickets drop onto the men's wrapped heads, there are wails of terror. The men grapple with panic. Through the camera I see two hit the ground, struggling.

That's when the snakes move in, when the guards are down. One wraps a man's feet and legs, while another moves from floor to shoulder to pounder. Pulls the weapon away.

Scallop trumpets orders over the stream. Curses, verbal flagellations. That makes me smile.

The two bots directly in front of me—both humanoid RX models—get pounded simultaneously. The head of one comes spiraling back, giving me barely enough time to duck. The other falls clumsily to the floor, partially blocking my path. I order the ranks to close and the obstruction removed, but the process is slow enough that I feel a window of full exposure. It is enough to remind me of the danger. I must not forget that. Or relent.

We're down to almost half the armed men now. I notice on the stream that there is another, smaller band of armed men headed toward the detention center—toward the imprisoned crew. Without a word, I stream a dozen bots to break off from the blockade and intercept that second group.

Looks of puzzlement strike the features of the men that notice my reassignment, my bots suddenly stopping and skittering away. Perhaps they think Scallop has found a way to control them, a way to stop me.

He has not.

Speaking of Scallop, where is he?

The larger members of my group have now met the enemy. Arms, both humanoid and not, reach out to grasp, tug, and prod. To the men it must seem like being pressed in by a many-horned rhino. To them, a robot revolution is an impossibility—a nightmare. They shoot and shoot, but we continue to advance. Crickets drop. Snakes slither in silence. Tiny maintenance bots ram forcefully into un-guarded shins.

I close my eyes to the chaos temporarily, check on HardCandy again. She isn't responding. I send her a gentle message. A digital nudge. But still nothing. My gut aches. I swap through camera images again, notice my bots engaging the group near the prisoners. So far, so good.

Finally, I find the image of Hard's cell. She is lying on the floor, motionless. "I'm okay," she stream whispers. "I can handle it..."

I feel the full weight of my fatigue. I start to swoon, but the bot behind me catches me, holds me straight. "A-not-A cubed be praised," it says.

Wish I felt that confident. I force my eyes open, take stock of my current surroundings. Only three guards remain in this group, and they are fully engaged. One has a cricket hanging above and two snakes at his feet. Within moments the snakes have wrapped his legs up to the knee. He struggles against falling, but does so anyway.

The second glimpses me through my robot shield. With a howl of "A is the greatest!" he shoots at me repeatedly.

Bots splinter and fall all around me. I duck so low one knee touches the floor.

A cricket drops on the guard's back. "Aaayeeeh!" he screams and goes careening down the hall. Distracted, he trips over a boxy maintenance bot, and drops headlong. Snakes envelop him. Bind him. Servbots shuttle him away. We're not killing people here, after all.

The third is now similarly contained. A humanoid servbot holds his arms back, removes his nanopounder. "What should I do with this?" the bot asks.

"Smash it," I say.

I get a camera glimpse of Scallop. He's two passages away, entirely on his own, and running. He still holds the controller, and is gripping it like a sponge he's trying to wring dry.

I get an occasional clipped moan from HardCandy, so I know she's still being affected. I have to get him.

I break into a run, ordering the bots to constrain the guards. Move them toward a nearby room and seal the door...

I check on the prisoners again. The band of guards has shrunk considerably, but so have the bots. In raw numbers they are about even. The men are more intent on reaching the prisoners than steadily fighting. That's the problem. They may make it.

I switch to the view inside the detention center. The nanoshield is still in operation, so I order it lowered. The four crewmembers—Handler, TallSpot, and the two scientists I have yet to meet—all still in their space suits and helmets—step forward out of their cell, puzzlement evident in their slowly turning heads.

I send a message directly to the audio devices in that room. Tell them the situation. "You may need to fight," I say. "I did what I could..."

All four bubble-heads acknowledge with a nod. I'm confident that at least Handler can make a showing of himself. He was strong when we were young, anyway.

I check on Scallop. He is still running, and I know exactly where he's headed.

WHEN I GET THERE, the first set of doors have already closed. Through security cameras I can see Scallop beyond, though. He still has the controller in one hand and a pistol-sized nanopounder in the other. He is in the long hall leading out of the station and toward the lift. Fifty meters beyond him are the nasty machines.

He is leaving, that much is clear. Typical Abdul leader. But I can't let him go.

I stream open the door and hurry forward. I enter the sliding walkway, but instead of slowing to let the walkway do its work, I continue my pace, using its motion only to accelerate me. I glance at the row of windows to my left. Even with my perceived speed, the stars remain fixed, unmoving.

I see DarkTrench there too, that silent angel. The messenger that changed my life.

Scallop is up ahead, at the place where the passage begins to curve. As he enters the curve, he must notice the motion behind him because he turns and fires at me. I throw myself against the handrail, barely missing the impact. Fortunately for us both, nano-pounder shots are inherently limited to the confines of the station, programmed to disperse at the right time. Otherwise he would've just opened the hull.

I realize now how foolish I was to chase him without a weapon of my own or my bodyguards. Even though his pistol is meant for extremely short range, he still might get lucky.

I hear Scallop laugh. "Almost!" he shouts.

I make a quick check of the nasty machines ahead. They are all on, set to stop anyone from leaving.

"Turn back!" I shout. I search the stream for the loudspeakers above. "Throw down your weapon," I say through them. "And I won't hurt you."

Scallop has left the walkway now and is running on his own. My heart is pounding. My breathing sounds like I'm wearing a spacesuit. Plus I'm dead tired. But I still must catch him.

HardCandy is completely silent now. All attempts I've made at contact have gotten no response.

What seems an eternity later, I too exit the walkway. Scallop draws up and pauses at the start of the nasty machines. The inhibitor's claws have lowered, and within another step or two they will commence their wailing menace. He turns to look at me, indecision written on his face.

I glance up and, seeing one of the station's venting ports, call for the nearest crickets to assemble. Moments later, three exit the port and line up beside each other on the ceiling above. Ready.

"You are dangerous," Scallop says. "Infected!"

I shake my head. "No," I say. "I'm healed."

I urge some larger bots to join me. I get in-progress navigation reports from five in the vicinity of the inner doors. Another six are already on the walkway behind me.

Scallop takes a step back, and the inhibitors begin to whine. Wincing, he drops the controller and brings a hand to his ears. With the other hand he takes unsteady aim at the ceiling. After a number of failed attempts he manages to strike the claws with the pounder, mashing them into the surrounding surface. Smiling, he turns to look at me again.

The humanoid servbots have reached me now. Together we slowly advance.

"You must tell me," he says. "What really made that bot go mad? Tear itself apart."

"You," I say. "Modifying it. Making it more like us. Making it more stream aware. More cognizant. Trying to replace us."

Scallop nods, takes another step backward. "I must admit, we did. It was foolish to think you wouldn't notice." A smile. "But then, you weren't going to leave the station anyway."

I guessed as much. That's why I was given no information before arriving at the station, but had free access once I arrived.

My group continues to advance. We're now to the point where the nasty machines begin.

Scallop hurries backward. The emerald tubes that dispense nano-bubbles emerge. Noting this, he raises the gun. He takes two shots at the leftmost tube, destroying it, but needs only one shot to dispatch the other. He looks at me again. "That still doesn't answer my question. About the bot?"

"The DarkTrench crew encountered a stream in space," I say. "Not unlike our own. A conduit for carrying communication, carrying instructions. There was code on that steam. Programming that, given the proper interpretation, the proper mechanism, can bring about changes in human behavior. A sense of their place in the universe. Their meaning.

"The crew received those instructions, and their effect was felt, but the crew lacked the mechanism to sense the actual stream. They felt the wind, you might say, but could not view its source. The bot, on the other hand, could sense the fullness of the stream, could understand its source, but, lacking a human brain, normally wouldn't have been susceptible to the instructions it contained, and so wouldn't be reprogrammed."

Scallop takes few steps more. Pauses, watches as my group closes the extra distance. "But it clearly malfunctioned..."

"Bots have rules," I say. "Inherent rules, like I used to have stops. They are based on our assumptions about the world. We gave them to them—the humanoid models—so they could function in our society. They are based on the same rules and beliefs we follow every day. Was that entirely necessary? Probably not. But some Imam decided it was a good idea, so it was done. So complete were we in our assumption about the universe, about how it should behave, that we made sure everything we made believed that too. We wound it into the tiniest interaction.

"But somehow, in your experimentation you made this bot special enough, debugger enough, that he *could* interpret what the meaning of the source of the stream meant—to him. This all happened in a nanosecond, I'm sure, but somehow the bot's implant-enhanced brain got stalled. It couldn't get over the central inconsistency it was presented with."

"Which is?"

I frown. "That A is not A."

Scallop grows quiet for a moment, staring at me and my group, pounder at hip level. He then breaks into laughter. "Preposterous! And blasphemous at the same time." He shakes his head. "All the more reason to bring this entire experiment to an end." He takes another, hesitant look at the set of double doors, which are now five meters away. "I intend to decompress the secure portion of this station when I leave." He bolts for the doors.

I instruct my group to move in, to converge as fast as possible.

The crickets above take an early lead, yet as they reach the remains of the emerald tubes, another door drops from the ceiling, slamming into the ground with a weighty *Clong!* Scallop is beyond it, separated from us.

I hit the stream, singing out for the doors that have just closed. They must be stream-aware, must be. What I get instead is a response from the door beyond, the one that Scallop is now standing beside. The one that leads to freedom. It is tightly locked still—immovable. And Scallop, sans communicator, will not be able to open it. He must've known that...

I hear pounder shots, followed by a desperate hissing sound. I rush to the door, look within. Scallop stands there, grimacing. What is he doing? On one side of the containment room another—smaller—door is opening. Beyond it, all I can see is darkness. The pinpricks of stars.

Will that decompress the station?

I feel spent, like all the blood has left my body. My energy completely sapped. I bring up the station map, start paging through specifics, search blindly for a solution.

My eyes widen, I shake my head. The room Scallop is in. It is the final inhibitor, the final protection against an unauthorized exit.

"Scallop!"

I press myself against the glass in time to see Scallop pulled to the door, then torn into the void.

The muted roar continues as every last bit of oxygen escapes the chamber. The small door snaps shut then. Its containment chore finished.

It is mine to avenge; I will repay. In due time their foot will slip; their day of disaster is near and their doom rushes upon them.

My knees buckle. I drop to the floor.

But there is no singing.

I AWAKE TO SEE a white cone hovering over me. Near the top third of the cone is a small circular mirror with a hole in the center. In the center of that circle I see a mechanized red eye, and within that eye I see one lens swapping for another, and another. Finally the cone raises away and, sliding on a telescoping neck, stretches itself upward.

It is a strange way to wake up.

"The DR is conscious," the medbot says.

I rise to find myself in the same examination room I had repaired the servbot in. White walls, white cabinets. Framed blue planet.

I've even been placed on the same cushioned table, I think.

Next to me, on a separate but similar table, is HardCandy. She's unconscious. Alive, yes—I can see her chest move—but way, way out.

Standing two paces away are TallSpot and an Abdul I haven't met before—a slight man with fine features. A simple stream touch tells me who he is: Grackle, one of the remaining DarkTrench crewmembers. A scientist.

Neither man has a helmet on. TallSpot's wheat-like hair is perfectly groomed and his face looks as if it has been recently steamed clean. Handsome as always.

As for Grackle? Well, let's just say it is good that Abdul marriages are arranged.

Turning, I sit to face them, with my legs dangling over the table's edge. "Is HardCandy okay?"

Grackle nods, a knowing smile on his lips. "Yes, she's fine. Sedated, but fine. We discovered her in an interesting location. And, might I say, it was a delight to try to convince her guardians we wouldn't hurt her." He glances at TallSpot. "I was going to sedate you as well, Sandfly. You clearly need rest. But there are important matters to discuss here first."

The weight of the last few days hit me hard, forcing me to recall all that has happened. I look around the room. No one else is here. Where are Handler and the other crewman? Where are the bots? More importantly: "The security guards?"

"They're confined," TallSpot says. "Awaiting our decisions." He sets his teeth. "Where is Scallop?"

I frown, feeling a touch of freehead guilt. "He took a walk."

"A walk?" Tall looks at the nearest wall, as if glimpsing the death beyond. "You mean, in space?"

I nod, still frowning. "It wasn't my doing," I say. "He expected the worst from me, and he *was* being chased. He felt suicide was the best option, apparently."

Tall reverts to silence, looking thoughtful. "There's precedent for that in our society," he says. "Especially when confronted with fear. Even the founder considered suicide at one point."

I nod, aware of the story. Scholars still wrestle with the implications.

The door slides open to reveal the stocky form of Handler—his head also free of the helmet. Behind him is the other scientist, BlueTrain. He is dark complexioned and trim looking.

"So he's alive?" Handler says, smiling. "Still functioning?" He rushes into the room and actually bear hugs me. If I wasn't so tired, I might resist. All I can do is act embarrassed.

TallSpot chuckles. "I don't think he's used to that, Handler."

"I'm not used to anything that is happening here," I say. "But maybe that's not so bad..."

Handler backs away, smiling broadly.

Grackle steps forward. "Yes, we're quite interested in what has happened to you, Sandfly. We saw bots overwhelm three guards. We assume that was your doing?"

I shrug, unsure of how to explain. Unsure about a lot of things.

"Really, debugger," BlueTrain says from doorway, "what happened?"

I feel the need to giggle, but push it away with a simple smile. "I don't know if you can call me *that* anymore..."

I explain everything that has happened, starting with my trip to Scallop's office and ending with his exiting the station. The crew remains silent throughout. Even after I've finished, though they must have questions, no one says a thing. They just stare at me. Which I'm sort of used to.

Handler looks at the others. "So, no more suits then?"

"I guess not," TallSpot says, still staring at me.

"That's great, because I'm getting an awful rash." Handler touches a circular spot at his suit's shoulder. Immediately, the suit splits there and goes slack, exposing Handler's bare shoulder. A small mountain of hair. Something I really don't want to see.

"So, what to do now?" TallSpot asks, scanning the others. "No one on the outside knows what has happened here. Should we take advantage of that opportunity?"

"And you have no stops at all?" BlueTrain asks me, eyes narrowed. "Not even from a controller?"

I shake my head. "Last I checked, nothing."

TallSpot's eyes widen. "Imagine what that could mean," he says. "The safety it might ensure."

Grackle crosses his arms, scratches absently at an elbow. "Yes, but to what end?" he says. "Our goals must always be remembered."

I frown. "What are you Abbys talking about?"

Grackle looks at me, hands now entwined. "Our invasion, of course."

From behind him, Handler huffs loudly. "Invasion? Who said anything about an invasion? I just want to go home..."

"An invasion by proxy?" I ask.

"Think of it more as a movement," Grackle explains. "Or an enhancement." He smiles softly and his hands separate, now moving as he speaks. "Whether we like it or not, we *have* been affected by our experience at Bait al-Jauza, and by what we learned. We have been changed. Given revolutionary—even dangerous—knowledge. But keeping it a secret goes against the scientific method."

"You found more than you expected," I say.

Grackle shrugs. "As a semi-regular variable star, Bait al-Jauza is most peculiar. We anticipated something unusual there certainly, but not of this nature."

"But did you *see* anything?" I ask.

"We saw many things," Grackle says. "Wondrous things."

BlueTrain snorts, happily agreeing. "But if you're asking if we saw a bright light," he says, "or a burning bush, then the answer is no." He shrugs. "There is more to exploration than what can be seen, of course."

I nod. "Always seeing, but never perceiving…"

Blue's eyes narrow again. "What was that?"

I shake my head. "I'm not sure, actually."

The words came from nowhere, freehead. I swear.

I smile, attempt to shrug it all away. "There is lots of random in my head," I say. "By design." A memory strikes me, pushing my thoughts a different direction. "The bot said something about the stars pouring forth speech…"

Grackle nods. "An astute observation. I believe Bait al-Jauza to be a portal of some sort. Or a conduit."

"A conduit," I say. "Of a superlative stream?"

Grackle brings a finger to his lips thoughtfully. "Is that your own terminology?" he asks. "Because it may prove accurate…"

I shake my head. "Something from the bot."

He nods again, slowly. "I wonder if I might borrow the phrase for my treatise on the subject?"

"I doubt he would mind." I think of the bot's body parts, now sown to the darkness. Small satellites of Earth. There is no sorrow—he was a machine, after all. I do feel loss, however.

What else would he say if he were still here and functional? Maybe *he* was the conduit…

"Regardless, this experience, this revelation, has serious repercussions," TallSpot says. "It flies against everything we've ever known. The knowledge that there is another entity out there claiming to be A and yet—"

"Not A," I say. "He is specifically not A. He is both master and servant. And He has His own agenda here."

"But that alone," BlueTrain says, eyes flipping between Tall and me. "We need to tell people, enlist them to our cause."

"They're not going to like it," Tall says. "The masters, the Imam..."

Grackle shakes his head. "I'm afraid there will be a war. If not of weapons, at least of ideology." He looks at me hard. "But I fear it will be the former."

"So, we should take Sandfly with us," Tall says. "Sneak down the lift among the tourists, try to enlist others to our cause, build plans, an army, and strike at the system. Free the people. Free the streets."

"Yes," BlueTrain says. "That is a good plan."

Grackle stares at me, hand perched at his chin. "Unless..."

"What?" TallSpot asks. "Don't you agree?"

"Oh, I agree a change is necessary," Grackle says. "I welcome it, in fact."

"But...?"

Grackle wags a finger in the air. "Sandfly is important, I think, and not just as a defensive weapon."

I'm really tired, Abby. Got woken after only two hours of sleep. I want to go back to bed.

"So, what are you suggesting?" I say.

"Someone needs to return to Betelgeuse," Grackle says emphatically. "Someone needs to study the source of the stream more closely. Fully understand what this new entity—this A~A³—wants of us."

Handler has been undressing the entire time we've been talking. He's down to his undergarments now, I can't help but notice. It is like being in the locker room again. "So we should return, then?" Handler asks, face sorrowful. "Put the suits back on?"

Grackle shakes his head. "I doubt *we* would find anything new. We don't have the proper equipment."

Handler looks from Grackle to me, then raises a finger. "But Sandfly..." His finger touches his scalp. "He does. I get it."

My eyes go wide. "Me? In space?"

TallSpot smiles and turns his palms out. "Why not? You said the stream had a message for you personally. You had your stops removed."

"I'm still not right," I say. "I still don't know why I was affected like I was. It doesn't make sense."

Grackle smiles. "What better way to find out?"

Deep dread returns. "I don't know how to fly anything."

"DarkTrench does the flying, really," Handler says. "We pretty much go along for the ride."

"And it is stream-aware," Grackle adds. "Fully."

I shake my head. "But one implant to handle an entire ship? Alone?"

"You did pretty well with that army of bots," BlueTrain says.

Grackle's hand caresses his chin thoughtfully. He glances at Hard's still resting form. "Actually, I wasn't thinking alone."

Now I'm really freaked. "HardCandy come with me?" I say. "She'd never go for it."

"At the moment she doesn't have a choice."

I notice the planet picture again. My old friend. What planet is that, exactly? I touch the stream, look for something that visually matches that picture. In a few nanoseconds time, I have it.

It is Neptune! Good old Nep. One of the outer Jovians. A monstrous gas giant. The first to be discovered purely by mathematical means. Astronomers knew something was out there, because Uranus was behaving curiously in its orbit, being moved in strange ways. Neptune's presence was felt, but they could not see it directly.

I smile, shake my head. Part of me wants to experience what the bot did. To see things a little more clearly. DarkTrench makes it easier. If it were any other ship...

"You're right about Hard," I say, looking at her. "Her stops would probably tweak her if we woke her to ask. But unconscious like this..." I get a tweak. Not in my head like before, but in my midsection.

He has sent me to proclaim freedom for the captives.

"It's decided then," Grackle says. "We will clean things up here and then go down to wait, to plan. You will take the ship and discover A~A³, find out what He's about."

"And the guards?" I ask. "The others on the station?"

"You'll instruct the bots to release them after we're gone," Grackle says. "There was so much confusion here, I doubt any of them got the full story."

Concern shows on TallSpot's face. "The only thing I worry about," he says, "is keeping everyone alive until you return. Our story isn't going to be welcomed. And the ulama controls the flow of credits."

It takes me only a second. Yes, of course.

I reach into my pocket and pull free the coin. I hand it to Tall-Spot, who immediately lifts it to his eyes, turning it, examining each side closely.

"I've been told it is worth many credits," I say. "Many, many credits."

"A rare coin like that?" Grackle says, amusedly. "I'd guess it is worth thousands."

"Hmm," I say. "I could've known that too, I guess. If I'd bothered to check."

I think of my head wound and remember. "I need you to do something else for me, TallSpot," I say. "I need you to look in on an old friend of mine. Make sure that he's safe." I tell him of GrimJack, and where he can be found. I also mention Hard's spot under the bridge, where a little more truth can be found.

Tall forms a fist around the coin. "We will do that" he says. "Good tech men are hard to find." He bows and flashes a sheepish grin. "I have something for you, Sandfly, as well."

AFTER THE CREW EXITS the room, I give the medbot new instructions. With a simulated nod of its head (more an up and down slide of its neck, actually) the bot affirms my request and extends one of its appendages to sink a syringe into HardCandy's arm. A few minutes later I see her eyes flutter. She moans softly and brings a hand to her forehead. She then squints my direction.

"Sand..." she says giving me a weak smile.

I move closer to her table. She grasps my arm at the elbow.

"Is everything all right now?" she says.

I nod. "On the station, and with the crew, yes."

Her smile broadens. "I knew you would do it," she says. "You being highlevel and all."

I sniff , and shaking my head, lean in closer. "Listen, I have something to ask you." I give her the highlights of my talk with the crew. The decisions we reached.

Hard looks at me a long moment, then glances at the other examination table, where the crews' spacesuits now lay folded, along with two helmets. She frowns. "You could've just let me sleep," she says.

I feel a twinge of guilt. "Sorry, I know you're probably tired. I know I am—"

She squeezes my arm hard. "No," she says. "I mean you could've done whatever you wanted. Put me on the ship with you." A flare of her hand. "Taken me out wherever."

I shake my head. "Probably, yes...I could have. But I realized it would make me as bad as my master. Forcing you to do something regardless of how you felt."

"You *are* a master now, Sand," she says. "Of this station, of the bots onboard. Even those Abbys in the crew listen to you now."

I shrug and self-consciously study the tiles in the floor. "Liberty isn't everything it seems," I say. "It demands a lot more than you might think." I force myself to look at her face, to study the beauty behind the eyes. "So, about the trip..."

She looks at the suits again. "So do they smell?" she asks. "I mean, they wore them for a *long* time..."

"We probably don't have to wear them," I say. "Just have them around for emergencies. And I think there are more in the ship."

"The helmets look tight," she says, frowning.

"I don't know," I say. "I mean, Handler...he has a big head."

She laughs heartily, a glorious sound. Then, as the laughter dies, she grows thoughtful, shyly looking between my face and the wall below her feet. "A trip sounds good," she says. "But I doubt I can go. I doubt my head will let me."

I smile. "Let's not ask your head then." Feeling moved, and fighting years of tweaks, I somehow manage to touch Hard's forehead with my lips.

Her eyes go wide for a moment, but the smile returns. I stream assurances to her and signal the bot, who produces another syringe.

"Pleasant dreams," I say.

IT IS EARLY MORNING. HardCandy and I are safely aboard DarkTrench. Somehow we managed to launch the thing. Got away from Earth. From there, the ship took over. Now we're traveling in a tunnel where no darkness is visible.

I know what you think, freehead, I know you think that's not possible in space where only night reigns. But in the kind of space we're moving through it is light that rules, you see. The darkness gets compressed. It is stars one after another now.

Last night I got my first real sleep in days. Turns out, even though DarkTrench doesn't have any cinder chutes, it can act like one all on its own. Remember, the stream is placid here, tranquil. DarkTrench mutes everything except the good stuff. In fact, I think it specifically lets more of the good through. All I know is that the dreams are bright, and I'm as happy as I've ever been. Happier, I think.

I have lots of questions, as I'm sure you do too. I'll find the answers, though, because that's what debuggers do. I've had my one unsolvable problem already. Passed it. Lived to tell. But I don't intend to have another. Can't afford to.

I have three things to help me now. First, I've got DarkTrench. I've only done a little sniffing around, but I can tell that the designers left more here for debuggers than they did any human. Maybe they knew what was in store for them, I don't know. But there's lots of good stuff here, lots I can use.

Secondly, I have HardCandy. Her implant hasn't buzzed her, even though she's awake and out here with me. But how could it?

She didn't disobey any direct command. Technically, she's been brought here without her consent.

She and I haven't talked much since we got onboard, not physically talked. But, as I've told you, that's secondary for us. We've said bunches really. More than I've said to anyone since being implanted. More than I could ever say on Earth.

Freedom! Bliss!

And finally, I have the headchip Tall gave me. That's right, that crafty Abdul was holding on to it the entire time. It was the bot's original chip. It wasn't destroyed, but it looks awful. Whack ninety-nine would've done it in for sure. There was no way for me to know, because once those things get their shell broke, they're like eggs. They dissipate, dissolve. This chip is still functional. Enough that I can probably learn a little more. Until we get there, that is.

There are two ways to see code change—to observe the code or to observe the behavior. It follows then that, if the behavior is good, so is the code. That's what we aim to prove, anyway.

But what is good?

Well, I'm starting to learn that, I think. "Good" is in this song I heard, but more than that. Much more.

He stoops!

Plus, freehead, we're going there. We've got DarkTrench and we're headed straight toward that big old semi-regular Betelgeuse. In our tunnel of light. Going back to go forward.

And when we get there?

Only A~A^3 knows...

JOIN SANDFLY IN HIS NEXT ADVENTURE!

Sandfly is free of the rules and free of Earth, but now there's a new mystery to solve.

With his female companion, HardCandy, and a secret ship named DarkTrench, he travels across time and space to find the source and meaning of the transmission that changed his life.

But what he most wants to know is why is he seeing things no one else can see. And where is the song that started their journey—or its singer?

Where is the Superlative Stream?

Grab *The Superlative Stream* and find out!

YOU CAN MAKE A DIFFERENCE!

Word-of-mouth marketing is the best kind. Not only does it ensure that good books get noticed, it also helps bring the right books to the people who will enjoy them most.

If this book met or exceeded your expectations in any way, please consider telling your friends and/or posting a short review.

Your help is greatly appreciated!

ABOUT THE AUTHOR

Kerry Nietz is a refugee of the software industry. He spent more than a decade of his life flipping bits, first as one of the principal developers of the database product FoxPro for the now mythical Fox Software, and then as one of Bill Gates's minions at Microsoft. He is a husband, a father, a technophile and a movie buff. He is the author of several award-winning novels, including *A Star Curiously Singing*, *Freeheads*, and *Amish Vampires in Space*.

If you'd like to get an e-mail alert whenever Kerry has a new book out or has a special on one of his already-released books, sign up here: http://nietz.com/EmailList.htm.

ABOUT A STAR CURIOUSLY SINGING

This was supposed to be my last novel.

In the fall of 2003 my first book—a memoire entitled *FoxTales: Behind the Scenes at Fox Software*—was published, and I hoped it would smooth the road for me to become a published novelist. Anyone familiar with the publishing business knows that few first books (or second books, or third books) breakout enough for a writer to have publishers knocking on their door. Few books, in fact, sell more than a couple hundred copies. But alas, I was both naïve and optimistic.

Over the course of the next five years I wrote a handful of novels, corrected them, and queried publishers about them. I had a few nibbles, but ultimately nothing happened. I'd written a lot of words, but none of them were going anywhere.

By the winter of 2007, I'd reached the conclusion that my dream of being a novelist wasn't going to happen. I'd tried a lot, learned a lot, but the road now looked like an unplowed field.

Still, I had this story idea about a computer programmer of the future. I also wanted to experiment with writing an entire novel in first person present tense. I'd written the prologue of FoxTales that way and wondered whether I could maintain it for an entire novel.

I decided I'd write one last story...for me. I didn't care if anyone ever read it. I didn't care if I even corrected it or queried about it. I was simply going to write it for my own enjoyment. Then quit.

So, while waiting in an airport one day, I pulled out my laptop, created a new document, and wrote:

It is hard to describe, this buzzing in my head. It wakes me, obviously. But it is hard to clarify for someone like you—at least the type of person I assume you to be—someone with a free head.

Almost fifty thousand words later I had a first draft. I read it over. I knew it wasn't perfect. I knew it was a little short. Yet there was something about the book, tentatively titled *2000 AP*, that I thought was truly unique. I decided to find a second opinion.

I knew of a guy, Jeff Gerke, who had just started his own publishing house. I knew he also worked as a freelance editor. One of his editorial services was a complete read through of a manuscript along with an opinion as to whether it was publishable. I hired him to perform that service with *2000 AP* in the spring of 2008.

Months went by.

Finally, in the fall of 2008 he sent me a message. "I'm reading it now. I love it."

He concluded that the book needed a better beginning, a revised ending, and a handful of other changes. "If it had all those things," he said, "I would publish it myself."

I spent the better part of a year making those additions, and in the fall of 2009 the book, now titled *A Star Curiously Singing* was published. My first last novel. There have been five last novels since.

• • •

Now a few words about content.

Speculative fiction is by nature controversial. It exists to take an idea from the here and now and extrapolate it into a potential tomorrow. It doesn't intend to predict the future*, only to ask the "what if?" question, and attempt to answer it. For some people, however, merely constructing a *possible* is akin to predicting it. And so, the controversy: Prophets are rarely liked, even when they're right.

My setting was born as the result of a handful of books written by sharia survivors. It was also influenced by Mark Steyn's demography-laden book, *America Alone*. My ruminations on how beliefs affect behavior, and how belief systems differ, clearly played a part, as well.

My goal was to be as true to the characters of my potential future as possible. How would someone who is controlled by an implant in his head feel and think and act? What conclusions would he reach? And why would he reach them?

So, if you think I've failed that goal, or missed the mark in any other way...

Write your own future.

* That said, when *A Star Curiously Singing* was written there were no caliphates under sharia law, nor was anyone talking about brain implants. Now both are regularly discussed. No one was writing in first person present tense either! Now it seems everyone is. *The Hunger Games* beat me by a month. A month!

95750621R00152

Made in the USA
Columbia, SC
17 May 2018